Ple
You
nor
or b
Plea

LIFE ACCORDING TO LUBKA

Life According to Lubka

LAURIE GRAHAM

ISIS
LARGE PRINT
Oxford

First published in Great Britain 2009
by
Quercus

Published in Large Print 2009 by ISIS Publishing Ltd.,
7 Centremead, Osney Mead, Oxford OX2 0ES
by arrangement with
Quercus

British Library Cataloguing in Publication Data
Graham, Laurie, 1947–
   Life according to Lubka.
   1. Music trade - - Fiction.
   2. Commercial agents - - Fiction.
   3. Female friendship - - Fiction.
   4. Large type books.
   I. Title
   823.9'14–dc22

ISBN 978–0–7531–8468–4 (hb)
ISBN 978–0–7531–8469–1 (pb)

Printed and bound in Great Britain by
T. J. International Ltd., Padstow, Cornwall

To Coach O'Halloran

CHAPTER
ONE

I did lunch with Lisa. I hadn't seen her in months and she said she had some big news to tell me. I was hoping she'd split up from that humorless dyke she's been with forever but no, *au contraire*, Lisa and Toni are going to be mommies.

They've used this agency in Knightsbridge, really, really exclusive. You can say what eye colour you prefer, stuff like that, and they guarantee the donor is high-end, not some jerk-off on welfare. They're getting twins, one of each. I'd have expected them to order two girls, considering how Toni feels about guys, but I guess it'll be different if the boy's made from a Lisa egg. And Toni'll make sure he doesn't grow up oppressing women. Twins, though. That's not going to do her figure any good. Such as it is.

She's four months along now so they're picking out the nursery drapes and everything. That sounds like it could be fun. You can buy some really neat stuff for kids. I could do it if I wanted. It'd take some thinking about though. A baby is a very big decision. And an expense. I read this report that it costs 300,000 dollars to raise a kid, and that's probably if you go for the Economy Plan. That's probably if you get a stroller with, like, wooden wheels. I could do a lot with that kind of money. I could get a time-share on St Barth.

Two hours I sat there listening to all this stuff about spinals and soy baby formula, *and* I picked up the check, and she never asked me a damned thing about what's going on in *my* life. She never even mentioned my new neck. I've noticed this happens when people get pregnant. They become completely self-obsessed.

So we're coming out of the Wolseley and I run into Hunt Madson.

"Buzz, Buzz," he says, "You are looking fly! Are you ready for the Urbies? Ready to do or die?"

Comet and Starburst both have bands up for Best Industrial Album at the Urban Musical Awards. I have Spam Javelins, he has Banana Bubbles.

I said, "Give it up, Hunt. This year it's ours."

"Not a chance," he says. "Better start practising your Cheerful Loser face. See you in Seattle. You staying at the Waterfront?"

Then he says, "By the way, I heard a whisper on the street you might not be going home empty-handed. You got any information you'd care to share?"

I thought he must mean Best Extreme Metal. We've got Mach 10 nominated although frankly they're the underdogs, but he says, "No. I mean Lifetime Achievement. Course, there's a lot of talk this time of year. It could be a red herring. A lot of people think Ed Rix should get it before he goes tits up. He's on oxygen now, you know? Carries a tank when he goes out. It's such a tragedy. But you also got to say, it'd be nice for an award like that to go to somebody at Comet. You know? Before you all die of old age? They put any of those stair chairs in your building yet?"

Hunt Madson is such a butt hole. Still. Lifetime Achievement.

I didn't go back to the office. I had a couple of new bands to see later and anyway I wasn't in a going-to-the-office kind of mood. I got a shoulder rub and an express facial, picked up a prescription from Dr G. Then I hit Rubber Queen where I found this eat-your-heart-out, single spaghetti strap, watermelon red, mid-calf, tube dress. I already got a Hector Munro cropped pants suit, kind of hibiscus shot with tangerine, but I find you need at least two outfits for the Urbies. You wake up the day of the awards, there's no telling who you'll feel like being.

I get home and the cleaning girl's sitting with a duster in her hand watching *Oprah*, so she's fired, and there's another whiney message from Felix on the machine.

"Hi. It's me. I wondered if it'd be okay to pick up the rest of my stuff, maybe Sunday? Only I need my old trainers."

He should have thought about that before he walked out. A guy decides he's leaving, so be it, but he'd better plan ahead a little, he'd better have his bag packed. Otherwise he's liable to find that the sneakers he left under *my* bed and the ten-buck sucker-dart crossbow and that pathetic so-called CD collection have all gone down the jolly old chute.

3

A&R asked me to look at two bands they thought might be worth signing so around nine I go all the way out to Acton to take a look at Party Susan and the gig's been cancelled. Somebody's time of the month, probably. Girl bands are more trouble than they're worth. So then I got a cab down to Brixton to check out the Understains. Three more bozos who wear their baseball caps sideways but they made an interesting sound. Kind of dubstep with a lot of bass. Worth a second look at any rate. We might be able to do something with them.

I didn't get home till two and of course I'm still up, up, up. That's the thing about night work. Sometimes lately the Mebaral doesn't even touch me. Plus I'm wound up about Felix. I mean, we were a good combo. He was uber-cute without any distracting extras, like opinions. That's how I like them. I do the choosing around here. I'm the one with the money and the address book. I took him to places — I mean, without me he wouldn't have been allowed in to hand round the canapes. Then I'm gone for three weeks, shopping for Japanese bands, and when I get back he announces he's been thinking. Beginner's luck. He's decided he's got age difference issues. The fucking ingrate. I notice he waited till I bought him the diamond ear stud before he started thinking.

And as if the Felix thing isn't enough I've got this Lifetime Achievement story going round and round in my head. Like, I always thought of it as an award for the walking dead. Ed Rix definitely has to be a candidate, but Spinks got it one year and I think he's still around.

It'd be so great to get something like that. All those sad people back home, used to call me names, used to forget to invite me to their sleepovers. That'd show them. Not that they'll be up to speed on the business I'm in, but if I get Lifetime Achievement the news'll be like, everywhere. Even losers who never made it out of Pittsburgh'll get to hear about that. Then they'll realise their error. Lifetime Achievement is like getting your footprint outside of Grauman's Theatre.

Anyhow, I have all this shit going on and I can't sleep. So I try a Tylox and a Jack D and then I'm just starting to relax and the goddam birds start up. Five-thirty in the a.m. I mean what's that about? This is the Docklands. This is the city. You don't pony up half a million for a sub-penthouse in a prime urban development to get birdsong. If you want Nature and stuff you buy a place in Vermont.

I guess I managed about three hours, then I woke up with such a tension headache I couldn't even stand the noise of the juicer. Mornings like that the only thing to do is take things nice and steady. So I get in to the office around one and when the Muffin Top sees me she actually exhibits a couple of vital signs.

"Yesterday," she said, "after you went out to lunch and didn't come back, somebody called."

I'm kind of between interns right now. Candidates for an opportunity like that, to work for an industry legend, you'd expect to get the pick of the bunch, but it's surprisingly hard to get the right guy. You don't want a total doormat, obviously, but then you don't want somebody who's going to have a nervous breakdown just because you occasionally throw a phone at them. We're in a high-pressure business here. So until I find young Mr Right I'm relying on the front office to field my calls. It's no wonder I'm stressed.

There's a nameless temp who mainly goes out for the coffee orders. There's the Muffin Top, who claims she's doing No Carbs and yet every time I see her she has her fist in a bag of candy. And then there's Mal. He's been with us a couple of months now. He looks about fifteen, weighs around ninety-five, wears Buddy Holly glasses and deeply uncool zippered knitwear. He does call me Ms Wexler, however. I like that.

The Muffin Top, though. I'd dearly love to know who hired her. I've asked many times but nobody ever owns up.

So, somebody called for me. Yesterday. In the p.m.

I said, "Is this a quiz show? How many guesses do I get?"

She said, "It was a woman."

I said, "And of course you put her through to my voice-mail?"

"No," she said. "She didn't want me to. She said she didn't like talking to machines."

Aha. A vital clue.

She said, "Anyway, I wasn't even sure it was you she wanted. She asked for Beryl Wexler."

Got it. A female, who is pathetically phobic about technology and who refuses to respect certain life choices I have made. Well, given that Mom's been out in Ridgelawn cemetery fourteen years now there's only one woman that could be.

The Muffin Top said, "Is that your real name then? Beryl?"

A stupid smirk on her dumb ass face.

I said, "No. But if this person calls back I'll speak to her. And by the way, fruit chews are carbs."

There were some okay names around in '61 when I was born. Mom and Dad went to the movies, they even read *Time* magazine. They could have named me Jackie or Marilyn, or something unusual invented with Scrabble tiles, but no, not my folks. I guess they said, "Seeing we've been blessed with another little daughter after so long a time, seeing she's come along and queered things just when we were free to go polka dancing every night and not need a babysitter, let's choose carefully and saddle her with the ugliest name we can come up with. Beryl Eunice Ermengild Wexler."

I'm just sitting thinking we might have some kind of situation developing back home for Dorothy to call me, and my phone rings. It's Dave Corcoran.

"Buzz, dear," he says. "A minute of your precious, if you'd be so kind."

CHAPTER
TWO

I don't like going up to Dave's corner kingdom. You have to walk past the water cooler and all those open doors. Everyone knows where you're going. It makes you feel like you're reporting to the principal's office.

He was playing with his stress balls.

"Pull up a pew," he says. "I tried to catch you yesterday but nobody seemed to know where you were."

I said, "I was in a lot of places yesterday. Tell you who I saw. Hunt Madson. He asked me if I'd heard anything, a rumour?"

"What?" he said, "What'd Madson say?"

Really kind of jumped on me, like he'd heard something too.

I said, "Just some whisper he heard about the Urbies, about a Lifetime Achievement Award. Someone at Comet?"

"Really," he says. "No, I didn't hear that. That'd be nice."

He's trying not to smile, I can tell. I've known Dave too long for him to fool me. Which gets me thinking, maybe it's not me. Maybe it's him. The Urban Music Panel has been known to get things wrong. Every year they find new ways to goof. Well, if Dave Corcoran gets Lifetime Achievement I'll quit. I mean, that would be so not right. The only smart thing Dave ever did was to listen to me once in a while.

Who was it told him Hardcore Emo was going to be the big trend in '89? Who was it told him we had to get ourselves a boy band? Hellfire, I didn't only launch Backdoor Boyz. I *found* them for him, I groomed them. There's nobody to touch me in this business, everybody says so. Angry Belgians, Not the Andrews Sisters, Lime Twist. Those were all *my* babies. Lifetime Achievement for Dave Corcoran? It totally cannot be.

He said, "I haven't heard anything, I swear. But I'm sure if anybody at Comet is going to be so honoured we'll soon hear about it."

He didn't know how much notice they give people for an award like Lifetime.

He said, "What's up? You worried you won't have time to write your acceptance speech? Worried about what you'll wear?"

I said, "I never worry about what to wear. I always look fabulous."

He said, "You do, Buzz, you do. Knockout. Now listen, I've got something to run by you. Something that's not your usual territory but I think it has your name on it. It's a World Music band."

I sat, waited. World Music is the Mojave Desert of Comet Audio. It's Ulan fucking Bator. I don't even know which floor their office is on and I have no interest in finding out. Besides, I never return Dave's first serve.

He said, "We've got a group coming over. We signed them last year and they're something rather special. The Gorni Grannies. Bulgarian ladies of a certain age. Their first album's just out and they're booked to do a promotional tour. Five UK venues with a show called Balkanalia — that's with an exclamation mark — then ten days in the States. But their Artist Rep's in quarantine. Holly. She picked up something nasty in Mozambique."

He pushes a CD across the desk. *Singing the Harvest.*

I said, "Not me, Dave. I do cutting edge not cutting corn. Plus, I don't go on the road unless it's something very, very special."

"Exactly," he said. "And this is. Would I waste your time on any old? Music-wise these ladies are off the screen, you never heard anything like it. Plus, they've never been out of Bulgaria. They're tour virgins. As far as I can make out, they don't even have a manager. Well, there's some relative of one of them kept calling Holly about security, but basically they're on their own. They need taking care of, giving a bit of direction. All those bands you did it for, way back. You had the magic touch. And don't tell me you don't miss the thrill of the road. I know I do."

I said, "Then you take them."

"Buzz, Buzz," he says, "they're old ladies. They need a woman out there with them."

There's a girl in Finance who's into that folksy shit. I heard her talking about this guy she's dating, plays traffic cone in some band, everything recycled, banjos

10

made from old broiler pans and stuff. I told Dave, he should give it to her. Call it an interesting career development opportunity.

He said, "It's not like this is completely new ground. You did a terrific job with those Bhangra Boys. I mean, who'd have thought?"

Well the Bhangra Boys were hip-hop. These are crones.

I said, "Look at them. And this is when they've made an effort for a photo shoot. These women are older than God."

He said, "Not all of them. There's one of them is only forty. Remind me, Buzz, how old are you?"

Bastard. I look great and he knows it. With this new neck I'm thirty-five.

He said, "You may not know this but World Music is our fastest growing division. We've almost doubled our list in the past twelve months. Have you thought about it?"

I said, "Thought about what?"

"Changing markets, changing times. I know you like to be where the action is."

I said, "I *am* where the action is."

They're lined up for the photo, arms linked, all wearing long skirts and aprons and those babushka scarves tied around their heads. No bras. Not many teeth. And they're all smiling. I mean, who *smiles* on an album cover? But it's one of those dumb things, you look at the picture and you can't help but smile back. Radical.

He said, "I see the flicker of a smile. Is that a Yes?"

Then he shows me the itinerary. King's Lynn, Stoke-on-Trent, Burnley. I never heard of those places. Chicago though, that's okay. Reno's fine. LA is great. But Pittsburgh? Of all the places on my travel no-no list, year upon year, welded into the Number One spot. And brought to mind twice in one day too? Uh-oh. That's not good. That really spooks me.

I said, "Why Pittsburgh?"

"Search me," he said. "But I'm sure there's a good reason. World Music has its hotspots. Maybe Pittsburgh's one of them. Holly knows what she's doing. And you'll note that you finish the U.S. leg in Mendocino, California. Convenient for a quick hop up to Seattle for the Urbies. I'll bet it's only a couple of hours."

It'd be fun to be back in LA. It must be three years.

I said, "This is a one-off, right? If I do this you're not going to land me with a bunch of Berbers that play camel bells? No Solomon Island nose-flutes?"

He laughed.

He said, "It'll be more like a holiday than a band tour. Just think. No groupies sneaking in, hiding under the beds. No broken toilet bowls. And remember what I said. World Music is the Next Big Thing."

Well actually, Grime Beat is going to be the next big thing. Evil Marsupial are going to be the next big thing, but what does Corcoran know. I see things coming practically before they even started down the turnpike. I have this extra sense, like horses know when there's going to be an earth tremor. It's a gift.

12

I get back downstairs and the Muffin Top is counting coins, tongue sticking out, heavy breathing.

She said, "Would you like to give something? It's for flowers for Holly. She's in the Hospital for Topical Diseases."

"Tropical," Mal says. "It's tropical diseases."

"Now you've made me lose count."

I said, "I need something on Bulgaria."

I get the dead fish look.

"Bulgaria is a country."

She said, "You going on holiday?"

I said, "We have artists coming in from Bulgaria. Holly's artists as a matter of fact. Call World Music, get me anything that might be useful."

She said, "I haven't got time to do it now. I've got to organise these flowers and take the card round for everybody to sign. I can't be expected to do everything."

And Mal says very quietly, "Or even *anything*."

He says, "I'll do Bulgaria if you like, Ms Wexler. Actually, I've been to Bulgaria."

And lo, the clouds parted, angel choirs sang and the front office was bathed in a golden light. Little Mal has been to Bulgaria, on vacation.

I said, "Where is it, exactly?"

He said, "You keep going straight till you get to Romania, then it's first right. If you get to Greece you've overshot."

The Muffin Top said, "Are the clubs any good?"

He said, "I don't know. I was bird-watching."

She said, "What do you mean?"

13

He said, "Which bit didn't you understand, 'bird' or 'watching'?"

The Muffin Top says, "You mean like an old anorak? You mean hiding in the grass with a magnifying glass, like an old perv?"

"Yes," he said, "or even with high-powered binoculars. I look at their legs and their breasts. And their beaks. I'm a beak man, really."

She said, "You're weird."

I said, "Why Bulgaria? Can't you watch birds in, like, Hyde Park?"

He said, "Not if you want to see a pygmy cormorant. Not if you're hoping to see a masked shrike."

Just this once I think the Muffin Top may be right.

I said, "Well I'm not going to Bulgaria. Bulgaria is coming to me. I just need bottom line. For instance, what do they eat?"

Kebabs, he reckons. Kebabs are okay. Any time I get the deeply urgent late night munchies I order me two doners on pitta with hot sauce, hold the salad.

He said, "Yogurt's very big there too."

Yogurt I can handle. As long as they won't expect like, chicken's feet or goat brains. Artists can be very temperamental, especially just before a show. When Tartan Fairies were playing Helsinki their bass guitarist had a conniption fit because he'd ordered crunchy peanut butter and they sent smooth. Put his fist through a mirror. We realised afterwards he'd forgotten to take his beta-blocker but still, it was a useful lesson to me.

With performers the little things can make all the difference.

I said, "What about bathrooms? Will they know how to flush a john?"

He says it depends. The hotels he stayed in had all mod cons but out in the wilds he saw a lot of squatters.

He said, "I can also tell you off the top of my head Bulgaria's into Round One of the UEFA Cup. But you probably don't need to know that."

I called Corcoran.

I said, "I've found the perfect minder for your singing Grannies. He's right here in the building. Mal."

He said, "Who?"

I said, "Mal. He's in the front office. Little skinny kid but he's got a great attitude, and he knows everything about Bulgaria."

He said, "Buzz, *you* are doing the Grannies. These ladies are special. We're not sending them out with some kid, and they don't need an expert on Bulgaria. They need somebody they can relate to. They need somebody to show them the ropes. Why are you trying to offload this? I thought we had a deal."

I said, "A *deal* suggests we both get something out of this. Right now I see zero benefit to me."

I hear one of Dave's big sighs.

He said, "I'd have thought you'd be glad to take a little time out, slow down for a few weeks. This is a business that can burn a person up and you've kept up the pace longer than most."

The age thing again.

I said, "Hauling a bunch of old ladies half way round the world isn't time out. A sun lounger in Martinique is time out."

He said, "You've had rather a lot of sickies this year and we shouldn't ignore the warning signs. Let's not forget what happened to Luke."

Well, Luke was plain crazy. He was out of control. He'd buy stuff any old place. I mean, you have to have a hundred per cent reliable supplier. With me, if it didn't come from Dr G, I won't touch it. And I have not had "rather a lot of sickies". I've had flu three times and a migraine attack in Amsterdam, which was hardly my fault. That bottle of schnapps was off. Kind of oxidised or something.

It's about four-thirty and the Muffin Top splutters back to life.

She said, "It's that woman again, asking for Beryl Wexler. Her name's Mrs Luft."

Mrs Luft. My sister, Dorothy.

"Beryl," she said, "is that you? I must say you're not the easiest person to track down. Now we really have to talk. It's about our father."

Oh yes. Our father, who art in Troy Hill.

CHAPTER
THREE

Dorothy never really felt like a sister. She was out of her trainer bra by the time I came along. She was dating Les Luft by the time I was in first grade and I was flower maid when she married him. Nineteen sixty-seven. They flouted international law and made me wear a crinoline in band-aid pink, to match the patch over my lazy eye. I believe I've destroyed all the photos except the one Dorothy keeps on her night table, and I'd have gone to the trouble of lifting that one by now too, but she's in Butler, Pennsylvania so it's not like it's going to be seen by anyone who matters.

Les died in '97, got a thrombosis after a procedure for a bunion. He was a Fuller Brush man, always suffered with his feet. As far as I know Dorothy manages okay. I don't imagine Les ever made very much. She drives a school bus, helps at Girl Scouts, calls me two or three times a year to remind me where I've gone woefully wrong with my life. Plus she has Kenny and Janine, grown up now of course. Kenny works at a correctional facility in Waynesburg, married, three kids. Dorothy sends me a picture of them every Christmas. I don't know why. I can never remember their names. Janine sells leather jackets at an outlet mall in Grove City. She has allergies and seems to be unlucky in love. Not the brightest bulb in the tanning bed, Janine. They all meet up at some Eat 'n' Park for Sunday dinner, hardly ever miss a week. I'd shoot myself.

She starts right in. No, "Hi Sis, how are you? What's going on in your life? Been tipped to win any top industry awards recently?"

She said, "Don't you think it's about time you visited Father? You never call him, you never visit, you never write."

How am I supposed to write to him? He doesn't have email.

Dorothy started calling Dad "Father" after Mom died. She said it sounded more dignified. Personally I think she's trying to put to rest all that icky "Daddy darling, Sugar Plum" shit that used to go on between Mom and Dad. She's just buried it so deep it'd take years of therapy to bring it to the surface.

I said, "Is he sick?"

She said, "He has water pills for his kidneys. He needs patches for chest pain. He wears elastic socks for his ankles."

Ask Dorothy about health, you get the full organ recital.

"Also," she said, "he's gotten in with some people and he just goes along with any crazy thing they say."

Gotten in with some *people*? Dad? I don't think. He worked thirty-five years as a sorter at UPS. Okay, he's a charter member of the Sharpsburg Polka Dance Club but I'm sure that was at Mom's urging. Ted Wexler is a man who rarely leaves the crawler lane.

I said, "You mean like, the Moonies?"

She said, "Don't be ridiculous. I'm talking about warehouse clubs. He joined three."

This is a new one on me.

I said, "What's a warehouse club? It sounds like Garage for Seniors."

"You see," she said, "how out of touch you are? A warehouse club is a warehouse club. BJ's. Costco. You get a discount card, so you can buy everything in bulk. Don't they have anything over there?"

A discount card sounds right up Dad's street. He always loved a bargain. Mom had to wait till January for her Christmas gift, so he could buy her one of those Evening in Paris bath coffrets when they put them on sale.

I said, "So what exactly is the problem? Is he over-spending? Does he need money? I can send him money."

She said, "Beryl, Father is eighty-two years old. He lives alone. He does not need a gallon of blue cheese dressing."

I don't quite see what I'm supposed to do.

I said, "Is he confused? Is the house dirty?"

"No," she said, "*I* make sure of that. But you can't move for all the canned goods and he can't put his car in the garage any more. It's stacked with paper towels and beer and dog kibble."

I said, "He got a dog? When did he get a dog?"

She said, "He didn't. He's storing stuff for one of these people he's gotten in with. And that's another thing. Stockpiling items like that he's liable to attract vermin. The neighbours won't thank him for that."

I said, "Are the Hootens still next door?"

"No," she says, "Mr Hooten died, Mrs Hooten's in the Methodist Rest Home and Shirley's in Turtle Creek with husband number three. Father has foreigners next door. As you would know if you ever visited."

I said, "I'm just trying to understand, what's the problem here? He's got a few old guy complaints but it sounds like he's happy. Does he still go to the Polka Club?"

"Not very often," she said. "He's too busy buying stuff he doesn't need. If he carries on this way he's going to have to be evaluated. He leaves his car out in all weathers because of some stranger's kibble, it snows, he falls, breaks his hip, gets pneumonia, who's going to take responsibility?"

I said, "Dorothy, it's May. It's not going to snow."

She said, "That's not the point, Beryl. Father has two daughters and there's only one of them watching out for him. I visit with him every week. What if I wanted to go away?"

I said, "Do you?"

She said, "I'm just saying. What if I did?"

I said, "Couldn't Janine keep an eye on him?"

She said, "Janine has a life of her own."

That's not been my reading of Janine's situation.

I said, "As it happens I have to come to Pittsburgh on business. I'll be in town June 11 and 12 so I'll drive out to Troy Hill and see Dad. Give you a breather."

She said, "Two days? Is that all you can spare?"

Two days! What does she think I'm going to do? Go through the photo albums? Sit drinking Sanka and listening to all that shit about what a perfect woman Mom was?

I said, "Are you nuts? I'm not staying with him for two days. It'll be more like two hours. I'll have work to do."

She said, "Doing what? Blessed if I know what they pay you for. Every time I phone they say you left early. The girl I spoke with yesterday wasn't even sure you still worked there."

My sister has no idea about my life. What does she think? That you make things happen in this business sitting behind a desk? She should see my diary. I'm out four nights a week, minimum. I'm totally gridlocked for lunches. And it's not like Dad's dying or anything. She had me over there three times for Mom, swore she wouldn't last the week, and then when she did go I was at the airport, actually at the gate, after another false alarm.

I said, "You know what, Dorothy? Two hours is perfect for me, and for Dad too. That way we have time for all the dumb questions and it's over before I feel the need for a full and frank about my damaged childhood. And while I think of it, will you please quit calling me Beryl. My name is Buzz. There is no Beryl Wexler."

She said, "It's the name God gave you."

Not God, Dorothy. Don't pin this one on God.

I said, "No. Mom and Dad thought it up all by themselves. And I've rejected it."

She said, "After everything they did for you."

Yeah. Like sending me to school dressed for a '50s costume party. Like porking me out on deep-fried Velveeta and giving me lifelong food issues. And stinking up the house with hot Oleo. It's no wonder nobody ever wanted to come home with me after school.

I said, "Let's not go there. Times must have been different when you were a kid. You think you grew up in paradise. That is not my recollection. You didn't have to share a closet with Mom's polka skirts. Just tell Dad I'll visit."

She said, "I'm not saying a word about it till I know you're in town. I know what you're like. You'll cancel and then he'll be disappointed."

I said, "Are you dating yet?"

"None of your business," she said.

So now we're getting to the bone. Dorothy's dating. That's what all this "what if I wanted to go away" crap is about. Well that's fine. That's good. I wish her well. None of my business if she's overdone the dutiful daughter thing. None of my business if she's made a rod for her own back. Anyhow, she doesn't have to go over to Dad's every week. Where is it written she has to do that?

This whole family thing, genes and stuff, I read an article about it in the Sunday supplement. It's just chemicals, just nucleic acids. They get shook up, in the end you have something that bears no resemblance to its constituent parts. Like a Black Martini. You have the same nucleic acids, it doesn't mean you have to get along. It doesn't mean you'll have anything to say to each other. Dorothy could drop the visits down to once a month and Dad probably wouldn't even notice.

I said, "I think you should look on the bright side. Dad's independent and it sounds like he got a new interest in life. Plus, one of these days he could go out to the garage to fetch a can of beer, set off a landslide of dog kibble and meet a merciful end. There are many, many worse ways to go."

"Beryl," she said, "you are a horrible, horrible person."

CHAPTER
FOUR

I played one track of the album. *Singing the Harvest. The Gorni Grannies*, the notes say, *discovered in a tiny forest-fringed village south of the capital, Sofia, by ethnomusicologist Dr Gwendolyn Robertshaw.* Crazy names. Lubka Lilova, Kichka Nikolova, Stanka Stoyanova, Mara Petkova, Zveta Borisova. I really don't know what I can do with this. It's a different sound certainly, and I'm used to different, but I can't see this filling any arenas. One thing for sure, it ain't Jimmy Jam Harris.

I walk outside for a cigarette and who do I see coming out of the elevator but Knifey-Spooney, all four of them.

I said, "What are you doing cruising the corridors? Am I expecting you?"

Big M says, "Not you handles us now, Buzz. We dealing wiv Sasha now. Din' vey tell you?"

One of the suits was in with Corcoran. He took one look at my face and he was out of the door faster than you can say "spreadsheet."

"I'll run the numbers, Dave," he says.

Corcoran's half out of his chair like he's filling his pants. He should have been.

I said, "Knifey-Spooney."

"Ah," he said. "Yes. I meant to talk to you about that."

I said, "Knifey-Spooney just met with Sasha. What's going on?"

He said, "Sasha needs to start building a list. She's ready."

Not with my bands, she doesn't.

I said, "Let her find her own list. Let her do the rounds of the clubs. Let her go all the way out to some church hall in Mitcham after she's put in a long, hard day."

He said, "You make it sound like you work in a coal mine. Okay, you've brought in some great bands, I'm not denying. But you've got a very big list, Buzz, and we're none of us getting any younger. We can't keep everything to ourselves. We have to bring the next generation on. Give them something to do."

I said, "You mean something to do when you're not schtupping her?"

He said, "I am not sleeping with Sasha. Anything she's been given is entirely on her own merits."

Right. Well, maybe not *sleeping* with her. Let's face it there probably isn't room for his fat gut in her kiddie starter bed. He probably just tucks her in with a glass of milk. After he's schtupped her in the back of his Jag.

I said, "Who else did you give her?"

Gilgamesh.

He said it so quiet. Well there it is. Dave Corcoran finally loses the thread.

I said, "This cannot be. Gilgamesh are Doom Metal. About which Sasha knows jackshit. She's a child."

He said, "She's twenty-two. You're not. You've done it all. You've so 'done it all' there's a rumble about you getting Lifetime Achievement."

I said, "So you did hear something?"

"Just a rumble," he says.

Just a rumble.

I said, "She's not touching Spam Javelins. You give her Javelins I'll personally kill you."

He said, "I haven't given her Spam Javelins. Now please, let's not fight, Buzz. Go have some fun with the Grannies. Relax. Be well."

Not looking good, old Dave. He sweats too much. He should get botox shots in his armpits.

Sasha's at the photocopier as I walk by.

She says, "Hi, Beryl."

That Muffin Top is for the high jump.

I said, "Hi, Sasha. Play nicely in the sand tray now."

So here's the math. I lose Knifey-Spooney and Gilgamesh and in exchange I get three weeks on the road with a Bulgarian freak show. Plus a whisper about a Lifetime Award, maybe. That is not a fair trade. I think there's something going on. I feel the ground shifting a little beneath my feet. Time to make some calls, take some meetings. Howie Schlepper at Store Front is going to be very interested to hear from me.

I'm out of Advil and the front office is deserted. It's like the Marie fucking Celeste out there. So I'm rooting around for medication and I see this sheet of paper in Mal's desk drawer:

The Wexler Mood-o-Meter.
1. WEIRDLY CALM
2. WELL-LUNCHED
3. DEEPLY OKAY
4. TOTALLY WIRED
5. NO CALLS
6. APPROACH WITH CARE
7. DEFINITELY HOSTILE
8. PARANOID
9. HURRICANE WARNING
10. LOCKDOWN. REQUEST BACK-UP

I have it in my hand and Mal walks in.
I said, "I was looking for aspirin."
He said. "You have to see a first-aider for aspirin."
He never took his eyes off me.
I said, "This is fun. I imagine everybody's got a copy?"
"No," he said, "just me. That's my drawer."
I said, "But where did you get it? I'd so love to know who wrote it."
He said, "I did."
I said, "You don't have to cover up for anyone. If it came from upstairs I'd just like to know, that's all."
He said, "It didn't. I wrote it."

I said, "Anybody else seen it?"

Just Jessica, he says. The Muffin Top.

I said, "But she probably like, photocopied it, to pass it around?"

"No," he says. "She didn't understand it. Am I fired?"

He started putting his stuff in his backpack, getting ready to leave. Friday evening. It was two Fridays ago when Felix walked. We were going to the opening of a new club on Earlham Street. Saturday we were meant to be getting some fish and a tank, then we were going to a gig out of town. He really didn't need to screw up an entire weekend. And I hate it when it's Friday and I'm the last one left in the office. It makes me feel like I'm sitting in one of those Hopper paintings.

I said, "You want to get a drink or something?"

So we go round to the Moon and Sixpence. He drinks orange juice with lemonade.

I said, "Is it because of your religion?"

"No," he says. "It's because I'm on my moped. I park it at the station."

He lives with his dad and his gran in Thornton Heath. It's somewhere in the 'burbs.

I said, "You feel like seeing a movie?"

The Day After Tomorrow was showing at the Curzon.

He said, "I can't really. I'm meeting some friends. We're going skating in Queensway."

Skating! So retro. I used to go to the Roller Palace a bit in the '70s but I didn't realise people still did stuff like that.

He said, "But you can come with us, if you fancy it."

I said, "Your friends probably wouldn't like that."

He said, "No, they won't mind. Anybody can come. Can I just ask you something? Does this mean you're not going to fire me or are you going to torture me slowly first?"

I'd never said anything about firing him.

He said, "I'm sorry about the mood-o-meter thingy. I'll put it through the shredder on Monday."

Too late. I memorised it.

I said, "It's okay, Mal. I'm Code Three."

There were five of them. They ride in on the train together every morning, two guys and three girls. It seemed like one of those Youth Fellowship things Dorothy used to be into: table tennis, picnics, light necking, no tongues.

We get to this Queensway place and it's not like the Roller Palace at all. It's *ice* skating, on real ice. And I'm in linen cut-offs and a trail shirt, freezing my ass. They rent you the boots but you don't get any choice of design or colour or anything and getting around on them isn't so easy. Everybody's shooting past me doing circuits. There are some really cute-looking stewards who're supposed to pick you up if you fall but I didn't get a lick of help till Mal came and towed me round a few times. That was wild. Then I took them all for pizza.

It's the start of the weekend and there I am, hanging out with five virgins. Who'd have thought? But this is one of the many reasons I'm so great at what I do.

When kids look at me, they don't see, like, a figure of authority. They see someone who's on their wavelength. I caught one of the girls looking at me a couple of times, in kind of total awe. I mean literally, jaw-drop amazement. I'm sure she never met anyone like me before.

CHAPTER
FIVE

Saturday I bagged up Felix's comics and wind-up toys and threw them in a builder's skip. Sunday afternoon I took a bennie and called Dad.

I said, "What's this I hear? You're riding around in buses with strange women? Buying Cream of Wheat by the pallet?"

He said, "Some people say Sam's is better but I like Costco. I know my way around. I like Wal-Mart too. Where do you shop?"

I said, "I don't. I eat out."

"Oh that's not good," he said. "That costs a pretty penny. And you never know what you're getting. Give you an example. These Chinese eateries? They say they use rats and pass it off as chicken. You wouldn't catch me. I cross the street. I won't breathe the air on their sidewalk. Those Reds are out to poison us, take over the world."

Communists are about the only subject that ever got Dad riled. He lit into Shirley Hooten one time I remember, just because she was wearing a Che Guevara T-shirt. Asked her what she was thinking of. Asked her if she'd be as willing to wear Adolf Hitler on her shirt. Hell, she only got it at a yard sale. She was only twelve. She didn't even know who Che Guevara was.

I said, "You're not still worried about Communists?"

He said, "When they change, I'll quit worrying. Won't ever happen though. You heard it here. Because a leopard can't change his stripes."

I said, "What about IHOP? You still willing to eat there?"

Dad always rated International House of Pancakes.

He said, "IHOP's okay. Who's buying?"

I said, "I am. I'm coming to visit you."

He said, "You don't need to do that. Matter of fact, I don't have room for visitors."

I said, "So I hear. Dorothy says you can't move in your place for canned goods. She's threatening, if you don't start behaving she'll get you evaluated."

He chuckled.

He said, "She told you that? She told me that too. I don't know what this 'evaluating' is but you can bet your last dime it costs money. They don't give anything away. I already told her, no thank you."

I said, "Well I'm going to visit you anyhow. It's been a while. But you don't have to put me up. I'll be staying in a hotel. I'll be in Pittsburgh on business. So we'll just get the breakfast at IHOP and then I'll be out of your hair. June 11. Write it down."

He said, "I'll write it on my calendar."

I said, "Anything you need? Anything I can bring you?"

"I don't know," he said. "What do you have?"

I said, "You okay for money?"

He chuckled again.

He said, "Who is this? You're one of those radio shows, right? Bagdarnit, you nearly had me there."

I was born in the West Penn Mother and Baby Hospital. There could have been a mix-up with the cribs. You hear of it happening. I could get a DNA test, nail it once and for all, but I choose to leave the question open. I don't need a cheek swab to tell me I was right to make a run for it at sixteen. Wexler gravity can be very powerful. If you don't break out while you're young and strong you'll never get away. Look at Dorothy. And Mom and Dad didn't mind my going. I'll bet they were relieved. I'll bet they celebrated.

"Have another helping of Tuna Bake, Daddy Darling. The cuckoo has flown the nest."

"Gosh darn it, Sugar Plum, I thought she'd never go. You open the beers. I'll call the locksmith."

I'm going through the file World Music sent down:

ONE WORLD PROMOTIONS, FAR SHORE MUSIC and COMET AUDIO
present
Balkanalia!

Balkanalia! brings together for the first time three leading exponents of the folk music of Bulgaria: The Ursari Wedding Band, the Tutrakan Trio and the Gorni Grannies.

A wedding without a band is unthinkable in Bulgaria and like many wedding bands Ursari are a Rom group, from the capital city, Sofia, where they are much in demand for all kinds of celebration. The Ursari create their unique, fast-moving sound with clarinet, trumpet, accordion, saxophone, violin and bass drum while the younger and nimbler members of the troupe dance the flamboyant *ruchenitsa* and *kyuchek* wedding dances.

The Tutrakan Trio featuring Anastas Popov on *gudulka* lute, Ioan Draganov on *gaida* bagpipes[1] and Valentin Asenov on *kaval* flute, evokes the musical melting-pot of Greeks, Turks, Bulgarians, Russians and Jews who have peopled the vast Danube plain that sweeps eastward towards the Black Sea.

The extraordinary Gorni Grannies represent the very best of the close-harmony singing from Shope region, where vocal skills are passed from mother to daughter. Their repertoire includes songs sung at work in the fields and the winter songs sung at women-only sewing circles. Lubka, Stanka, Kichka, Mara and Zveta have the ability to make five voices sound like ten.

Publicity-wise what has been done? Zip has been done. No special appearances, no interviews, no welcome party. The first venue is the Corn Exchange, King's Lynn, in the county of Norfolk. It seats seven hundred, which explains why I never was there before. When my bands do UK tours they play big spaces, fifteen, twenty-thousand seaters: the Manchester Arena, The

---

[1] All goatskins used for Ioan's bagpipes are obtained humanely.

Sage, Gateshead. This is small change. It's going to be like Amateur Nite. Why am I doing this? Sasha could do it. Even the Muffin Top could probably manage it. Five weeks on the road. Who am I supposed to talk to? I always hang out with my bands when we're travelling, after the show. I'm one of them. What am I going to do with this crew, join the knitting circle?

They're flying into Heathrow on Thursday. You should see the mug shots. They're all going to need a lip wax as soon as we get to King's Lynn. No picture of the interpreter. Oleg Ilievski. Sounds Russian. He might be fun. Russians can be very hot. High cheek bones and those side-button Cossack shirts that are *asking* to be ripped open. Oleg. Yeah. He sounds like he could very well be cute.

CHAPTER
SIX

My name is Olga Ilievska. I am Bulgarian interpret of qualified success. I am graduate of Plovdiv Institute of Interprets since 1982, certifiable in English and German and did interpret many high cadre visitors in Bulgaria, examples Secretary General of Lignite Miners' Union and world-known dart champion Len Norris. Also I did interpret in other lands such as Isle of Wight and United States of America for world towers of finest Bulgarian music.

Under Chairman Zhivkov dance and song of Bulgaria took big leaps. Songsters of highest level were trained at institutions to make authentic People's Music. Only very best were permitted to make world towers. Now situation is different. Now we have freemarket any person can make world tower, such as Gorni Grannies who give no damn of authentic People's Music. Gorni Grannies make non-advanced music of yesterday year. Also they do not smile or wear beautiful uniforms. But recording disk conglomerate Comet insists to make a tower so I will go with them. I do not like to travel with primitive songsters but with freemarket I have no celery from Institute of Interprets.

On Thursday we fly to English city of Heathrow where we will meet us high-ranking recording disk executive Buzz Wexler. Mr Wexler does not speak Bulgarian. Bulgarian is not yet world language.

Gorni Grannies will stay in de-luxe Sofia hotel one night before we make departure. These persons have not maximated benefits of Bulgarian world-leading education system. Thus I must correct their thinking and make their orientation for travel to West. This will be a big project.

Leader of Gorni Grannies is Lubka Lilova. I did not yet speak with her. She does not have telefon in place of residence. Thus I did speak with Stanka Stoyanova who has mobilfon even she is olderly Granny with seventy — five years. In my opinions this is too old for major cultural tower. It can be she will die and make big work for me.

Gorni Grannies must come to Sofia Sheraton Hotel on morning of Wednesday without failures. We have many preparations to make. Stanka Stoyanova says they will come in Moskvitch car of Grigor Nikolov, son of Kichka Nikolova. I have telled her, certainly five persons with baggages will not go in one Moskvitch car.

"Ne, ne," she said. "Grannies will go in car. Baggages will go in behind-trailer with boy sheep."

I did explain her, boy sheep cannot come in United Kingdom. It is not permitted by regulation of animal product.

She have said, "Is not problem. First boy sheep will go to Zheleznitsa to be husband with lady sheeps. Then Grannies will come to Sheraton Hotel."

But at ten o'clock has arrived Moskvitch car with four persons only. Lubka Lilova, Kichka Nikolova, Zveta Borisova and non-expected person, Dora Gavrilova.

Where is Mara Petkova, I have asked to myself. Where is Stanka Stoyanova?

"Because of her ages Mara Petkova does not come in this journey," have replied Lubka Lilova. "Instead comes Dora Gavrilova. Stanka Stoyanova, comes in car of idiot son. Except gangsters kill her she will arrive."

This talks of gangsters is not pleasuring my ears. Also, in Moskvitch car is baggages only of three Grannies. Instead valise, Dora Gavrilova wears many many garment, like matrioshka doll, so baggages-worker cannot steal.

I have told her, "English baggages-worker does not interest himself in old lady cloths."

"Not English person" she says. "Bulgarian person."

"But what of personal requisite?" I ask. "What of soaps? What of teethsbrush?"

Lubka Lilova says, "No need of teethsbrush. Dora Gavrilova has no teeth. And deluxe hotels give soaps. International interpret must know this."

Then have arrived Stanka Stoyanova in Mercedes limousine of son Gogo Stoyan. At once this Gogo Stoyan arises my suspicions. Why he does park in No Park zone? Why he does demand best room suitable of high-level dignities, not necessary for olderly lady. I must keep close eyes on this people.

Now all is prepared for on-time departure, except Zveta Borisova has swelled face, perhaps of teethache. Also she does tremble. I have ensured her, to fly in aeroplane is no danger. She will see demonstration of safety features, she will enjoy beverage and light snack, no charge, she will read interesting magazine, then in twinking of an eye she will arrive in city of Heathrow.

Kichka Nikolova did say, "I will tell you why this Zveta Borisova does tremble. I will tell you why she has swelled face."

Lubka Lilova has said, "Be silent, Kichka Nikolova. Go about your business."

For sure these are not no-trouble Grannies. They have incorrect ideas concerning up and coming tower in United Kingdom. I have telled them, Gorni Grannies must be ambassadors of Bulgarian culture. They must not make bad behaviors to high echelon record disk executive Mr Buzz Wexler.

CHAPTER
SEVEN

I was in the office by ten, caught them all rubbing the sleep from their eyes. The temp's just sitting, glowering at her computer screen. The Muffin Top's eating a bacon baguette and seems to have got as far as Saturday afternoon in a blow-by-blow of her weekend. Mal's watering the *ficus*.

I said, "It's plastic."

He said, "I know. I just like to pretend."

The Muffin Top says, "He's *supposed* to be taking the post upstairs."

I said, "Mal, my office. Right now."

He said, "Thanks for the pizza and everything on Friday."

I said, "Remain standing and give me your CV. The thirty seconds version."

He'll be twenty-two in August, went to a poly in north London, dropped out of something called Media Studies because it was crap, spent six months selling bagels at Victoria station, started at Comet in March. Preferred music, cheesy pop.

I said, "You've made a study of me, Mal. What qualities would you say a person needs to work for me? As my intern."

He was looking at the Angry Belgians tour poster, deciding how to play it.

He said, "Well, nerves of steel would be good. Combined with inner calm. Ability to work under pressure. Willingness to follow orders but also to show initiative."

I said, "Not too much initiative."

"No," he said, "Hardly any, come to think about it."

I said, "What about loyalty?"

"Yes," he said. "Total, brown-nosed loyalty."

I said, "Anything else that might recommend you for the position?"

He said, "I have excellent personal hygiene, I don't forward chain letters and I'll never show you pictures of my children."

I said, "You have children?"

He said, "No. But if I did I wouldn't. Also, I know how to perform CPR."

I said, "I assume you'd like the job?"

He was hesitating.

I said, "It might mean more money. Almost definitely."

He said, "Will there be any unusual duties?"

I said, "You don't have to sleep with me, if that's what you mean."

He turned scarlet.

He said, "I didn't mean that. But Jessica said your last intern had to give you shoulder rubs. I don't do shoulder rubs."

I said, "Jessica's wrong, as usual. I have a shoulder rub guy who makes house calls. Do you need time to think about this unlikely to be repeated offer?"

"Okay," he said, "I've thought."

His tasks for today: to list all media within shouting distance of the UK Balkanalia! venues, establish friendly first-name contact with The Person Who Matters, find out their hopes and dreams, get them on the hook; to confirm all hotel reservations; to re-schedule the feng-shui consultation regarding my office layout; to pick up my dry-cleaning and take my Pedro Garcias to the heel bar.

Questions? Will he be accompanying me on the Bulgarian Grannies tour? Affirmative. Even to the United States? Yes, provided he has a current passport, a clean police record and a set of non-tragic luggage.

Does this mean he no longer has to take orders from Jessica? It does. And will there be anything else?

I said, "Yes. Who cuts your hair?"

His gran cuts his hair.

I said, "Go to Beak Street, ask for Stash. Tell him you're my new intern and the sprouting palm tree has to go."

He said, "It's because I have a double crown."

I said, "Never mind. Stash can work wonders."

The Muffin Top is in my doorway approximately ten seconds after she hears the news.

She said, "I should have been considered for that position."

I said, "You were considered, Jessica, but you're way over-qualified."

CHAPTER
EIGHT

I get to the airport Thursday morning and Mal's there ahead of me. He's in a brown suit.

I said, "I hope you didn't buy that specially?"

"No," he says, "it's what I had for my cousin's wedding. My gran said I'd better wear it, seeing these artists are older-type people. Is it all right?"

It was a better look once he'd dumped the cat-puke tie.

He's brought a document case too, for all the Balkanalia! papers and a little Bulgarian phrase book. He'd highlighted a few sentences he thought I might enjoy. *Can you tell me where I need to get off? What do I do if my kayak capsizes? Do you have space for a two-man tent?*

I said, "Were you by any chance a boy scout?"

He used to belong to something called the St John Ambulance Brigade. They go around to country fairs reviving fainters but he quit. He said he really only joined so he'd be able to get in to Crystal Palace free but it turned out they never sent cadets to soccer games so he's kind of lapsed.

I said, "I've been thinking about this tour. Are we likely to get anyone trying to defect?"

"Well," he said, "from King's Lynn, possibly."

I said, "Seriously, it used to happen all the time. You'd get like, whole chess squads begging not to be sent home."

He said, "But I think Bulgarians can come and go as much as they like now. I think Ryanair fly there."

We've got two drivers, Jerry for the tour bus, beer-belly, comb-over, thinks he's God's gift, Floyd for the luggage van.

First the flight's half an hour late, then an hour ten. I'm trying to make some calls. Mal's talking to somebody at King's Lynn and I've got Jerry and Floyd yacking about road works on the M25 and what the Special-K's bass player got up to in the luggage van last week, and there's this guy eyeing me up, about thirty, blonde buzz cut, black leather bomber, great shoulders. I mean, he is *built*. Every time I think I'll say something he wanders off.

Mal says, "Ticket sales for tomorrow night are slow but encouraging, considering."

I said, "Considering what?"

Considering there's a lot going on in the area. *Calendar Girls* is showing at the Arts Centre and Alvin Stardust is appearing live at a theatre in Hunstanton. People in King's Lynn have choices. Las Vegas had better watch out. Meanwhile, what is the rep from One World Promotions doing to make sure things swing in our favour? Sitting on her tuchus in Edgware, apparently.

So then the plane lands, the board says the baggage is in the hall, and Shoulders reappears. He has company. He has two guys with him make him look like he has a wasting disease. Jerry gets out his Meet 'n' Greet card. It says COMMIT AUDIO. Moron.

I tell him to go borrow a magic marker and change it but Mal already has a card in his bag. It says ГОРНИ БАБУШКИ. Which is Gorni Grannies, in Bulgarian.

I said, "How did you do that?"

"Internet," he says.

Awesome.

Meanwhile Shoulders and his minders have grabbed pole position at the barrier and we're all waiting, waiting.

Jerry said, "Do we know what our artists look like?"

I said, "It's a young guy plus five old ladies who've never been off the farm. Don't worry, we won't miss them. They'll be the ones with the rooster lashed to the luggage cart."

Shoulders is listening in. He laughs. Nice cologne he's wearing, kind of woody. Could be Fahrenheit.

Then the flight disappears off the board altogether, like everyone's collected their bags and gone home, thank you and goodnight. Still no Grannies. And I start to get this little flutter of excitement. Like maybe the whole thing had been called off, or they missed the flight. Mal says maybe he should go get a message put out on the PA. That's when Shoulders finally opens his mouth.

He said, "They'll be here, no worries. They were on the flight. My people verified that."

I said, "Excuse me?"

"Gorni Grannies," he says. "They definitely arrived. You're from Comet, right?"

He offers me a stick of gum, never takes his eyes off the Arrivals door.

I said, "And you are?"

"Security," he says. "Personal security for Mrs Stoyanova."

Mal whispers, "That's the one called Stanka."

I said, "I'm Buzz Wexler. I'm running this tour."

"Yeah," he said, "I know."

He dips into his inside pocket and gives me his card. Boyko Stoyan, Security, Insurance, International Real Estate, Foreign Exchange. An address in EC1.

I said, "Am I missing something? This is World Music. We're not expecting any hysterical fans. We're not expecting any screwball stalkers. Why the extra security? Is there something I should be told?"

Shoulders chewed his gum for a minute.

He said, "We live in a crazy world. Stoyans are high-profile, I don't have to draw you a picture, right? Mrs Stoyanova is family and Stoyans look after their own. My boys here are going to make sure nothing happens, God forbid some piece of shit should try anything."

I said, "Mal, do we have accommodation booked for security?"

Shoulders says, "We makes all our own arrangements. Just co-operate, okay? If it should happen that a situation develops, you just do what my boys tell you. Vilk and Nosh. They're the best."

Vilk and Nosh. Two heavies for one Gorni Granny.

Then the doors swoosh open and there they are, luggage carts piled high. Plastic shopping bags, a couple of cardboard boxes, suitcases tied with string.

Floyd says, "I knew it, they forgot to bring the mattress."

No rooster either. It seems they're travelling light.

Four of them are in wool coats and headscarves and Nurse Matilda shoes. It's kind of a heavy look for May. But one of them, tiny, white-haired, has a Hermès scarf round her neck and a Louis Vuitton Monogram Keep-All in her hand. They could be good knock-offs of course. And bringing up the rear there's a chunky little number in an electric blue skirt suit. She has a file folder under her arm.

Then Shoulders starts yelling, "Baba! Baba!" and the little old lady with the Louis Vuitton breaks into a sprint. Tears, hugs, Shoulders swings her off her little feet. It's Stanka Stoyanova, and he's Boyko Stoyan, grandson in charge of personal security.

The woman in the bad suit makes straight for Mal. Her sleeves are too long. The skirt's kind of groaning at the seams. The whole look says budget airline ground crew.

She says, "You are Executive Buzz Wexler of Comet Sound Recording Company? I am Olga Ilievska, official interpret."

Not Oleg. Oleg was a typing error. Instead of Oleg in a Cossack shirt I've got Olga. Cheap ankle boots and a face like a jelly donut.

I said, "*I'm* Buzz Wexler. This is my assistant."

She said, "I am very sorry of this mistake. I did expect person in business suit."

She couldn't take her eyes off my shoes. I was wearing my tortoiseshell Louboutins. Mal's already introducing himself to the old ladies.

"*Zdrasty,*" he's saying. "*Kazvam se Mal. Zdrasty.*"

Olga says, "First I must explain you our delay."

There'd been a problem with stuff they had in their bags. Pig products.

She said, "I am sorry of delay. This persons do not accustom themselves with international travel. Even I explain with care what is forbidden, still they disobey. Thus sniffydogs of border police did make great barks and *lukanka* sausage of Kichka Nikolova have been arrested. Also *panagurska* salami of Dora Gavrilova."

Mal said, "Who's Dora Gavrilova?"

We don't have a Dora Gavrilova on our list. We have Kichka Nikolova. Check. She's the one with braided hair. We have Stanka Stoyanova. No question. We have Zveta Borisova. Check. She's the younger one, very pale, looks like someone gave her a fat lip. We have Lubka Lilova. Check. Tall, thick in the waist, clearly in charge. And we have Mara Petkova. Except we don't. We have a toothless cannonball called Dora Gavrilova.

Olga says, "If there is problem is not my error. All documents was in order. You must ask of Lubka Lilova."

She heard her name.

She said, "What you must ask of Lubka Lilova?"

I said, "Whoa! You speak English?"

"*Da*," she says. "I speak."

I said, "Do the others?"

Olga cuts right in.

"No," she says, "none grannies does speak correct English."

Lubka says, "*Ne*, I speak good as you, Olga Ilievska. I have Berlitz book. I have movie channel."

Olga says, "Howandsoever, I am official interpret of this tower."

I said, "The problem is this, there should be a Granny called Mara but we seem to have somebody called Dora instead."

Lubka says, "*Da*. Mara did not come. She did not wish. She is at eighty-five years."

I said, "But we have a contract, Lubka. Mara's name is on the album. It'll be on the programmes."

She shrugged.

She said, "Dora Gavrilova is good singer. And she only is at sixty-five years. I think is better."

I said, "Suggestions, Mal?"

"Yes," he said. "Pretend it escaped our notice."

Floyd's trying to get the luggage together but Vilk and Nosh won't let go of Stanka's bags.

Boyko Stoyan says, "My boys have got transport outside."

I said, "You mean she's not travelling with the rest of the group?"

"Right," he said. "She's going in one of my cars. I like plenty of steel between my gran and some of the idiots you get on the roads. And if she gets sick, I don't want her in any crappy NHS hospital, you understand? I got contacts. I know the best clinics."

Stanka didn't want to go with her minders, you could tell. She wanted to stay with her pals.

I said, "This is not a good start. Look at her. She's miserable. I need happy, smiley Grannies. They have a show tomorrow night."

He says, "She's not miserable, she's tired."

I said, "Look, if you're so concerned about security why don't you just come along yourself? You look like you can take care of yourself."

That made him purr, but he said, "You think I keep guard dogs and do the barking myself? I'll be there for the Burnley show. I got business in Manchester."

Then he kissed Stanka on the top of her head and he was gone, just disappeared into the crowd and so did Stanka, Nosh on one side of her and Vilk on the other.

Mal said, "I think there's something I should tell you."

Olga's sticking to me like glue so he shows me what he's written on the back of his yellow pad. M-A-F-I-A. Then he wrote STANKA.

I said, "You're not serious?"

He said, "I don't mean the actual, *actual* you-know-what. But something similar."

So then while we pretend to be checking papers he whispers to me what he's read. How there's a lot of gangster money sloshing around in Bulgaria these days, building contracts, porn movies, drugs. People disappear, people turn up with a hole in their head. Security's a major industry.

I said, "Now you tell me this? You give me all that baloney about yogurt and lesser spotted nutpeckers and you don't happen to mention we could be dealing with Mafia? You call yourself an intern?"

He said, "I thought it was just going to be five old ladies. I didn't see any point in worrying you."

Worried! I'm not worried. I'm considerably thrilled. Except of course, Boyko Stoyan could just be acting the bigshot. He could be minor league. I mean, what kind of gangster gets tears in his eyes when he sees his grandma come through Arrivals? Great eyes though. Kind of light caramel, like a lion.

CHAPTER
NINE

We're on the way to the car park and they're starting to settle into their natural positions. Lubka's the leader. She's striding out with Mal, head and shoulders taller than him. The other three are huddling along behind her, clutching their purses. Kichka, Zveta, and Dora who should have been Mara but isn't. Olga's bustling along at my side, telling me how much in demand she is as an interpreter, how she usually works to a much higher level than people like the Gorni Grannies. I don't know where they found Olga but twice I told her "tour" isn't pronounced "tower" and she still doesn't seem to get it.

As we're getting into the bus Lubka says, "You are mama of this Mal?"

I *mean*. Do I look like a girl who has a kid old enough to drink in bars? I do not.

I said, "No, Lubka. He just works for me. Matter of fact, poor Mal doesn't have a mama."

"Ach!" she said. "I will be his mama."

As soon as we're moving Jerry starts playing an Abba CD. He drove them in 1980 and never got over it. Give him one minute and he can manoeuvre any topic of conversation around to Abba or, at the very least, to Sweden.

So I'm explaining to Olga what the rest of the day holds. We have to drive to King's Lynn, check into the hotel, record a piece for the local radio station, get dinner. Tomorrow we'll go to the venue for a sound check, do a piece for local TV, play the gig in the evening.

Lubka says, "Also go in shops."

I said, "Sure we can go shopping. What do you want to buy?"

She said, "I will buy all nice things what I can buy."

The others are quiet. Dora and Kichka are just looking out at the traffic, Zveta has her eyes closed.

I said, "Is Zveta okay? What happened to her mouth?"

Olga says, "Is allergia."

Lubka says, "Is not allergia. Is husband. Boomf," and made a fist.

I said, "I have something will fix it for her."

Dr G gave me some great herbal stuff when that collagen shot went haywire. A bad, bad scene that was. Core Meltdown were getting presented with their gold disc and I had a top lip that looked like a boiled frank.

Lubka grinned. If I were Lubka I'd spend my first royalty check on tooth veneers.

She said, "How you can fix for Zveta? You kill husband?"

Mal hands round a bag of Gummi Bears and the thaw sets in. Olga's humming along to Abba, like Jerry needs that kind of encouragement, and Lubka and Mal are conducting a Getting to Know You session in Bulgarian and English.

"Nem is Dora Gavrilova."

"Nem is Zveta Borisova."

"Nem is Kichka Nikolova."

"*Kazvam se Buzz.*"

Easy. Everyone should learn languages.

I said, "Lubka, how long have you been singing?"

She says, "Of course from age of baby."

I said, "And when did you all get together? When did you decide to start the Grannies?"

She looked at me, kind of puzzled.

Eventually she said, "Grannies did not start. Grannies was always. In Gorni, where is ladies, is singing."

I said, "But you're *the* Grannies. You're the ones who recorded the album."

"*Da,*" she said, "I will tell. English professor did come in Gorni with record machine. Daktor Gven, very nice. Two times she did come. She has made record of all Gorni ladies. Now some is already dead, some does not want to sing for record machines, even you give them money. They say, 'Why shall I sing for foreign peoples? Why foreign peoples cannot sing for their own selfs?' For record of Comet company five Grannies only did sing."

I said, "So Mara did the recording, but she didn't want to do the tour?"

She said, "Is long journey. She did not like to go away from her house in case she becomes dead."

I said, "What about the money Comet paid her?"

She said, "She gives to Dora Gavrilova. Mara has all things what she needs. If she does not, I will give. Mara is sister of my mother. I will take her care. And this is good thing for Dora Gavrilova. Now with money of Grannies' record she can get new teeth."

We stop at South Mimms to get coffee and sandwiches and I'm in the restroom when I hear the sound of hysterical Bulgarians. Screams, laughter, then more screams. It's the motion-activated faucets. Lubka's figured out how they work and she's giving the other three a demonstration.

"An! Aff! An! Aff! Varter! Stop! Varter! Stop!"

Zveta's blouse is soaked, Dora's backed herself into a vacant stall, seems to think it's all the work of the Devil and by the look of Kichka's bulging pocketbook she's cleaned the place out of paper towels. This tour could turn out like a first grade field trip.

The road to King's Lynn is all motorway till you get to Cambridge. After that you're out in the sticks with nothing to look at but fields. The funny thing is though, the sticks-ier the view gets the more they like it. Corn, green stuff, potatoes. More green stuff. They're shouting out the names of vegetables, so excited you'd think they were spotting faces at the Oscars.

I said, "Mal, tell me about this city we're going to."

He said, "It's not really a city. It's more a small regional centre of knob-head culture. But there's an award-winning multi-storey car park."

I said, "We're staying downtown, right?"

He thought "downtown" meant a bad neighbourhood.

I said, "It means the throbbing heart of the place. So that after the show, when we've tucked these girls up for the night we can hit the clubs."

He said, "Actually, that might be a really bad idea. They don't like foreigners in Lynn."

I said, "I'll let you do the talking. Who told you they don't like foreigners?"

He said, "My friend Jase, who came skating with us? His cousin got decked last year, outside Zoots nightclub. He needed twenty stitches."

I said, "He got decked because he was from London?"

"No," he said. "Because he was from Wisbech."

We pull in to the hotel. Single storey, newish looking. It reminds me of an eatery on an Interstate service plaza. Nothing else nearby except a couple of box warehouses and it's raining the kind of rain you just know is never going to stop.

I said, "What are we going to do to entertain these people?"

He said, "Don't you think they'd like to rest for a while? They've had a long day."

Lubka says, "I will not rest. I will see English shops."

I said, "Is there a mall?"

"Not as such," he says. "I think it's being redeveloped."

I said, "Call the Muffin Top. Tell her I want a cyanide capsule, Guaranteed Next Day Delivery. Get one for yourself if you like."

The only other vehicle in the car park is a sparkling new Beamer, licence plate BOYK 02, and sure enough Stanka's checked in and installed in a family suite. Boyko's goons have the next room with a communicating door between, so they can just walk right in. It reminds me of the tour I did with the Loobylous in '99, when Looby started having rationality issues and we had to keep her shrink within hailing distance 24/7.

Everybody's milling around in Stanka's room. She's demonstrating the trouser press and they're gazing into her closet like it's the eighth wonder of the world, and then I realise Lubka's deciding the sleeping arrangements. She's worked out that Dora can share the double with Stanka. Kichka and Zveta can have the pull-out couch, and she'll put the two armchairs together to make herself a cot. Then Mal explained.

"All this only for Stanka?" she kept saying. "All this?"

We're trying to parcel out the rooms but it doesn't matter what we do, the crowd doesn't get any smaller. We settle Zveta in her room but she won't stay put. She wants to tag along and view what everyone else is getting. Same with Kichka. There's an art to cutting one animal out from the rest of the herd but it's not the kind of thing they taught you in Troy Hill.

I'm starting to match the names to the faces. Dora's the one with the moon face, no teeth and no suitcase. She's apparently wearing everything except for the embroidered aprons they wear for special occasions. They're in a plastic shopping bag with a pair of bedroom slippers, a comb and a shaker of talcum powder. I hope we're not going to find ourselves in a compromised personal freshness situation with Dora. She got very anxious when Lubka was playing with the faucets at the rest stop and when we took her to her room she just kind of peered round the door into the bathroom. You could see her thinking like, what if they turn themselves on in the night and flood the room and drown me?

Kichka's a whole other story. I don't think she'll be losing any sleep over faucets. She has this real don't-fuck-with-me face. Good bones, dark eyes, grey pan-scourer hair with a centre part and a coiled braid. She went straight for the little bottles of shampoo and stuff in her bathroom, wanted to know how much they cost. When Olga told her they were free she started pricing everything else in the room. How much for the TV? How much for the desk lamp? Come check-out time I think we may have to pat Kichka down.

Zveta's hard to read. She hasn't spoken, hardly looks up. The lop-sided way she holds her head, trying to hide her mouth, she looks like a Modigliani model. She's perched on the edge of her bed, still holding her purse. Olga's showing her exciting features of the room, like the electric kettle and the teabags, but all Zveta wants to know is how to lock the door.

Lubka takes a quick look at her room and then the caravan moves on. Olga's, Mal's, mine. That's all, folks. They have an hour or so, to rest and freshen up. Ten minutes and Lubka's back, tapping at my door. She looks younger without the headscarf. Strawberry blonde, a bad home permanent, a lot of sun damage to the skin, but she's nifty for her size. Good legs.

I said, "Something wrong with your room?"

She said, "Ne. Is very nice. But I have question. Does Boyko Stoyan pay my room?"

I said, "No. The promoters of the show are paying."

She said, "If Boyko Stoyan pays I will have different room, not so big, not so nice."

I said, "Boyko Stoyan's not paying for anything, except for those men he has guarding Stanka."

She said, "Then I am happy."

I said, "Do you know Boyko?"

"Pah!" she said. "I know him when he is at fourteen years. I know him when he is thin boy, like Mal Cleaver. Now he is big idiot *mutra*. How to say?"

She puts on a tough guy face and does a Boyko swagger.

I said, "Is he a gangster?"

She says, "*Da!* Gangster. Is good name of Boyko Stoyan."

I said, "What about Vilk and Nosh? Do you know them?"

"*Ne,*" she said. "I do not know. They are *borcheta*. Idiot *mutra* must have idiot *borcheta*."

Bodyguards.

I said, "Does Stanka really need those guys?"

She said, "She does not need. Stanka Stoyanova is good person, no trouble person. But she has son, Gogo. Gogo has son, Boyko. Both they have bigshot money, bigshot autos. What can she do? It is family."

I said, "Shall I tell Boyko to get rid of the *borcheta*?"

"He will not," she said. "Please, I will not make trouble. Only I am happy he does not pay my room."

Mal was wearing his "is this a good moment?" face.

He says, "I have some good news and some not so good news."

There's been a misunderstanding with KL-FM. They already recorded a piece with one of the other acts, the Ursari Wedding Band, to be broadcast this evening, so they cancelled the piece on the Grannies.

I said, "There hasn't been a misunderstanding, Mal. They're fucking you around. I'll bet you were all meek and mild with them."

He said, "I don't think it hurts to be polite."

He has a lot to learn.

I said, "Forget polite. You want one thing — air time, they want a number of things — interesting material, topicality, and for you not to be calling them every five minutes until they come to their senses. Go figure."

He said, "But the really good news is that Anglia TV wants to film the Grannies in the market place tomorrow morning."

They're doing a special report on organic produce so they can work in a nice link to five women with soil under their finger nails. That is good. That I like. I told him to make some calls, hire some like, hoes and pitchforks and stuff, to give them the right look.

I said, "And tell Lubka they're going to need a suitable song. Does it have to be about vegetables?"

"No," he says. "It has to be about two minutes."

60

I suggested to Olga we all meet in the bar before dinner.

She said, "I will meet you. I am accustomed with Western business method. But Gorni Grannies is not accustomed. In my country womens do not drink in hotel bar except they are sex slaves."

CHAPTER
TEN

Mal and I were discussing how many teeth a human is meant to have. He thought it was thirty-two. I'd say the Grannies are averaging half that. Zveta's missing about four teeth, bottom front. Dora has nothing. Lubka has interesting random gaps. In fact the only one who seems to have a full set is Stanka and she's obviously had work done. Her mouth looks like someone jammed it full of chiclets.

He said, "Lubka's nice."

I said, "You'd better watch out. She may apply to adopt you. Besides, what are we supposed to do with 'nice'? Does 'nice' sell tickets?"

Take Knifey-Spooney. They're all borderline personalities. You probably wouldn't want to find yourself alone in a subway car with any of them. And *that's* what fills arenas.

He says, "Well, King's Lynn isn't exactly an arena. It's more a medium-size venue. Anyway Cliff Richard's always been nice and he's had more Top Twenty entries than any other recording artist ever."

Something else he has to learn. There's an important difference between facts and figures and the gift I have. When a band has what it takes, I can't explain if I smell it or taste it, or if it's like something just scuttled over my grave. I just know, that's all.

There were a couple of sorry-ass salesmen swapping war stories. Otherwise we had the bar to ourselves. Stanka was the first down, with her minders. She's carrying this really cool alligator evening purse. I'm starting to think those Stoyans have some serious money.

Mal says, "What's the protocol? I suppose Nosh and Vilk'll expect to sit with us."

No way. I've learned to be very careful about fraternising with support crew. I mean, they can dream. But you have a few drinks with a guy one night after the show, maybe even hook up, hey we're all grown-ups, but then he starts getting above himself. Plus, I didn't want Jerry running away with any ideas. He'd been creaming himself from the minute he saw me at the airport.

I said, "They can sit with the drivers."

And the one called Nosh says, "We sit with ourselves. We get bar menu. Watch door."

Then the rest of the girls appear. They're all wearing hand-knit cardigans except Olga, who's decided it's a dress-up night. Frosted eye shadow, a beaded top, another skirt with seam-strain. I wonder if you can get dexxies in Bulgaria? I could let her have some, help her drop a few pounds, but I wouldn't want to start her on something she can't keep up.

Lubka's rearranging the furniture so we can sit in a big circle. And at the risk of being mistaken for hookers, would they like a little drink before dinner? The heads are shaking but the mouths are saying "*Da!*" This is the single most important thing to know about Bulgarians. When they nod they mean no, when they waggle their head they mean yes.

They're all looking for a drink called *rakia*. The barman has every other liquor known to humankind. He even has that sweet blue stuff you need to mix a Monica's Dress, but no rakia.

Lubka says, "Is not problem," and she brings a bottle out of her bag. It's home-brewed liquor, a kind of Bulgarian cousin to grappa, which takes a wet Thursday night in King's Lynn and bathes it in a not-unpleasant shimmering haze. Lubka makes hers from plums. Kichka and Dora use peaches, Stanka makes it with apricots. They've all brought bottles in their luggage. We've a long, long trail a-winding but you only get one glass each, before dinner, so I guess we'll have enough to last us to Mendocino. If supplies run out we'll just have to switch to embalming fluid.

There's a discussion going on about the bowl of potato chips. Then Lubka says something to Kichka, who goes off to fetch something from her room. Dora goes with her, which must shorten the odds they'll get lost.

I said, "What did they go for? What do you need?"

Lubka says, "You will see."

The rakia is supposed to go down in one shot, with a chaser of Sprite and something to eat. Potato chips don't count. I had a quick Jack D while we were waiting, to keep the barman sweet. Eventually Kichka and Dora come back with a Mason jar of cornichons.

Olga says, "Is piggles. In Bulgaria we make best piggles of world."

Lubka says, "In Gorni we make best piggles of Bulgaria. Now we can drink."

I'm afraid I palmed my piggle, dropped it into my bag. Nobody noticed.

Mal says the restaurant's holding a table for us so we ought to go in. Holding a table for us! Like it's the frigging Ivy. There's this patterned carpet everywhere and it's kind of vibrating and really disturbing my balance. I'm going to mention it to the front desk. They should get it changed. I mean, on this occasion it was only a few potato chips that landed on the floor but it could have been worse. They could be sued.

We get into the restaurant and Mal's trying to get the girls seated but they're going round shaking everybody by the hand: the waitresses, the chef who's come out to see what all the noise is about, and this one lonesome couple hiding behind their menus, who look like they'd been hoping for a quiet evening. It's probably their wedding anniversary or he's got something to tell her, like he's boffing his secretary, and suddenly there's this crowd of grinning hags bearing down on them, wanting to shake their hands. Suddenly they're in the middle of one of those, like, Breughel paintings.

Olga says, "In Gorni these persons do not go in restaurants. They are country pumpkins."

For sure they don't understand the concept of choosing something from a menu. I ordered for them.

Chargrilled chicken breast with lightly herbed mashed potato and sunkissed tomatoes under a drizzle of balsamic vinegar. A couple of bottles of Valpolicella. I could have ordered grilled cheese sandwiches and chocolate milks all round, they'd have been just as happy. These are low maintenance artists. The rakia's helped them relax, feel at home. Even Olga's starting to loosen up a little. She's sitting next to me, wants to tell me the story of her life.

"I am born, city of Kozlodui," she says. "Home of world-known nuclear plant. My father did build this plant. Also my mother. It was highmost engineering achievement."

She's six weeks older than me. Single.

She said, "I am career woman."

Sure, Olga. It's just you didn't find the right niche yet.

I notice Dora keeps asking Stanka the time. Stanka's the only one wearing a watch. Lubka tells me, what it is, Dora has this sheep, aged thirteen which is getting up in years for a sheep. It sleeps in her kitchen, and she's worried it's going to pine for her while she's gone.

I knew some guys in LA who got a potbelly pig. They had it in diapers and everything, and when they split up it cost them thousands in lawyers' fees, arguing about where the pig was going to live and visitation rights and stuff. A sheep though. That's different.

I said, "Is the sheep home alone?"

No, the sheep is home with Dora's husband but they don't get along.

Lubka says, "Is no problem. Stanka Stoyanova will help. You will see."

Eventually Stanka gets out her cell phone. She's got these gnarled, shaky old lady hands but she's fast-dialling Bulgaria. Lubka says she's phoning her husband, Danil Stoyan, to tell him to take *his* cell phone round to Dora's place, check on the sheep and then call back. Stanka gets through and she's shouting into the phone, "Danil, blah blah, blah. Blah, blah blah, Danil."

I guess Danil doesn't hear so well. Then he's gone. We wait, we wait, we wait some more. I order another bottle of red. Stanka's phone's on the table and everybody's looking at it. Finally it rings. It's the sheep for Dora.

I said, "What's its name?"

Lubka whispers, "No name. Is sheep."

Dora's chatting away, recounting her day, I guess, about flying to England and the demon faucets at South Mimms rest stop and the hotel and everything. The sheep doesn't seem to be saying a lot. Everyone's quiet, listening in but respectful. Dora wipes away a tear. And then Lubka started to sing.

There was no warning. She just opened her mouth and sang. Her voice seemed to start from some place high up in her head, kind of behind her nose and it felt like it had a closing speed of ninety miles an hour. She sang a couple of lines and then the others leaned in towards her and joined in. She'd got Zveta and Dora on one side of her, Stanka and Kichka on the other.

Sometimes they sounded like one big voice, sometimes I could hear the different threads. Kichka was easy to pick out. A smoker's voice, although according to Lubka she only smokes one roll-up a day. That Bulgarian tobacco must be something. Stanka's voice is husky too, but a softer old-lady kind of husky, Dora's is sweet, younger sounding than you'd expect from looking at her. Zveta's is high and hard, like a glass cutter. But Lubka's voice is the one holding it all together, like a steel cable. And if you closed your eyes and somebody said, "one guess, where are these girls from?" you'd probably say Africa. Especially when Zveta did that sliding "yip!" at the end.

The waitress was just standing there, six sticky toffee puddings balanced up her arms and her mouth hanging open.

I said, "Was that for the sheep?"

Lubka said, "Ne. To say the truth sheeps does not understand. I can say in English. Dora will not know. A cattle can understand. To take milk of lady cattle is better you sing with her, else maybe she will not give you milk. But sheep, not. This song was for you, was for Mal Cleaver. It was to say thank you for welcome of us. Please, now you will sing."

Not me. Not even after Lubka Lilova's plum rakia. I haven't sung since third grade, not since that homeroom bitch told me to shut up and just pretend. Plus one time Mom threatened if I didn't stop singing the Lambchop song she'd put me in the dog box, but

68

that could have been more because of the song than the singing.

I said, "I don't sing, Lubka."

She said, "Do you have pain in voice? You must eat *med*. How to say? Bzzzz. Bzzzz."

Olga says, "*Med* is honey of bee. Now I will sing."

Lubka says, "*Ne*. Mal Cleaver will sing."

I said, "You really don't have to. It isn't in the job description."

"No," he says, "I don't mind. We sing "Glad All Over" at Crystal Palace matches but it's not very good as a solo. I'll do "You'll Never Walk Alone"."

He's a kind of light tenor. Not bad. They loved him. Dora gives him a big whiskery kiss. Lubka's shaking her head, "*Da! Da!* Bravo! Song of movie *Carousel*. This song I know."

Olga says, "Now I will sing."

Lubka says, "Olga Ilievska, what you can sing? Only you know Komsomol songs. We do not wish these songs."

But Mal said it was only fair to let Olga sing and she stood up, back like a ramrod, arms straight down at her side.

She said, "I will sing song "In Our Land We Have Everything for Happiness"."

Catchy. It seemed to have an awful lot of verses, and while she was working her way through it Jerry and Floyd wandered in. They'd been in to town for burgers.

Jerry says, "What's this, karaoke night? I'll go next."

He did "Knowing Me, Knowing You" and "Money, Money, Money" and there might have been no stopping him but he noticed Vilk and Nosh watching him from the doorway and that seemed to put him off his stride. Boyko's heavies are going to have their uses after all.

I said, "Are you boys going to give us a song?"

They laughed, nodded, faded back into the bar.

Lubka says, "Tomorrow, after honey of bee you will sing."

I said, "Not me. I never sing."

She said, "But how you can make jolly party?"

Well, that's between me and Dr G. I make jolly party just fine.

Olga said, "In Bulgaria many people sing to topmost standard, else folkloric song, else patriotic songs of Motherland. In this way we achieve promotion of good postures, healthy bowls and correct ideas. In this way we do pleasure our own selves, also others."

I could tell it was only a matter of time till Jerry gave us "Dancing Queen" so I suggested we have a nightcap and turn in. The bar was closed of course.

Lubka whispers to me, "You will come in my room. I have special bottle. Also Mal Cleaver will come. But not Olga Ilievska."

Throwing off Olga isn't so easy. We have to say goodnight, close our doors for a few minutes, then tiptoe out again.

I said, "Just one drink, Lubka. Tomorrow's a big day."

"Da, da," she says. "Big day. One drink. Is rozina. Nice drink of Bulgaria, is made of flower."

She's really nested. She's brought a pillow from home, kind of folk art embroidery, and two Jesus pictures painted on wood. They're set up on her night table with a little red glass candle lamp and a framed photo of a guy with a moustache.

I said, "Is that your husband?"

"*Da*," she says, "Here is Lord Jissus, here is Mother of God, here is Lazar Lilov, best husband of world."

And as she names each one she picks it up and gives it a big smacking kiss.

CHAPTER
ELEVEN

Now we are sconced in de-luxe King Lynn hotel. At end of first day in United Kingdoms of England I have many events what I must report.

Comet Sound executive Buzz Wexler is not English Mister. She is American female. When we arrived this have made me great surprise. Also she does not wear smartsuit of business person but clothes of Western sex slave. Perhaps she is ladyfriend of chief of Comet buro. Perhaps she did not rise in this position by excellence but only with sex flavors. I will observe her.

With Buzz Wexler is pleasant young man, Mal Cleaver, who does give aids to her and to all people what need it. Even he has learned traditional Bulgarian greeting. Like my ownself he has gift of tongues. Also, there is other nice person, very sexy, but I will not write his name. I will discover if he has wife.

We have arrived from Sofia in city of Heathrow with delay of ninety minutes. The blame of this was operational reason. Immediately from meeting with Buzz Wexler we have traveled in luxury mikrobus to fabled city of King Lynn where Gorni Grannies will make their spectacle tomorrow. Name of this spectacle is Balkanalia! This is made-up word.

In Balkanalia! spectacle also will appear Ursari Wedding Band and Tutrakan Trio. Ursari Wedding Band is gypsy band of Rom people. Under Chairman Zhivkov anti-state gypsy music was not permitted. Now gypsy persons can go there and here and it may be they will give bad impersonation of Bulgarian people. In my opinions it is good they will stay in karavana, not in hotel, else who can say what havocs may arise.

Gorni Grannies also is not persons of highmost quality. Already they make problems, examples,

1. Containing in their baggages non-permitted item of pig.

2. Sporting with sanitary equipage.

3. Saying opinions what should not be said. Who can say what ears is flopping? Lubka Lilova must close her mouth. Also she does believe she knows English, but she does not. She does not have diploma. Thus she makes many error.

I do not enjoy to work with this Grannies. For sure Kichka Nikolova has disease of brain. She does makes juju doll to kill wife of son. She says non-intelligent son, Grigor Nikolov, did choose wife with bony chests from village of Gabra. Now this wife makes bad luck magic on plum trees and on Kichka Nikolova, that she may die soon and bony-chest wife will get goose feather mattress.

Lubka Lilova says plum trees of Kichka Nikolova does not have bad luck magic, only fly and cattypillar. She says also, if Kichka Nikolova prays to Protecting

Veil of Mother of God, wife of Grigor Nikolov cannot kill her, even not with gun. She is person without education but she has highmost opinions of her own self.

Stanka Stoyanova did not go with us in our journey to King Lynn. Instead, at airport arrival have awaited her grandson, Boyko Stoyan with lifeguards. Quickly she was taken away in limousine. I do not like this. Why must village songster have this lifeguards? Why she must travel in limousine like wife of Party official? It can be this Stoyans is people of bad connection that will make trouble. I have made many cultural towers, and no person did ever make trouble except and only Krazimir Kozlek, world-known perpetrator of Bulgarian dance who have been kidnapped by American secret police and wash-brained.

King Lynn is historical market city of Eastern Anglia. It has been habitated already one thousand years, with much inns and ancient monuments, also high-class shopping at Vancouver Centre. Chiff products of King Lynn is seefood, examples cockle, wrinkle and muscle. Tonight we have enjoyed characteristical dinner of region; prawn and cocktail, chickens with selection of vegetable, toffee pudding with choice of ice cream else gustard.

In this hotel we are guests of organisation One World Music. Even we can enjoy breakfast buffet without voucher. Tomorrow after soundchecks of Corn Exchange Auditorium and interview for television program in Market Square we will make leisured strole of embankments of River Ooze and be soaked in atmosphere. Also there will be shopping opportunity and time at leisure. For television interview I shall wear red costume with gold chain and black court shoe.

CHAPTER
TWELVE

The fire alarm went off about six-thirty. I could hear people opening and shutting doors, discussing whether to leave the building. I figured I might as well stay put, seeing my brain's slamming round inside my skull like a pin ball, seeing I've been robbed of Knifey-Spooney and Gilgamesh and my life is over anyway. Then everything went quiet and I was just cutting loose into a very mellow place when the phone went. It was Mal.

He said, "Panic over."

I said, "I wasn't panicking. Whatever it was, I don't want to know."

He said, "Okay, I promise I'll never reveal what Stanka was trying to cook in the kettle."

I said, "I thought they had everything confiscated at the airport?"

He said, "I suppose eggs are fairly easy to hide. Oh. Now I've told you."

I said, "And Stanka? I'd have thought she'd expect room service. She think this is a bring-your-own kind of tour?"

"Yes," he said, "I think they all do. I was worried when you didn't come to the emergency muster point."

I said, "I don't do muster points, Mal. They're for the herd."

"Well you should," he says. "Most people would survive a fire if they'd follow evacuation procedures."

He's a stitch. I'll bet he was hall monitor in school.

I told him to get me a masseur immediately. Ten minutes and he calls again, extra loud. People who've never suffered from tension headaches have no idea how to modulate their voice.

He said, "Reception doesn't have the number of an actual masseur."

What numbers do they have, I wonder? A veterinarian? A euthanasia service?

I said, "Code Six, Mal. Approach with care. Seriously. I'm going back to sleep."

But I was awake by then. So I get up, brew me a double Nescafe, pop an Advil plus one of my little blue friends. I'm in the shower and the ideas start fizzing. I'm thinking about Dora's sheep. I'm thinking we can do something with this. Like, hire a sheep for the tour. Or maybe we could set up a live link to Gorni. It could be a very cute angle indeed, particularly if we can get the sheep to say something.

We go round to the venue for a sound check and the promoter's rep just arrived, fresh off the train from London. Serena from One World Promotions. A pony club type. I guess she must be somebody's daughter. She nixed my sheep idea without even listening to it.

"Gosh, no," she says. "We couldn't possibly. Animal welfare regs are terribly strict."

I said, "We wouldn't be giving it electric shocks. We wouldn't be dressing it up in a headscarf and boots or anything."

Although, now I think about it, that is another cute idea.

She said, "We absolutely can't do anything like that without a permit. It could get the whole tour closed down."

The English go on and on about this great, like, *empire* they had but I don't understand how they ever got past first base. They're such scaredy cats. Anyhow, Serena's dashing back to London after tonight's show so there'll be plenty of opportunities to go off script.

The Corn Exchange isn't a bad venue. It's some kind of historic monument but they fixed it up, kept it looking quaint on the outside and spiffed it up inside, made it into a multipurpose space. So we go in and there are three guys on stage, I'd guess mid-fifties but when people come from disadvantaged countries it's very hard to say. They're wearing old-fashioned suits and ties and the colour of their faces is Dark Roast. This is the Tutrakan Trio. They'll be opening the show.

One of them is playing a pipe, one is scraping a fiddle, but not tucked under his chin. He's just holding it upright. The third guy seems to have some type of headless animal under his arm and he's kind of blowing into it and then squeezing the air out. If you tortured a goose I imagine it might sound something like that.

I said, "Serena, if we're not allowed to have a live, happy sheep in our section, how's this going to go down?"

She ignored me, but I'm telling you, if they get any fur-coat protesters in the audience, there could be real trouble ahead when that Tutrakan guy starts playing his headless goat. Then she says the Grannies have to wear mikes.

I said, "These girls do not need amplification."

She said, "We mike all our artists."

I said, "Okay, Serena. Have it your way. Although strictly speaking they're *my* artists."

So the girls get miked, they sing a few verses, strip the paint off the inside of the sound booth and what do you know, Serena's too busy taking calls to crawl across the floor and kiss my ass. But that's okay. I can be big about stuff.

Then we go backstage to take a look at the dressing rooms. The Ursari Wedding Band already staked their claim and moved in. They're a big group, must be twelve of them at least. I'm standing in the doorway and the atmosphere is like, 99 per cent testosterone. I see some ugly faces, I see a quantity of chest hair and I see some badass sunshades. Plus, the crowd parts, I see two pairs of leather pants, and the guys who belong to the pants are tens. I mean: They are awesome, beefalicious TENS.

Mal's at my side.

He says, "You're not going to be happy."

The TV show has a breaking story. An oil tanker's run aground so all the outside broadcast crews have been diverted to the shore. The farmers' market piece is on the spike and so are we. Of all the goddam days of the year to have an oil spill.

I said, "You didn't tell me we were close to a shore."

He said, "I'm releasing information on a need-to-know basis. I thought that's what you prefer."

I said, "Well what about later? Can't they reschedule? How long does it take to film an oil slick?"

Mal says, "It's what they call a developing situation. People'll be worried about the sea birds and everything. I think they're probably almost definitely not going to film the Grannies."

I told him, fuck the sea birds. He almost winces when I use the F-word. I don't know if Mal's cut out to be a grown-up just yet.

I said, "This is a Buzz Wexler tour. We think on our feet. Where the cameras are looking for oil, there shall they also find Bulgarian grannies. We can be environmentally concerned too. I've given to Save the Panda and all that shit. Tell Jerry he's taking us to the shore. Olga, tell the ladies."

Lubka says, "When we will go in shops?"

I said, "Later. The shops will still be open. First we have to get you girls onto TV."

Jerry says he can take us to a place called Hunstanton. We can be there in half an hour.

Lubka says, "Where we are going?"

I said, "To the ocean."

"*Dobry*," she says. "I will like to see this ocean. In Bulgaria we do not have."

Olga says, "We have Black Sea. *Cherno more*. Very, very beautiful."

80

Stanka beamed when she heard the words *Cherno more*. She's been there.

I said, "I thought none of you had ever been outside of Gorni till now. That's what Olga told me."

Lubka says, "Olga Ilievska is *nevezha*. She does not know our life. All Grannies has been from Gorni. Stanka Stoyanova was three times at *Cherno more* at town of Golden Sands. At Golden Sands Gogo Stoyan has many hotels. All friends of Stanka Stoyanova can go in this hotels if they wish but I will not. I did already tell you my reason."

Mal says, "So did you ever see the sea, Lubka?"

"*Da*," she said, "In movies I have seen. In *Poseidon Adventure*, also *Jaw 1* and *Jaw 2*."

Jerry said Hunstanton was a resort. I guess Jerry was never in Atlantic City. Hunstanton is a town you can hold in the palm of your hand. There are some gardens and a kind of boardwalk, with a little tractor-train. There are tea shops and places that sell cotton candy and on the beach there are some, like, miniature horses kids can ride on. But there are no casinos, no spas, no big-name showrooms. And there is no ocean.

You ask people and they look at you like you're nuts. They say, "Tide's out."

Well I'm sorry, but that was beyond "out". I'm not big on oceans, personally I prefer a saltwater pool with bar service, but I do know you're supposed to be able to see the ocean, even when the tide went out. This didn't appear to bother the girls though.

Lubka says, "No problem. We will find." And she's off across the sands. Anywhere Lubka goes, the others follow and anywhere Stanka goes, Nosh and Vilk are supposed to follow, but I can see them hesitating, worried about mussing up their shoes.

Olga says, "I also will not frolic on this bitch. I do not have correct attire. I will remain in mikrobus with Jerry Driver."

Then a helicopter comes wup-wup-wupping overhead. Mal's rolling up the cuffs on his pants. He says, "Uh-oh. I think Boyko's taking this security thing a bit too far."

But it was just the coastguard. No sign of any TV crews.

I said, "Mal, I hope those people at Anglia weren't just kissing you off. This doesn't look to me like an unfolding environmental catastrophe."

He said, "No, there's definitely been an oil spill. Jerry heard it on the radio. I'll go for a wander, shall I, see what I can find? Comb the bitch?"

They've all taken their shoes off, wiggling their toes in the sand, squealing and laughing and holding their skirts down in the wind.

Lubka says, "I like this ocean."

I said, "But you can't see it."

She said, "I can smell. In Gorni I cannot."

Zveta was picking up seashells.

I said, "Her lip's better today."

"Yes," she says. "Is better."

I said, "Her husband? Does he do that very often?"

She shrugged.

I said, "Was it because of the tour? Didn't he want her to come?"

"Ne," she says. "Tour is not problem. Money is problem. With record of Gorni Grannies Zveta has money. Dimitar Borisov wants she will give him these money. He wants he can open Sexy Shop in Sofia but Zveta will not give. She gives to Citibank. And when she will not give, boomf. You think is okay?"

I said, "What? That her husband boomfed her?"

"Ne," she says. "Is okay to give money to Citibank."

Shit, poor Zveta. No wonder she wanted to know how to lock her bedroom door.

I said, "Is he likely to come looking for her?"

"Dimitar Borisov?" she says. "Ne, ne. Zveta did give him little money. He will drink vodka, sleep, wait when she returns, boomf."

Man, that is sad. Personally I never had any trouble like that from guys. My memory's a bit hazy but I think I might have smacked a few myself, years ago, if I caught them thieving from my stash or renting out my bed. With Felix I just stopped his cards.

Kichka's up by the boardwalk, poking around in a trash can. Dora and Stanka are watching the kids getting the pony rides.

I said, "You all have kids back home?"

"Some," Lubka said. "Dora Gavrilova has daughter in Varna what she does never see. Zveta Borisova has daughter in Chicago, America. She is movie star, only I cannot find this movies with my television. Stanka Stoyanova has son, Gogo. Kichka Nikolova has two son, Nikul and Grigor. Two baby one tummy. How to say?"

Twins. Like Lisa and Toni are getting.

I said, "But not you?"

"*Da,*" she said. "I had. God did send then he did take away."

I said, "I'm sorry."

"It can happen," she said. "Now it is many years. What is name of your husband?"

I said, "I don't have one."

She said, "Is because you do not sing. Song is life. We will teach. Then soon you will get husband."

I said, "I don't need one."

She said, "How old you are?"

Forty-two years and six months.

She said, "For this number years you are very beautiful. Why you did not find husband? Why you did not make baby?"

I said, "Too busy. I have a career. I have a lifestyle. Anyway you don't need a husband to get a baby."

I tried to explain to her how it is over here now. How you can order the guy stuff from the clinic and just kind of add an egg. Like a Betty Crocker mix. She didn't get it though. I didn't go into thermometers and turkey-basters and stuff. I guess you still have to do things the old-fashioned way in Gorni. Grind the corn, chop the wood. Date the guy, meet his folks, register your pattern.

She said, "After tour, you come in Bulgaria. I will find you husband."

I said, "What, in Gorni?"

"Not Gorni," she said. "In Gorni is only old mens and *alkoholik*."

My phone rings. It's Mal.

"Okay," he says, "Get them ready. I've found a TV reporter. There's no sign of any oil so they're getting ready to leave. He says he'll give us two minutes if we make it relevant. We're on our way."

I said, "I'm going to get one of these guys with the donkeys, for added atmosphere."

He said, "Do they have a suitable song?"

I said, "Does this reporter understand Bulgarian?"

He said, "I see what you mean."

They can sing two minutes out of the Sofia phone book. Who's to know?

The donkey-minder says the girls are all too heavy to sit in the saddle, though God knows I've seen grade school kids who weigh more than Stanka. I wave a pair of free tickets under his nose and he agrees one of them can hold the bridle. And across the sands four ants are developing into Mal Cleaver and the crew from *Eastward Ho!* Gareth Timms, presenter, plus cameraman and furry boom microphone man. I see Olga scrambling out of the van. Then Vilk and Nosh realise something's going on. Suddenly the whole world is converging on the Gorni Grannies.

Timms says, "We have here five musical ladies all the way from Bulgaria and I'm told the song we just heard was about Mother Nature taking care of the environment. Very nice. Let's hope Mother Nature was listening."

"Lubka Lilova's the group's leader. Lubka, how would you describe the state of the beach today?"

Vilk and Nosh have arrived and they're kind of crowding the donkey, trying to get themselves into the frame. I'm hoping for the donkey's sake it doesn't make any sudden moves. I have a feeling those boys are packing heat.

Lubka says, "Is very nice. We like very much. We have enjoyed your fresh hairs. You have ticket for our spectacles? Buzz Wexler will give you ticket."

He said, "So to any viewers worried about conditions on the beach, what would you say?"

She said, "I will say come, is no problem. I will say come then to Balkanalia! show, hear Gorni Grannies sing. Is tonight at seven and half clocks at King Lynn theatre. Very good spectacle."

Fifty-eight seconds. It was in the bag and Olga was still floundering across the sands in her kitten heels.

I said, "I'm going to call you One — take Lubka!"

"Yes?" she says. "Is bad name?"

CHAPTER
THIRTEEN

It's just after seven, there's a dribble of people coming in to the auditorium, mainly older women and I'm backstage babysitting Zveta because she's having some kind of nerve crisis. I've given her a Xanax but she still won't put her apron on and Kichka's not helping matters, keeps saying things to her, needling her.

I said, "What's going on?"

Lubka said, "Is nothing."

Olga said, "Kichka Nikolova says if Zveta Borisova does not sing all other Grannies must receive one quarter of her moneys."

I said, "What about the songs? Can you do them without her?"

Lubka said, "Of course. But Zveta will sing."

The others are dressed and ready to go. They wear cotton shifts, embroidered aprons, and kerchiefs on their heads. Everything is home made. Then usually they wear these *kindouri* slippers, kind of homemade ballet pumps, and thick knitted socks — Dora's threatening to knit me a pair — but tonight Lubka is wearing her new black fishnet anklets and her lime green Crocs.

Mal said, "Do you think it's the right look, Lubka?"

"*Da*," she says. "Is right look. Is jolly smart."

So far Lubka's the only one to lose her shopping cherry. The others did a lot of looking and Dora came close to getting Winnie-the-Pooh knee socks until Kichka talked her out of it. But Lubka's very decisive. I believe she has the makings of a really great shopper.

Tutrakan are opening the show, the Grannies are on second and the Ursari have top billing. Lubka wasn't happy when she saw the poster.

She said, "I think in England ladies goes first."

I said, "They're top of the bill because they're known. They toured here before. They have a following."

She said, "They should not come here. They give bad example of our country, Ursari is Rom. You understand?"

I understand a couple of them are supremely cute.

She said, "Rom is gypsy. They should go home, clean they front yard."

It's seven thirty-five and the house lights are still up. Zveta's nipping at the plum rakia, three of the Ursari still haven't turned up, last seen entering the Hogshead bar and the stage manager is having a cow. Then Mal calls me from out front.

He says, "I think you should know some men just arrived. A lot of men, actually. I think they're Bulgarians."

I said, "Are they armed?"

"Just with cash," he says.

I run down, and he's right. There must be a hundred of them, young guys mainly, and they're taking their time coming in, looking the place over, like they were never in a theatre before, trying out different seats. The stewards are trying to count heads but they can't keep track and the people in the box office are drowning in crisp, new twenty pound notes.

I said, "Where'd they come from?"

Mal says, "Two coaches dropped them off outside."

He's got his phrase book out.

"*Izvenete*," he says to one of them, "*govoriteh li angleesky?*"

And the guy says, "Yeah. We come up from London. Mr Stoyan sent us."

It's Boyko Stoyan's rent-a-crowd. He's papered the theatre for his gran.

I said, "Is Mr Stoyan here?"

"No," he said. "Mr Stoyan is a very busy man."

They're supposed to walk on in the order they stand: Zveta, Dora, Lubka, Stanka, Kichka. But Zveta's still not sure she's going anywhere, which throws Dora for a loop because she doesn't want to be first on. So Lubka's telling Kichka to reverse the order and Kichka's pretending she doesn't understand. In the end there's four of them out there, having this big discussion and not one of them is standing where they should be. It's like a Polish fire drill. And it brought the house down. That is a keeper. As Mal says, we just have to make sure the chaos stays natural-looking.

They opened with "Many Throats, One Voice", then "The Roosters are Crowing", then a couple of harvest songs. I'm standing off to the side with Zveta and I suddenly feel a change in her. It's like a chemical reaction. Xanax plus rakia plus time produces forward motion.

"*Dobre*," she says, and she walks out onto the stage.

When they sing the sewing songs they have to sit down. It seems they can't sing them any other way. These are the songs they sing on winter nights. They sit around in somebody's house, knitting, embroidering next season's aprons, and singing. In the old days the boys used to drop by later in the evening, to see which of the single girls was looking hot. It was like a dating agency at a sewing bee.

According to Lubka it was a good way to get a husband, because if you married a local boy you could stay in the village and be able to see your mom every day. There's no accounting for taste. If nobody local made you an offer then you'd have to marry "out", maybe go miles away to some other village, to some guy you hardly knew and move in with his folks. Kind of like Dorothy did. She and Les had a room with the Lufts in Kittanning when they were first married. All in all it sounds like Gorni wasn't a great dating scene, although Lubka says it isn't like that now. She says the kids are out of there the minute they graduate high school, off to the big city so they can do their own thing. Darn tootin'.

The chairs are in a little semicircle and they sit feet planted, knees wide apart. It's a good thing they wear those long, droopy skirts otherwise the front stalls could be getting more than the doctor ordered.

They sang "Beautiful Nedelya", "A Golden Apple" and "Go Down, Bright Sunshine". It's the second time I've heard "Go Down" and both times something weird has happened, like I was *this* close to tears. It could be something to do with the way their voices collide. I should look into that. Somebody probably wrote like, a Ph.D on it. Or maybe I just need a vacation.

They segue into "Trees in the Forest" and then Lubka stands up, the other four follow suit and they all pick up their chairs and walk off, still singing. I had to turn them round and make them go back on for their applause, and they looked so surprised. I think they'd genuinely forgotten there was an audience out there.

We're in the break and they're all drinking canned soda. The dressing room door opens and in walks this woman, shoulder-length hair with bangs and a centre part. As soon as Lubka sees her she starts shouting "Daktar Gven! Daktar Gven!" and then they're all hugging and kissing and blabbering away in Bulgarian. Kind of rude, if you ask me. You know? What am I, the fucking coat rack? This is Dr Gwendolyn Robertshaw, ethnomusicologist, fluent Bulgarian-speaker and strong candidate for a tit lift. A woman who thinks she owns the Gorni Grannies. *My* ladies, she calls them.

She said, "I saw the item on *Eastward Ho!* this evening and I must say I was very disappointed. One shouldn't trivialise these disappearing arts."

I said, "It was a great piece. Barefoot Bulgarians singing their hearts out. The cry of the birds, the howling of the wind. It was pure theatre."

She said, "But we must take this singing seriously. Do you realise how rapidly this tradition is dying out? Television is quite killing it. And of course you gave out completely inaccurate information about the song. It was a weaving song. Nothing whatever to do with Mother Nature."

I think it was the donkey she didn't like.

I said, "Well Gwen, this is show business. These girls are here to sell albums and fill theatres."

"Oh dear," she said. "I do very much hope you're not going to ruin them."

I said, "Were you out there just now? The audience loved them."

"Yes," she said, "but what does the audience really know? It takes years of study to understand this music. And Lubka, why aren't you wearing your *kindouri?*"

Lubka says, "I like this Crocs shoe. You don't like?"

"Not for singing, Lubkochka," she says. "Not for the custodian of a disappearing art."

Lubka's got her arms folded across that ample bosom. She's obviously not going to back down over the shoes but I can tell this woman's getting to her.

I said, "Disappearing art my ass. It's here in King's Lynn, whoever would have thought. Monday it'll be popping up in Manchester. It's going from Chicago to California and if Lubka keeps wowing them with her legwear, it'll be back next year."

She said, "But the purity of it will be lost. I shall reproach myself if I see commercialisation destroying their culture."

Yeah. If they make enough money from this album to afford an indoor john, that'd be a fucking tragedy.

The Ursari are all wearing red, easy-care shirts, unbuttoned, a little stiff in the armpit area. They might think of freshening them up some time. They start their set with a couple of slow pieces. The dancers do this Cossack knee bend routine, and then they bring out the big white hankies and start cracking them at each other in time to the music. There's just a sax, a clarinet and an accordion playing, but the audience are clapping along. Then they pick up the pace a little and the drums and the trumpet and the banjo join in. The dancers are in a line, each guy holding on to the belt of the guy in front, winding into a spiral and out again. It's fun. But it's only leading up to the *kyucheck*.

Kyucheck is the big wedding dance. It's wild and fast. The tens are stamping their boots and snapping their hips and shimmying their butts. The bling's flashing, the sweat's flying, the audience are out of their seats. King's Lynn is rocking. Tutrakan are back on stage but nobody's noticed, and then the girls come steaming by me, singing at full throttle before they ever reach the stage. It's war. It's like Pickett's Charge and Zveta's voice is the cold steel. How her husband ever had the nerve to smack her I don't know.

It's a great finale, like a sing-off to the death. The dancers are trying to bump everybody else and Lubka's flipping them the bird.

Mal says, "My gran'd like this. I think I'll get her a ticket for the Crawley show."

I suggested inviting the Ursari back to the hotel for a little R&R but everybody else was against it.

Mal said, "They're tired. They just want to wind down and go to bed."

He's such an old woman. He should tour with Spam Javelins some time. The minute they're clear of the arena they're passing the bottle and howling for fresh girlie meat.

I said, "Well I think we should get to know these boys. They look like fun. We can invite the Tutrakan too, if you like. And we can work out some new angles for the next show."

Lubka says, "What is angles?"

I said, "It's things you can do when you're all on stage together. Things the audience will enjoy. Showmanship."

She said, "I will not. I will not do showmanship with Rom."

She tells the others something and they're all nodding their heads. I can't remember if this means "yes, they don't want to party" or "no, they agree with Lubka." Basically, I need a drink.

I said, "Why don't you like Rom?"

She said, "Because all places they go they make big mess *mahalas*. In my country is big problem."

Olga said something to her and she shut up for a while, but she wasn't finished. She kept muttering things, under her breath, and Kichka and Dora were both shaking their head. She was like a dog that was determined to have the final growl.

Eventually she says, "Olga Ilievska says in our country is not any problem, even not Rom. But I think she will not like to live at Lyulin, else Filipovtsi."

Olga didn't bite.

Mal says, "What's in Lyulin, Lubka?"

"Rom," she says. "Is place of Sofia. Broken autos. Dirty childrens. *Naylonova* bags what fly in streets. You must not make party with this Ursari, Buzz Wexler. They must not come in deluxe hotel. They will rob chairs. They will rob all things what can be robbed. Better they go away. Let them go in Canada. There is plenty room in Canada. I have seen on TV."

So I figured this wasn't the moment to pitch my idea of getting a couple of Ursari to come on during the sitting songs and pretend they were checking out the talent. She liked the idea of having some real sewing to play with though.

"*Da*," she said. "We can do this. Else *pletene*. How to say?"

Olga was stumped for a minute, then she got it.

"Nikting garment of wools."

Lubka's running it by the others, about the nikting, and it seems to be going down okay. But Kichka's got a query and what she wants to know is, will they get extra money?

I said, "Here's how it works. If the tour's a success, the album will sell and in the long run you'll get more money."

Lubka says, "I understand this. Kichka worries always of money."

Mal said, "Is she very poor?"

"Ne," she said. "Not poor. Only she will like to be most rich lady in cemetery."

So the party poopers are all tucked up for the night with their warm milk and fresh straw, and I'm lining up the mini-bar bottles, deciding what the drinking order should be when the room phone goes and a voice says,

"I hear you had a good size audience tonight."

Boyko Stoyan.

I said, "Are you going to do this for every show?"

He said, "If I have to. I hope I don't. As well I did tonight though, hunh? What I heard from my boys, the place would have been half empty."

I said, "What do you expect? Just because it's your gran? This isn't exactly U2."

He said, "Company like Comet acquires a property, what do they do, wait for a miracle? Where's the advertising?"

I said, "World Music doesn't have a big budget for publicity. It's a word of mouth kind of thing. And don't give out to me. I took this on because the girl who should be handling the tour is sick. I'm doing this from a standing start and frankly the Grannies are lucky to get me. And by the way, we have a major daytime TV lined up for Monday."

He said, "I know. I'm the one who lined it up."

Men often get aggressive when they're attracted to me. I guess they feel they have to put up a fight. I could tell with Boyko the minute I saw him at the airport.

I said, "Anyway, you missed a great show. They were terrific. No nerves. Well, Zveta did, at the start, but she got over it."

He said, "She's the young one, right?"

I said, "She's a bit shaky. Her husband knocked her about before she left Gorni and I think she's worried he's going to turn up for Round Two."

He said, "You want him fixed?"

I said, "He's in Gorni."

"So?" he says. "I can still get him fixed."

Then he said, "The rest night, when you're in Burnley? You got any plans? I thought maybe dinner?"

I said, "Sounds good. Where?"

"My place," he says.

I'm just thinking wow this guy doesn't waste time when he says, "Salford Quays across from the Copthorne. It's called Baba's North, red and white awning. Tell your drivers to park at the Lowry Outlet Mall. They can come in if they like. And Comrade Interpreter. It's all on the house."

Five grannies, two drivers, Nosh and Vilk for sure, Olga, Mal. Not exactly a tête-à-tête dinner, more a group excursion. We could invite the Ursari too and the Tutrakan guys. We could invite the national football squad. But I know interest when I smell it. Boyko is definitely flirting with me.

I said, "Baba's North?"

"Yeah," he says. "I named it for my gran. It's country-style Bulgarian. I've got one in London, the original. Baba's, in Fulham Road."

I said, "Is it dress up? Casual?"

He said, "We don't have a jacket policy but personally I always wear a suit. It's a question of self-respect."

I knew it! He's just an old-fashioned grandma's boy. I'll bet he gets his shoes shined too.

I said, "I thought you were in security? I thought you were in insurance?"

He said, "There's a lot of opportunities in the world. I take them where I find them."

Message received and understood.

I get off the phone and I'm stripped down to my skivvies, trying to decide whether to shower and watch a movie or take a long, hot soak, when somebody taps on the window, right behind where I'm standing, just about gives me a fucking heart attack. I mean. I put the light out and then I can see him. It's the Ursari boy, one of the Tens I gave my card to. He's grinning at me and pointing into the room, wants me to let him in.

I opened the window and I'm trying to explain that I have to get my kit back on and come round to the entrance, that I'm going to have to sneak him in past Reception. He doesn't have a word of English. Then I'm groping around for a pair of pants to pull on and there he is. Up, over the sill and in. If you get my drift.

He was in great shape, not jacked, but lithe, like an alley cat. Black curls, awesome eyelashes. Just a kid in a big hurry really, still in his sweaty shirt and his Cuban heels. I didn't quite get his name. It could have been Chavo. He didn't even stay for a little nightcap. When we were done he was up, over the sill and out. Which is cool with me. Sleepovers can be a real bore. You wake up, want to get on with your day and there's this adolescent starfished under your comforter, refusing to wake up. If he's house-trained you have to share the bathroom. Well, I share my bathroom with no man. Frankly I'm glad he didn't hang around. I just hope Lubka didn't happen to be looking out of her window when he left.

So, Felix. Pushing it, am I? Showing signs of desperation, wasn't that what you said? Wrong, as usual. I still have what it takes. I can still pull. I can *so* still pull.

CHAPTER
FOURTEEN

Already we did depart from official schedule. Instead television interview in historic market of King Lynn we have gone quickly in ocean resort of Hunstanton, reason, disaster of oil tankard. Buzz Wexler have not explained me how this is concern of Gorni Grannies. Thus it was not blame of Jerry Driver if I have remained in mikrobus for pleasantries with him. If Buzz Wexler have explained me Lubka Lilova will make television interview in this place, I will have assisted. I am professional. Even I will go in sands with smart courtshoe. Without my assist I believe Lubka Lilova did make many errors of English. Also guards of Stanka Stoyanova have hoovered with dunkey in back ground at this interview. It was not their roll. It was roll of interpret, not of protectives.

Balkanalia! show has made satisfactory beginnings in city of King Lynn. It is not so pretty as spectacles of State Ensemble with beautiful costume but it may be audience will not care. English people does not enjoy elegant attire. Only they wear bluejean, perhaps with stains else wholes. Exception, Queen Elizabeth, monarch, who does not.

100

Suddenly has arrived at Corn Exchange Theatre many lackeys of Boyko Stoyan. I do not like this Boyko Stoyan. He is not good ambassador of Bulgaria. Only he has money. How did he get this money, I must ask my own self? I do not enjoy my replies. Jerry Driver also does not admire him. "Olga," he did say, "Boyko Stoyan is big winker."

Stanka Stoyanova says he is no-problem grandson, makes good import-export business in London. She says all is well except he have not yet found nice Bulgarian wife. Thus she have brought him many Bulgarian snicksnacks, examples *banichka* of spinach, also wall nut with frosting. She is old lady. She does not understand what person this Boyko can be. Only I will say she is more advanced than Lubka Lilova who has only forty-six years.

Lubka Lilova has incorrect opinions of Bulgarian Socialist Party. Also she makes sign-of-cross. Since 1945 this primitive behaviours was removed from Bulgaria but now they do return. When Lubka Lilova has arrived in hotel room, instead admiring modcons and pleasant view she have searched for place to make ikons corner. This is religion custom of yesterday year. I have explained her we will go in many different hotels. It is not possible to make ikons corner there and here.

She have said, "*Ne*, is possible. Without ikon of Mother of God, I do not sleep. I will give you ikon, Olga Ilievska. Ikon of St Olga of Kiev. I will buy with money of Gorni Grannies world tower."

But I have told her, I do not wish ikons. Give to Buzz Wexler who have said ikons is neat. This is colloquial word. With Buzz Wexler I hear many new words. As international interpret I like always to make advancement.

Then Lubka Lilova have said, "For sure I will give. Also to nice Mal Cleaver. I will give Holy Trinity ikon. I cannot give name saint. In Bulgaria we do not know this Saints Buzz and Mal."

Howandsoever, Lubka Lilova has not found ikons, even in worldknown Woolworth store. This is because United Kingdom is modern country, without trapping of old-lady believes and non-logical thought, example Holy Trinity.

Buzz Wexler is not healthy person. She wears sunshade glasses even in loungeroom of hotel. For breakfast she eats only candy bar and smokes mentholslims cigarette. Also she does take many tabletki. One tabletka she have given also to me but I have telled her, I do not need. I have no pain.

Then she did say, "Is not for pain. Olga, I observe you enjoy to eat hamburg and ships. I will advice you, with this pill you can be thin as me, also enjoy life. What size is your bottoms?"

My bottoms is 120 centimetres. In Bulgaria is recommended size. I will not take medication. Then she have asked me to tell her age. This is perhaps English partyquiz but I did not like to play this quiz because I did not know correct answer.

I have said, "Perhaps you have forty-five years."

She have replied, "Fug you, Olga. Look this all-new neck. You know how much this neck?"

Buzz Wexler is American person. She lives many years in United Kingdom but for new neck she returns in America. I have read of this procedures. Also is possible new bosoms, very large, but Buzz Wexler did not get this.

She have said, "We must stay young and beautiful, Olga. In my business, is dog eat dog."

In Bulgaria we do not eat dog.

CHAPTER
FIFTEEN

King's Lynn to Burnley, Lancashire is some trip. I never realised anywhere could be so far in this country. We even had to cross a kind of mountain ridge. Mal says they're called the Pennines. He's in a very happy mood. He began the journey reading to us from his book of useful Bulgarian phrases.

Molya, populneteh tozi formoolyar — kindly fill in this form

Nyakoy meh presledva — somone is following me

Surbee — it itches

Seegorno shte she opravite slet nyakolko dnee — it should clear up in a day or two

Mozheh lee da mee vurneteh pareeteh — can I get a refund?

Eemateh lee drook tsvyat — do you have it in another colour?

Then as we got into wilder country he started spotting birds.

He shouts "Magpie!" The girls shout, "*Svraka!*"

He shouts, "Goldfinch!" They shout, "*Kadinka!*"

Lubka said, "I like this England."

I said, "You have mountains like this back home?"

Olga says, "In Bulgaria we have mountains of three thousand metres. We have Rila mountains and Pirin mountains, also Sredna Gora and Rhodope. In Bulgaria we have all categories of great natural beauty."

Lubka said, "But we do not have shoes of this colours."

She loves her lime green Crocs. She should buy more. I'd like to see her get four or five different colours. When you find something you like, you should snap it up. She may never get another opportunity like this.

In Gorni, she tells me, they have just one store. It sells flour and beans and stuff, brooms, nails, tobacco, like something out of a cowboy movie. Anything else you want, you have to take the bus to Sofia. It's not far but it seems like it's a big deal. Lubka goes once a month, to buy knitting yarn for her Aunt Mara and magazines for herself. There's a coffee shop in Gorni but it's part of the general store, a little counter inside, a couple of tables outside, and it sounds like it's a guys-only kind of place. The old-timers hang out there while the women are picking up the house or if it's too wet to work in the yard. Not that there are that many guys in Gorni. If they're young they leave and if they're old they die. Sometimes even before they're old. Lubka's Lazar died seven years ago and he wasn't even fifty.

She said, "Is all right place, only there is not work for young peoples. You will see. You will come in Gorni for vacation. Stay in my house. We will make jolly party."

I hate to disappoint you, Lubka, but Hawaii's where I'm going. Kapalua beach here I come.

This is Lubka's day: she's up at six, lights the furnace, makes tea, strip-washes at the sink, gets dressed, feeds the hens, checks for eggs, picks up a can of milk from Dora, then she walks to her Aunt Mara's place to work in the vegetable garden. They grow beets, potatoes, cabbage, bell peppers, eggplant, tomatoes, spinach. If it's wet they do sewing or canning and stuff like that. She eats lunch with Mara, then she walks home and works in her own garden till it's too dark to see.

Evenings, about once a week they get together to sing and they take turns whose house they go to. Never Zveta's though, because her husband likes to watch football on TV, and rarely Dora's because her husband goes into his dying routine if she has people round.

If it's a non-singing night she has dinner on a tray and watches TV. *Columbo*, *America's Most Wanted*, the Cinemax movie. Unless they get a power outage, which seems to happen a lot, in which case she just goes to bed. No car, no telephone. She doesn't even have a bath tub. Wilma Flintstone has more than this woman.

I said, "Maybe you won't stay in Gorni. Now you're international recording stars maybe you'll leave."

She said, "But where will I go?"

I said, "I don't know. Into town, maybe? Get an apartment?"

"Ne," she said, "I will not. I already did live in Sofia. There is too much cars, too much crazy dogs. One time a dog did bite me."

She showed me the scar on the heel of her thumb.

She said, "And if I go away in Sofia who will help my Mara?"

She was quiet for a while, thinking. Then she said, "Will we have so much money?"

I said, "Could be. What would you get, if you could buy anything you wanted?"

Lubka's wish list so far: a button-tufted headboard for her bed and a kerosene heater for her john. So then we went around the bus. Dora wants to get her husband a set of dentures.

I said, "What about getting some for herself?"

Lubka says, "But is enough, one teeth. Grozdan Gavrilov is very old person. Soon he will die then Dora can wear this teeth."

I said, "What's the story? Is there like, a short supply of dentists in Bulgaria?"

Olga said, "There is not shorts supply. Under Chairman Zhivkov dentists was trained to highmost level of excellence."

Lubka says, "Under Chairman Zhivkov there was not teeths brush."

Kichka's desire is for a strip of land that's on her neighbour's property, except she doesn't really want to buy it because she says it's hers by rights anyway. But she might pay someone to put a curse on the neighbour, so he'll give the land back to her.

I said, "You can do that? Does it work? How do you find somebody to do that for you?"

Mal suggests Yellow Pages.

Lubka says, "If you are big fool for sure you can find old *znaharka* what will take money, make curse for you. But better you make contract, buy land and give money to neighbour."

All Stanka wishes for is a nice Bulgarian wife for Boyko. Jerry wants a weekend in some Swedish hotel where everything's made from ice and/or a cedarwood home sauna. Yeah right, Jerry. You think we're dumb enough to rise to that Scandinavia-loaded bait?

Mal said he'd like to go on a cruise to Antarctica but he'd get a Crystal Palace season ticket for his dad first and a home computer for his gran so she could have a Virtual Cat. They live in some kind of project housing and real pets aren't allowed. He says you can get dogs and hamsters and everything. I never heard of that. You can dial up, or whatever it is you do, and, like, play with them and groom them and stuff. Any time you feel like it. That is so cool. I am so going to do that. I'll get a Virtual Snake.

Lubka says, "What will you buy, if you can have any thing?"

Of course, my life isn't like that. I mean, I might go a little crazier than usual along Sloane Street and I might get my nose realigned. But basically, anything I want, I just go out and get it.

Olga says, "I also have all things what I require."

Betcha don't, Olga. Betcha don't have a flat panel TV and home theatre surround sound in *every* room.

I said, "What about Zveta? We didn't hear from her yet."

Lubka says, "Zveta only will like to go away."

I said, "Anywhere in particular?"

"Far," she says. "Zveta will like to go far away from all things."

I should introduce her to Dr G.

Lubka was quiet for a while, looking out at all that scenery. Then she said, "I will change my minds. Instead luxury bed I will get benzin generator. With generator, even there is snow, even there is thunder storm, I can see movies until they are ended."

She's seen bits and pieces of hundreds of movies and her favourite movie she's seen part of is *Pink Panther*.

She said, "I will like to meet this David Nivens."

I don't know. I have the strongest feeling David Niven already checked out. Mal's going to Google him. It's a cute idea though. Like, they'll be doing this Titch Marsh TV show next week and it'd be so neat if they could rustle up some old film star to meet them. Or anybody really.

I said, "Who else would you like to meet?"

She said, "I will think."

Mal said, "Tell us some famous Bulgarians."

Olga jumps right in.

She says, "Todor Zhivkov, First Secretary of Central Committee of Bulgarian Communist Party, years 1954 to 1989. Cosmonaut, Gyergi Ivanov. Hristo Stoichkov, winner of 1994 Golden Boot. Raina Kabaivanska, world — known songster. Many, many famous people of our country."

Lubka said, "If I cannot meet David Nivens I will like to meet most great American, President Reagan."

Ronald Reagan! I mean, wasn't he a bit of a joke? Didn't he dye his hair and stuff? Elvis Presley, now *he* was a Great American. Mom and Dad voted for Reagan but hell, they probably voted for Nixon too. Simple Republican folk. Thou shalt not and all that jazz. When you've lived in New York you have a more sophisticated perspective on the world.

I said, "Why do you want to meet Ronald Reagan?"

She said, "Because he did give us new Bulgaria. He did tell Gorbachev, open this door, fall down this wall. And it did fall down."

I remember that. The Berlin Wall. There was a guy in the Bowery had a sheet spread on the sidewalk, selling these like chunks of concrete with graffiti, supposed to be pieces of that wall. I don't know if they were for real. I should have gotten some though. They'd probably be worth something now.

I said, "Okay, so the Berlin Wall came down. What good did that do you?"

She said, "Then Zhivkov did run quickly away."

Olga didn't like that.

"Is not true," she says. "Chairman Zhivkov was already olderly person. He did already intend he will make his retirement."

Lubka said, "Ne, he went before we did shot him."

I said, "And life got better, after that?"

110

I mean that's like, fifteen years ago and this woman still doesn't have a telephone.

"Now is different," she says. "Next it will be better. Before I am died."

I said, "You know Ronald Reagan's a really old man now. I don't think he meets people any more. Too sick."

Mal's going to check but I'm pretty sure he's in a facility some place.

She said, "Then I am sad. I will like to shake his hands and say him thank you."

Shit, that would have made such a fabulous photo story. *Gorni Granny says Ronald Reagan changed my life.* I'm wondering though. Maybe we can get Nancy.

CHAPTER
SIXTEEN

Lubka's refusing to go to dinner at Boyko's restaurant. She says she'd rather stay in and watch a movie.

I said, "You can't stay in. They don't serve dinner here."

"*Da*," she says, "Is possible. I can have Lite Bite snack before hours of nine. Is better. In Gorni we do not eat big dinner so late. It gives me bad sleep."

I said, "But we'll be having real Bulgarian food tonight. Piggles and kebabs and all that stuff you like. Red wine. Plenty of rakia."

She said, "I have plenty rakia. I do not need to go in this gangster party."

It's the Boyko thing again.

I said, "Come on! Do it for Stanka. It's only dinner."

She said, "I will not. I do not like Boyko Stoyan pays my dinner."

I said, "Boyko's paying for all those phone calls to Dora's sheep. You don't seem to mind that."

She said, "Is different. Dora is old lady. We must be kind with her. She is nice person but she does not understand what is Boyko Stoyan, what is Gogo Stoyan. If she can be happy, let them pay. But I am not old lady. I know what is this Stoyans."

I said, "*I* don't know. What is this Stoyans?"
So she sits on the bed and tells me.

Stanka grew up in Gorni. She was in elementary school with Lubka's Aunt Mara but they lost touch for years. After the war, after everything was shared out and the Soviets got Bulgaria, people were on the move, leaving the villages to find work. Stanka went to a town called Mikhailovgrad, to work in a clothing factory. Which is where she met Danil Stoyan. He was the guy who fixed the sewing machines. They'd both joined the Communist Party, so they qualified for one of the new apartments that were being built, although Lubka reckons they never really took to city life. They always kept rabbits in a little pen in the living room and grew tomatoes on the window ledge, in case of food shortages. Then they had a son, Gyorgi. Gogo, as everybody calls him. He was born in 1951.

Gogo grew up to be a big strong boy, went into the army and won a lot of prizes for weight-lifting. Then he made the Olympic team for Montreal in '76. He didn't win any medals but while he was there he knocked up a Canadian girl and took her back with him to Bulgaria. That was Boyko's mom.

I said, "Is she still around?"

Lubka says, "She is not. Stanka never does speak her name. If she had good brain she has returned in Canada."

After the Olympics Gogo left the army and joined the border police. Apparently this was a recommended career path. Bulgaria took very good care of its athletes, allowed them to get accustomed to life's little luxuries. Came the day they were too old to make the team, they suddenly had a lifestyle to support and working the border checkpoints was a very good way to do it. They gave you housing, transport and a cool uniform, plus you got to carry a handgun and scare the shit out of truck drivers who might be in a position to top up your monthly pay check. Gogo did very well at it. And then when the Berlin Wall came down and Olga's Chairman Zhivkov was out with a boot print on the seat of his pants, everything was up for grabs. So Gogo did even better. Car dealerships, real estate, insurance, bars, hotels. Since 1989 he's had money coming out of his wazoo.

Lubka says, "Even he has farm. Even he grows *shraoos*."

Shraoos. I thought she must mean smack, or maybe coca.

But she says, "*Ne, ne*, not *narkotik. Shraoos* is big bird what can not fly. Tall as man, ugly bird what can kill you."

I said, "We call it an ostrich."

"Thank you," she says. "Yostridge. Stanka Stoyanova has eaten meat of this yostridge but I will not. It can be you will eat this meat tonight, in restaurant of Boyko Stoyan."

I said, "It's not a crime, Lubka, to have an ostrich farm. It's only like having a ranch. Ronald Reagan has a ranch."

She said, "I have heard this. When we go in America I will like to see this ranch. But Ronald Reagan does not have prastitoot. Gogo Stoyan has many prastitoot in his hotels. There is special rooms. There is electric bubbly bath and girls without undypant."

I don't know that I believe this. It seems to me it doesn't take much for a Bulgarian to mistake you for a hooker. Olga thought I was one.

That first night, in King's Lynn, she said, "You do not have hairs of businessperson. In our country only sex slaves has hairs of colour of cherrysoda."

I told her, welcome to civilisation. I pay £150 a pop for this at Kutz. I am styled and coloured by the creative director.

Anyway, Gogo hit the big time and Boyko with him. Envy, I reckon that's all it is with Lubka. She laughs at Olga, but in her own way she's just as bad. The world changed and people don't like it that a guy like Gogo was first out of the trap. He doesn't sound so bad to me. There's a market for this stuff. Like it's all going to go away if Gogo decides to run a soup kitchen and take up golf? Those girls are probably better off in Gogo's hotels than standing on street corners, getting into a car with a psycho and waking up murdered.

I said, "You must admit, they take good care of Stanka."

She already told me how Stanka and Danil only have to say the word and they could have a penthouse at the shore, but they don't want to move. Gogo's had their old place fixed up and that's where they want to stay. She sings, does a bit of sewing, cans fruit, he mends clocks, plays chess with Boyko by SMS. They sound like the Ted and Eunice Wexler of Gorni.

115

"*Da*," she said. "But even most devil fox is nice with his mama."

And that's her final word. She absolutely will not eat at Boyko's table.

Mal said, "As long as you promise to stay in the hotel, Lubka. You mustn't go wandering into town on your own."

Like she might find herself in Bed Stuy. Like she might turn a corner and whoops, she's wandered into the 45th precinct. I mean, Burnley?

I said, "Why not? She can take care of herself."

He said, "It's Saturday night."

And? *And?*

He said, "She might inadvertently look someone in the eye."

Such a drama queen.

Lubka says, "Do not worry of me, Mal. I will not go in this town. I will have ham tost sanvichi, put nightydress, watch movie."

Olga's really going for it tonight. She called me to see if I had nail polish remover and when I dropped it off she had this flesh-colour corset thing laid out on the bed, like Mom used to wear. I didn't realise you can still get them.

I said, "You're not going to wear that?"

She said, "It is our custom. In Bulgaria when we go in restaurant we make smart attire. I will wear cocktail dress of Boteek Mademoiselle in Sofia. For this I must also wear pantygirdle."

Personally, I'll be dressing down. Boot-leg jeans, a stretchy little vest and a great big cloud of Shalimar.

CHAPTER
SEVENTEEN

Salford Quays is Manchester's version of Docklands. They're still building but there's plenty going on. Restaurants, great bars, shopping, a theatre even. The Lyric. There were people streaming in for *West Side Story*. That's where the Grannies should be appearing. Not stuck out in Burnley. Mal says the Lyric would have been too big for them but I'm not convinced. The Burnley Mechanics seats seven hundred and it's nearly sold out, forty-eight hours still to go. We could be turning people away.

It was hot inside Baba's. They broil the meat right there in the dining area, over a big open grill. We walk in and Stanka gets an ovation from the wait staff. How do they know which one she is? Well there's a portrait of her on every wall for one thing, and then they have Boyko directing. She's smiling, shaking her head. They whisk her straight through to the kitchen for a tour of inspection. You get a restaurant named for you I guess you'd want to check they're not serving up any old shit. Stanka's a sweet little soul, never a frown, never a cross word. Every night she kisses me, left cheek, right cheek, I can feel that papery old lady skin. I'd love to be able to talk to her but she doesn't have a word of English.

The help are all guys. They wear a long, loose, collarless white shirt and a red silk sash, like an extra-wide formalwear cummerbund. Boyko's strutting around in a black single vent Armani.

He said, "You're one short. Who's missing?"

I said, "Lubka. She's tired."

Olga says, "Lubka Lilova is undisposed."

We would have been eleven but Vilk and Nosh went off for the evening. I have Olga next to me. She's feeling the heat in her polyester cocktail sheath, sweat beading on her top lip, a flush spreading up her throat. Mal's seated across from me looking at the decor. Cow bells hanging from the beams, carved wooden doodads on the walls and brass chargers, lambskins draped over the mezzanine rail.

I said, "First impressions?"

Confused Rustic, he thought.

The rakia arrived and the appetisers: sour pickles, salty white cheese, *sudjuk* sausage, a kind of eggplant dip, and something called Boyko's Salad which is the usual chopped tomatoes and cucumber but with hot oil. Cold soup, kind of yogurty, with more cucumbers. Then the meat starts arriving. Pork knuckles, lamb shish kebab, goat carved off the spit. It just keeps coming. And once he's satisfied no edible animal is missing from the table Boyko pushes Mal along so he can sit down next to his gran and eat.

He said, "So? What do you think?"

Mal says, "*Mnogo fkoosno.*"

Show-off. Boyko laughed.

He said, "Learning the lingo, are we? Nice touch. Ladies like my gran appreciate it. But I wouldn't work too hard at it, know what I mean? We're all learning English."

I said, "Mal was already in Bulgaria."

"That right?" he said. "In that case he knows it's a very nice country. Beaches, ski-ing, sunshine. It's got everything."

Olga says, "Many site of historic heritage. Also masked revel of spring."

"Yeah," he said. "That too."

I said, "It can't be that nice. You moved here."

He said, "I'm in business. We've got businesses in Bulgaria too but my dad takes care of that end. Real estate mainly, for foreigners. Investment properties."

Mal said, "I saw a programme about that on the telly. About English people buying houses there, really, really cheap."

Boyko says, "You interested?"

Mal said, "Not really. It'd be a long commute. And anyway I'm really, really poor."

I said, "How much are we talking about here?"

Boyko says, "In dollars? You can get a fixer-upper for twenty-five thousand. If you want a beach front apartment I can get you something off-plan for fifty."

He had to be shitting me. Twenty-five thousand for a house? You could spend that on a Rolex.

I said, "Where's your place?"

"Mine?" he said. "I don't have one. I've got some tasty parcels of land, but we've got hotels I can stay in.

Anyway, I'm never there. I haven't been back in three years. Too busy."

He's opening another restaurant later in the year, near Fenchurch Street station.

I said, "Opening a restaurant must be a fast way to lose money."

He said, "Not everything I do is about money. You got to have some fun too. It's going to be retro-Soviet. High-end, lunches only, waiters in Red Army uniforms. I'm calling it Ostalgia. The City boys are going to love it."

I said, "Is there any type of business you're not in?"

"Hey," he says, "there's a lot of me to spread around."

He has very pale eyelashes. I've clocked a lot of Bulgarian guys over the past few days and they've all been dark and sleek. Boyko's got an altogether different look, kind of solid, dark blond, a redhead's skin.

I said, "I guess you get your colouring from your mom?"

He said, "My colouring?"

I said, "Lubka told me your mom was Canadian."

"Lubka?" he said. "What the fuck does she know?"

Never even looked up, shovelling in the rice. He's going to have to watch his weight when he hits forty.

So then they're clearing the animal carcasses off the table and I'm thinking we must be finished, but this is just a breather before they bring on the baklava and the pistachio halva and the gurney-sized platter of watermelon skewered with ten inch, ooh-aah sparklers.

120

I had to go to the bathroom, to lighten the load a little, and I was on my way back to the table when I noticed that Jerry had snaked his hairy arm around the back of Olga's chair and was fingering her bra strap. At which sight I could have blown my cookies all over again.

We get back to the hotel and Lubka's waiting in her doorway, bright-eyed, jumbo rollers in her hair. She must have been listening out for us.

Mal said, "Everything okay, Lubka?"

"*Da*," she says. "Everything okay. But I must tell a private thing to Buzz. Is a lady thing."

Olga was hanging around.

Lubka says, "This night I have seen pornografski film."

I said, "Lubka, you're a surprise a minute."

She said, "In this film there was factory of irons and steels, like Kremikovtsi factory. But it happened there was not work. For all the men what was in that factory there was not work and they were sad. They could not buy glass of beer and they did ask their selves how can we have money? Then came in their head this idea, that if they will take off they clothes, if they will go in a place like Corn Exchange of King's Lynn to make dance without panties, ladies will give money. And they did do this and ladies gave them many quids to see they bottoms. It was English ladies."

Olga says, "In Bulgaria ladies will not give moneys for this."

Lubka said, "I will give. It could be I will give five lev if it is nice bottoms. I like this movie. I will like to see it again."

Olga said, "What is name of this movie?"

Lubka said, "Name is *Full Monties* but you cannot see it. Now it is finished."

Olga said, "Certainly I did not wish to see it."

CHAPTER
EIGHTEEN

Sometimes they just start singing. We'll be in the van and one of them will start up, Lubka or Stanka usually. They don't say anything. They just start, and then the others join in, like the song's a ski lift sailing by and they're hopping aboard when their turn comes. Sometimes they'll be singing, each one in their own little space and then their voices collide in this, like, far-out, harmonic crunch. I love it when that happens. It's like when you bite into a perfect pear. It's like the first blast of some really excellent snow.

I said, "How do you do that?"

Lubka says, "You can learn. I will teach. All womens must sing, else they are not alive."

I said, "I don't know the words."

She said, "Sing without words, sing with mouth very small."

I'm squashed in between Dora and Zveta, Lubka's opposite me. She sings a note, Zveta sings a major second, Lubka says, "Now you. Same sound as Zveta. Follow."

I said, "But I don't know how it goes."

She says, "It does not go. It stays."

It was a song about a girl getting her hair braided on her wedding day. I just kind of hummed with Zveta, just carried the same note all the way through. It's harder than you'd think. Doesn't matter what anybody else is doing, you have to concentrate and stick to your note. Mal said it sounded pretty good.

We're on our way in to Manchester, to the TV studios for *Good Morning, North West* and there's a big discussion going on about what they should sing. It would have been really neat if we could have gotten Dora's sheep on the phone again. People love an animal tie-in. But Lubka says it can't be done, with the time difference and everything. She's says a sheep can't stay in the house all morning waiting for a phone call.

"It must have fresh hairs," she says.

Well excuse me.

I think they should do "Go Down", or the fast one where Zveta goes yip! at the end, but Lubka says it has to be a morning song. Everybody's adding their two cents' worth. Then it all goes quiet.

I said, "So what did you decide? What's it to be?"

Lubka says, "When it is time to sing I will know."

They're something. They've all got their own ideas and the way Bulgarians discuss things is they all shout at the same time, but when it really comes to it, Lubka decides and everybody falls into line. Mother of pearl, I remember one time when Knifey-Spooney were having slight artistic differences, Lil' M ended up in the emergency room.

So while they're in make-up I go out to find an ATM and my Comet card doesn't fly. I try another machine, same thing. I call the bank, I'm waiting in a line for fifteen minutes listening to Johann fucking Strauss and when I get through they say the card has been stopped.

I said, "Who stopped it?"

She said, "I'm not able to say. If it's a corporate card I suggest you contact the company concerned."

Cards get stopped all the time. I wouldn't mind a dollar for every time it happened to me. But I had this real bad feeling, like my knees turned to Jell-o, and the production assistant's waiting to speak to me. I told Mal to call the office.

He said, "Are you all right?"

I said, "I'm fine. It's probably the magnetic strip. Tell them to bike a new card to wherever we'll be tomorrow night."

Tuesday. That'll be Stoke-on-Trent.

The PA says Lubka will be on right after the sports report. She just has to sit on the sofa between the presenters, answer a few questions, and then join the rest of the girls for one song. Whatever that may be.

I said, "Just make sure they get the information out there. Burnley Mechanics Theatre, tonight, seven-thirty. A few tickets still available."

Good Morning North West has two presenters, Susie and Steve or Sandy and Stuart or something, and they're actually, actually married. I mean. Plus, not only do they have matching hair-dos, they're wearing matching sweaters, one of those stripey patterns boring people wear so you might, for like one nano-second, think they have zany personalities. Olga's bent out of shape because she's been told she's not required. Lubka doesn't need her and the Sweaters don't want her.

She said, "It must not be permitted to speak without interpret. Lubka Lilova will make many errors and give out bad names to Bulgarians."

I said, "Olga, this is television. You think people watch this shit to see things go right? They don't. They watch to see things go wrong. The bigger the mistakes Lubka makes the more they'll love her."

She said, "Then I will return to mikrobus. I will wait with Jerry Driver. We will practise our conversations."

I said, "Okay. Just be careful what you say about me. I've got the van bugged."

And you know, for a moment there I think she believed me.

The Grannies are waiting to go on and one of the make-up girls starts whispering in my ear. Am I with the foreign ladies? If so, this is a bit difficult, but she has reason to believe some professional-quality lip brushes have disappeared into a deep Bulgarian Granny bag.

I said, "Let me guess, it was the one with the braided hair?"

I know Kichka cleaned her King's Lynn hotel room out of coat hangers and she pocketed a knife and fork from the table at Baba's.

Make-up said, "There is a lot of stuff lying around. She might have thought things were there for the taking. I don't want to make a fuss or anything but they're my own brushes. They're quite expensive."

So I'm in the green room and I'm watching Lubka on the monitor while I'm going through Kichka's bag. Three lip brushes, two mascara wands, a palette of eye colours, a lycra hairband, three raisin Danish wrapped in serviettes, a clipboard, two ballpoints, ten plastic coffee cups.

Mrs Talking Hair-Do's saying, "We have with us Luba, one of the Gorni Grannies who are appearing tonight at the Burnley Mechanics Theatre. The show is described as a 'mouth-watering musical Bulgarian feast' and we're giving away pairs of tickets to the first three people to call in with the correct answer to this question: Bulgaria, is it a) in South America b) in Eastern Europe or c) in Germany. The number to call is coming up on your screen right now, lines are open till nine fifty-five. So Luba, welcome, tell me, what do you think of the Manchester weather?"

What a doosie. I could do that job. Give me that job. I could do mornings if I had to. I could look great on a couch. I'll bet you get a car service too.

Lubka says, "Thank you. We have very nice time. Even it does rain, we are happy. At Burnley we have made visit in famous beer factory. We have T-shirt, can of beers and photo with boss. I do not know why he liked this photo. Perhaps Gorni Grannies is already famous in Burnley."

Mr Stripey Sweater says, "Of course you are. You're on *Good Morning North West*. Now, you're all ladies in your singing group. Do you ever get any gentlemen asking to join?"

Lubka laughed. She said, "They will not ask. They know they cannot."

He says, "You wouldn't get away with that in England, you know. That's what we call sexual discrimination. Equal opportunities."

Lubka says, "In Bulgaria also we have this, but still they cannot sing our songs. Even they come, bang down our door. Even they sing in our window we will not have them. Mens can do different music, what ladies does not do. They can blow trumpet, else play *gudulka*. To sing our music they must listen to voices of other persons. Mens cannot do this. Only they can hear 'how great singer I am, how big sexy man I am'."

You can hear the cameramen laughing.

Mr Sweater says, "Controversial stuff. Any gents out there got anything they'd like to say about that, give us a call . . ."

But Lubka's in full flow.

She says, "In this country we find ladies does not sing so much. How can English lady cut her grasses, when she does not sing? How can she make a naughty cattle go in its house? This is question to us."

It's a funny thing about Lubka. She's got this seriously bad home permanent and she needs to drop two dress sizes, three even, and yet she glows. The camera loves her. The producer loves her, the Hair-Dos love her. But it's time for the song and they only have time for two verses of "Roosters are Crowing" because we're going live to Cheadle Hulme for an attempt at a new world record for a bubblegum bubble. Twenty-three inches to beat.

Mal's waiting for me in the passage to the set and he looks ill; I mean, he looks like he just haemorrhaged.

He says, "Can I have a word?"

I said, "Did somebody die?"

"It's Comet," he says. "We don't exist any more."

It's Starburst. They took us over. That bastard Corcoran knew. He knew what was coming and he let me leave town.

I said, "What about my card?"

He said, "As far as she knows people are getting new cards. The ones who still have jobs."

"She" being Jessica, aka The Muffin Top. Well, *there's* a reliable source of information.

It happened on Friday, apparently. While we were chasing TV crews across East Anglia, unknown to me a wrecking crew moved in on my life. There's this very loud Bulgarian discussion going on about the green-room snacks and I'm trying to establish some facts. Like, who's in, who's out, and why did nobody call me?

I said, "First things first. Did she say anything about me?"

Nothing in particular, he thinks. What nonsense. People always say something about me. He says mainly she talked about the builders being in and that they're knocking down a wall to open up the front office.

So I'm thinking, apart from Madson who do they have in New Trends at Starburst? A couple of nonentities, that's who. No Buzz Wexler in that outfit. That's where Comet's always had the edge.

I said, "If they start rationalising they won't be interested in some chickenfeed intern. It's big people like me they go after."

He said, "Well if they're sending you a new bank card, that's a good sign."

How little he knows. They could just be trying to lull me into a false sense of security. Stuff like this happens in a company, it's like being on a sinking ship. Screw you, buddy. And excuse me if I step on your face. I just gotta climb into this last life raft.

CHAPTER
NINETEEN

Corcoran's phone was turned off and it took me till three to get Madson.

"Buzz, Buzz!" he says. "World Music, how goes it? Still on Planet Earth?"

I said, "Okay, Hunt, cut the crap. What's going on?"

He said, "Oh, nothing much. Only the industry's most exciting merger in years. Starburst, Comet, it was meant to be. These are very exciting times. We're going to be singing from the same song sheet now, Buzz. I'm kinda going to miss our little rivalries."

I said, "It would have been nice to find out some other way. You know? I'm out here doing the Lord's work, I go to the cash machine and find my plastic is declined."

"Oh that's bad," he says. "That's terrible. Talk to Finance. They'll sort it."

I said, "I've been in a TV studio all morning. I have a gig tonight. It would have been nice to get a call, at least."

"Yeah," he says. "Sorry about that, but you know how it is. First the Come to Jesus meetings, then as soon as the news was public everything went crazy. I didn't leave the office till midnight. But look at it this way, getting a call wasn't necessarily a welcome thing. Know what I'm saying? Some people had a long ride home."

I said, "Who's gone?"

He said, "You'll see a few changes. The suits, mainly. There are bound to be casualties. No organisation needs two sets of bean counters, right?"

I said, "What about Corcoran?"

"Dave?" he says. "He's on vacation."

On vacation, my eye. Corcoran's out. Which could be a very good thing for me.

Hunt says, "So, you're on the road again, eh? Albanians, is it? Always out there on the wild frontier, hunh? How's it going?"

I said, "They're Bulgarians, actually. And it's going great."

"Bulgarians, Albanians, same dogpatch," he said.

He's such a lunch head.

I said, "Not even close, Hunt. These Bulgarian girls make a unique sound. The tour's creating a huge amount of interest. Lots of TV coverage. We had star spot on the major mid-morning show for the north west."

"Terrific," he says. "You're really getting into it, I can tell. That's really terrific."

My first impression is things sound okay. If they were canning me Madson wouldn't have taken my call. Plus, he knew where I was, kind of knew what I was doing. That's positive. I think. And if there's bad stuff going down maybe I'm better off out of town. Sometimes, when the ocean gets rough, you're better off staying below the surface, just treading water and waiting for the storm to pass.

On the other hand I wouldn't trust Madson as long as he has a pulse. Even without one. He's the biggest fucking back-stabber in the business. I need somebody down there, reading the bones, keeping me informed.

Mal says, "Did he say anything about me?"

I didn't like to tell him, he's of no more significance to Hunt Madson than a bug on the windshield.

I said, "Relax. The ones who got terminated were told already. We just have to keep an eye on things, that's all, in case of after-shocks. I want you on a train back down there this afternoon. You're going to be my eyes and ears. And anything you think I should know, call me from outside."

He said, "You mean things like the locks being changed?"

I mean things like more bodybags being delivered.

Lubka says, "But why Mal Cleaver must go away? We like this boy. We will like him to stay."

I said, "He has to do something. You'll see him again, when we get to London. Now you and I have to talk about Kichka."

All the way back to the hotel Kichka was going through her bag, muttering, looking for the stuff she lifted from Make-Up. I did leave her the cups and the Danish, but this is a woman who obviously has, like, property issues. I've been through this kind of stuff before with artists. Big M could never go into a store without stealing a Zippo lighter.

I said, "Kichka takes things. Stealing is the word."

"*Da*," she said. "Only it is little things."

I said, "Makes no difference. She stole a chocolate bar when we stopped at the gas station. Mal saw what she did and paid for it, but if he hadn't she could have been in trouble. She has money. What's her problem?"

She says, "I will tell you of Kichka Nikolova. She is crazy person. She did not have good life. Is twenty years she does not have husband. Is twenty-five years her sons will not speak with themselfs. Only she is good singer. Now she is Gorni Granny perhaps she can be happy."

Lubka's only known Kichka since 1991 but her Aunt Mara remembers her when she was a girl and she says she was the best-looking girl in Gorni. I can buy that. She's still got a good face. Kind of chiselled. If they ever start filming Westerns in Bulgaria they could dip her in Ronseal and cast her as a Cherokee.

She was married to a guy called Nestor Nikolov and they had twin boys, Grigor and Nikul. Kichka drove a tram, Nestor was supervisor in a furniture factory in Sofia. And he was in the Communist Party, quite well thought of, which meant they got a nice apartment and shopping vouchers and all kinds of extras. Apparently belonging to the Party made all the difference. Lubka's folks never joined.

I said, "Why not?"

She said, "Because it was bad. It was all things wrong."

134

Which sounds to me like cutting off your nose to spite your face. Hell, if it means you can get the phone connected without having to wait ten years, why not go with the flow and join the stupid Party?

I said, "But surely all those other people wouldn't have joined if it was *that* wrong."

She said, "You think? You do not know."

So then she tells me the rest of Kichka's story. The Nikolovs were doing very nicely, getting all the pork chops they could eat, I guess, and their boys were both in the Pioneers, which would be like Campfire USA with added value, like fast-track career perks. If you were a good little Pioneer you were set to get a nice cushy job when you left school. But then Nestor was caught running some black-market scam on the side and everything came a-tumbling down. Except they gave him the chance to save his neck.

She said, "Else he can lose employment, else he can do special works."

She's whispering right up close to my ear, more Olga-style than the usual Lubka.

"To be *donosnik* for DS. For secret police."

The deal was he could keep his job if he became an informer.

I said, "And did he?"

She said, "It was years of '70s. Bad years. Many spy. In every place is people what listen, people what tell."

I said, "What kind of things did they tell?"

"All things," she said.

People must have been getting up to a lot more interesting stuff in Bulgaria than they did where I come from. You'd have a pretty thin time of it being an informer in Troy Hill.

She said, "Even you are good person, even you did never do nothing bad all your life, people can tell made-up story to DS. They will listen at your walls. They will look in *shpionka* hole in they door and see who comes in your apartment. Perhaps you can have American magazine in your house, perhaps you can give your dog name of Chairman Zhivkov, all this things *donosnik* will run to tell to DS. Then you will be sorry. Then you will have big problem."

But Kichka's husband didn't do it. He turned down the deal, lost his job, lost the apartment, got thrown out of the Party, and Kichka was so mad she never spoke to him again. She still cooked his food and washed his shirts but there was no talking. I imagine there are many married people who'd welcome that kind of arrangement but, from what Lubka heard, Nestor took it very hard. And then, as if he hadn't had punishment enough, the kids got involved as well.

The one called Nikul was expecting to go to college and of course Dad getting drummed out of the Party screwed that. All bets were off. But somebody told Nikul he could safeguard his future if he went to the Pioneers and disowned his dad.

She said, "Many Pioneer childrens did this. They can be teens-ager, else young. They can get different name. Then for mama and *tate* is bye-bye."

136

And that's what Nikul did. He made a statement in front of the other Pioneers, changed his surname and air-brushed his dad out of the picture. Then the other boy, Grigor, disowned Nikul. He said he wouldn't have anything to do with it, because his dad was his dad, right or wrong.

So Kichka and Nikul weren't speaking to Nestor, and Grigor wasn't speaking to Nikul and they kept it up for six years, till Nestor died. I imagine not talking to somebody who's always hanging around your living room must take a lot of effort. His dying must have left quite a hole in Kichka's life but the not-speaking brothers were both married by then so, as Lubka put it, Kichka had new people she could not to speak to: the daughters-in-law. And then it was only a few more years and the Communists were out anyhow, so the whole thing had been pretty pointless. That's bad. That's tragic. You trade your dad for a place in college so you can get an education, get a decent job, then you wake up one morning and the rules have been changed.

Nikul made professor. He teaches electrical engineering, but some months he doesn't get paid. Grigor's a potato farmer. It sounds like neither of them has a pot to piss in. The people who get ahead now are the ones who make their own rules. Guys like Boyko. He probably hardly even finished junior high. We're two of a kind. Too much energy, too much vision for any take-the-test pay-as-you-earn system. That's why we've clicked. He just didn't realise it yet.

Lubka says Nikul and Grigor still don't speak. I guess some things can never be fixed. Look at me and

Dorothy. We hardly speak and my only crime is I turned out to be a high-earning world-shaping phenomenon.

I said, "But I still don't understand why Kichka takes things. She has her Grannies money. Why would she steal plastic coffee cups?"

Lubka said, "Much things is changed in our country. Is new people what has big apartment, has new car. Gogo Stoyan who perhaps was not good communist has all things what Kichka had. More things. She did say to me one time, 'Lubka, now Bulgaria is full with thiffs.' Even she was not happy to make this tour. She is afraid when she is gone wife of son Nikul will come in her house, take cucumber, take best tableclothes. Wife of Nikul Nikolov is professor. Why does she wish cucumbers of crazy old lady? Ne. Kichka is thiff now, to be like rich people. But always she was crazy. To be good communist you must be crazy. I did tell her, 'Kichka Nikolova, if you do not come in this tour Comet company will give no money. Even they will take back money they already gave.' Then quickly she did prepare her baggages."

So Kichka got thrown off the gravy train. Come to think of it, Stanka Stoyanova probably got her seat. It's a wonder they're still friends. But then, there's nothing flash about Stanka. She's got a pair of blindingly white Nikes Gogo gave her, smart, comfortable footwear for sightseeing, but she hasn't taken them out of the box. I get the impression Stanka would give you the coat off her back. If Kichka hasn't already stolen it.

Jerry says two of his Abba CDs have gone missing. I'm saying nothing. If he finds out where they've gone, Kichka can take the rap. It won't bother her. And if they've disappeared forever, so be it. Even a kleptomaniac can have her uses.

CHAPTER
TWENTY

Now we are in world-known city of Burnley in top-nitch hotel. In this city we see many dark faces, also ladies in robe of Asia. Mal Cleaver says this people are of countries Pakistan and Bangle Desh but now they reside here. He did not explain me the reason of this. Upon our arrival at city of Burnley we have been guests of fabled beer factory. There we have enjoyed welcome drink and explanations of beer manufacture, very interesting.

Last night there was not spectacle, but evening of repose with Bulgarian dinner at restaurant of Stoyan family with candel and gay tableclothes, very suggestive. Thus Buzz Wexler have acquainted herself with typical dishes of our country, examples, salad of tomats, *shashlik*, spit of goats, roll of pig with insides. For this we have been guests of Boyko Stoyan, grandson of Stanka Stoyanova. Except only Lubka Lilova did not attend. For her own motives she have remained in hotel of Burnley.

Lubka Lilova makes bad names of Boyko Stoyan. I also have had this bad opinion but now I am reinsured. Boyko Stoyan is gone-ahead business person. He has already many enterprises, example, to sell characteristical houses of Bulgaria to English persons. Perhaps I will speak with him of opportunity for high level interpret.

Zveta Borisova have asked him, "In England I observe there are black people and brown people. Will these also come in Bulgaria?"

"It could be," he have replied. "If they have moneys let them come."

Then Dora Gavrilova did ask him, "Why do you do this? Let English people stay in their own houses."

He have replied, "In Bulgaria we have many houses what are empty. Youth of Bulgaria go away. They will not live in this houses. But English persons will pay good price, even for house without roof. In this way Bulgarian people will have money, can buy nice apartment. Perhaps you also would like this, *Gospozha* Gavrilova."

Kichka Nikolova have wished to know how much money. She has house of five rooms, also with barn and vegetables garden. Boyko Stoyan says this she can sell for thirty-thousands lev. Buzz Wexler have asked how much is this. In dollar is twenty-five thousand.

Then Zveta Borisova have whispered many things with Boyko Stoyan.

Kichka Nikolova did say, "Do not sell your house, Zveta Borisova. In apartment house where can you grow cucumbers?"

Dora Gavrilova have said, "I know why these English come in Bulgaria. I have seen their houses. In England houses are stuck together without fields so they do not have places for their sheeps."

Boyko Stoyan have replied, "English do not keep sheeps, except they are farmers. Most also do not grow cucumbers. They go in Sainsbury Superstore for this things. English buy Bulgarian houses to make vacations. Some go in Varna, for Golden Sands, some go in Bansko to make ski-ing vacation. Also some enjoy to repair fallen down houses. It is English custom. For sure some will come in Gorni, for beautiful sceneries."

Kichka Nikolova have said, "I will not sell today. I will wait. It may be I will get more than thirty-thousand lev."

Now I will write of my secret. At Stoyan restaurant Jerry Driver did sit next me. He have said, "Olga, I will sit with most beautiful woman in this table."

Jerry Driver is at fifty-one years but he does not have wife. One wife he did have but she returned with her mother. Another wife he did have but she was no-good wife what spended his moneys, also went with men. This can happen. Marriage is out-of-date institute.

He is high-rank driver with many famous stars, examples Harry Nillson deceased, Nana Mouskouri, Sweden songsters Abba. Because of this he has respect of my career of top-level interpret. Perhap he will like to learn of my language. Who can say what Bulgarian star he will ride in future to come?

At ending of dinner he have said, "Olga, how you are handsome lady. I will like to know you very well."

I have replied, "After tower of Gorni Grannies perhaps you will come in Bulgaria. I will show you my country. There is much to admire."

Then he did whisper, "Perhaps I will come in your room this night. Perhaps I will admire your sexy melons."

This is most great secret that Jerry Driver does love me. I will not tell Buzz Wexler this information. It can be she will be angry because he does not love her. She is alone lady. I think she will like to find gentleman nice as Jerry Driver to be her lovered one. Already after spectacle of King Lynn she have asked I will speak to Ursari Wedding Band person, that he will visit hotel bar with her for light refreshment. But this is not my duty. Only I interpret for Gorni Grannies.

"Fug you, Olga," she have cried.

Still I did not do it. Ursari are not as Bulgarians. I think they are not so bad like Lubka Lilova says, but they can be naughty. Buzz Wexler says Ursari dancer has cute buns. Buns is English cake, perhaps with fruits. Lubka Lilova says if Ursari boy has buns certainly he have stealed them from breakfast-buffet of hotel. Buzz Wexler says is not matter of cakes, is matter of sexy boy. This I did not understand. Ursari dancer has twenty years. Buzz Wexler has forty-two years.

Stanka Stoyanova have said, "You are right, Olga Ilievska. Buzz Wexler is too young. Send me this Ursari. I will teach."

Then all Gorni Grannies have laughed, even Kichka Nikolova who does never laugh.

This morning we did drive in city of Manchester. There Gorni Grannies have attended television show Good Morning! Once more again Lubka Lilova did speak without assistance of interpret and have made many errors. This gives me much worry. How can I give satisfactions if I am not permitted to do my work? Wow is me! I have fat experience of this work but Buzz Wexler does not listen to my advises. She goes here and there and does never sit still. At one moment she has gay smile without motive. In next moment she shouts at Mal Cleaver else Floyd Baggages when they try only to pleasure her.

Today at television studio Buzz Wexler did make many angry messages on mobilfon and Mal Cleaver have observed her with anxious gays.

I have asked him, "Is problem of tower?"

"No," he have replied. "Is no problem. Only it can be in Comet company we have new boss."

She did telephone to person called Corkoran but machine did answer. I did hear her say, "I know you are there, Corkoran. Pick up, you fugger."

But he did not. Now Mal Cleaver has departed to London and all Gorni Grannies are sad. He says only he must go in headquarters of Comet to make controls, then he will return with us. I hope he will come. When Buzz Wexler angers herself only Mal Cleaver can speak with her.

Jerry Driver says she is crazy druggy head. He wishes new Comet boss will her give her sacks (colloquial expression), then we can complete Grannies tower in peas. Howandsoever, I can be sorry with her. She is decadent product of rotten capitalist system.

CHAPTER
TWENTY-ONE

I'm in a thrift store trying to keep an eye on Kichka when Mal calls me with his first report. There's traffic noise. He says he's calling me from Soho Square because it's not easy to talk from the office.

I said, "Why, did something else happen? Are people listening in?"

He said, "No, but everything's being moved around. A lot of the phones are unplugged."

My furniture's in the corridor. I would take this to be an unambiguously bad sign, but The Muffin Top told him I'm being relocated upstairs. Which could be very good news if only the information came from someone who had the faintest.

I said, "Where upstairs?"

Third floor. That's okay.

I said, "Is it a corner office?"

I could be getting Corcoran's spot. That would be excellent.

He said, "I haven't actually seen it yet."

I said, "Then go see it, Mal. Go right now. What are you doing down there? I hope you're not wasting time covering your own hide?"

"No," he said. "But if you lose your job I'll lose mine."

I said, "Likewise if you feed me information from the Muffin Top without checking it for bogosity. I want the facts, Mal. Who's gone? Who are the new faces? Are there any messages for me? Did you check my mail? And make sure my Donna Karan trench coat is safe. I left it hanging in my office. And while you're upstairs, Dave Corcoran had a great leather recliner I could use, kind of tobacco brown. Put my name on it before Hunt Madson grabs it."

He said, "I'll call you again later. How are the Grannies?"

I said, "They're stripping a place called Quids In like a storm of locusts."

Lubka is their shopping maven. Where she leads, they follow. Stanka got Betty Boop socks, Kichka got hair ornaments. She tried to trade her complimentary brewery T-shirt for some other stuff she wanted but when the store insisted on hard currency she settled for one pound's worth of sparkling barrettes. Dora got a party kit with rabbit ears on a headband. The ears are meant to flash except the battery wasn't included but she doesn't seem bothered, and the edible panties came as a surprise bonus. Frankly I think it was the circumcised chocolate wieners she bought it for. I tried to explain what it was all about but I don't have a lot of confidence in Olga. Over here they call a bachelorette party a hen night. This was probably too much information because she got it into her head it's something to do with chickens. God knows I tried. I never got into these kind of dead-ends before, not even with Lime Twist, and their speech centres were pretty much burned out.

Lubka got a pink cowboy hat to go with her second pair of Crocs, leg-warmers, a pair of zebra-stripe leggings and a pack of bendy drinking straws. Eccentric, but okay. Some of the other stuff in her basket I just had to challenge. The scented kitty-litter tray liners? I mean, I never was in Bulgaria but I imagine kitties in Gorni would be made to like, do what they have to do outside. She put them back on the shelf.

She said, "Instead this cat toilet I will buy another angle-warmers for my Mara."

Then there was the pregnancy test kit.

She said, "Is not good price?"

I said, "It's a very good price. I just don't think you need it."

She listened carefully while I explained. And the can of WD-40 penetrating oil?

I said, "Do you know what this is?"

She said, "I do not know but it costs one quids only. It can be useful."

I said, "It's oil. For metal. You understand? Not for skin. Not to drink."

Last thing I need is a trip to the emergency room with these lunatics.

"*Da*," she says. "I understand. I will not drink. But baby test I will buy. In Gorni we do not have. It can be interesting souvenir."

Olga bought a discounted bottle of Mustang aftershave.

I said, "You do realise that's a man's fragrance?"

"Yes," she says, very crisp.

Fine. Just checking.

Jerry comes looking for me.

He said, "Okay with you if Floyd drives the bus tonight?"

I said, "You got a date?"

He said, "Yeah, well."

Floyd didn't mind. He said, "Fine with me. Let Jerry have the Love Wagon. Matter of fact he's welcome to it. It's not smelling too fresh. Soon as we get to Stoke I'm hosing it down. I'll sit backstage with the big boys tonight."

He's got a card game going with Vilk and Nosh.

Olga says, "Perhaps this night you do not need me at theatre?"

I said, "Sure. Perhaps we don't. I hear you have a date?"

A shy little smile.

She said, "Jerry Driver will like to take me in gourmet restaurant. Is okay?"

I said, "It's fine with me."

Not my affair if she wants to get it on with a loser blubbernaut.

"Thank you," she said. "I can ask you one thing? For this restaurant I shall wear smartsuit else cocktail gown? Please, I like your opinions."

Monday night, Burnley, I felt she could dress down a little, maybe the flared pants, persimmon jersey leisure two-piece and a high security padlock on her garter belt.

The Tutrakan boys were at the theatre ahead of us. They'd spent the afternoon in a bar and two of them were asleep in their dressing room, didn't even wake when Ioan started warming up his goat pipes. The Grannies don't warm up. They put on their aprons and their babushkas and just sit around shooting the breeze. Dora has a quick word with her sheep, then she gets back to her nikting garment of wools. Kichka's sorting coins into separate piles, sterling and Bulgarian: one lev buys you forty p, five stotinki buys you zip. Lubka and Zveta are studying the make-up adverts in a magazine.

Lubka says, "For television show at Manchester our faces was beautiful with made-up. We have had pink lips, same like yours. Now it is disappeared but yours is not. How you can do this?"

Well of course I have permanent lip outline. Also permanent eyeliner and a monthly lash tint. Most women aren't prepared to commit to that level of maintenance but I'm not most women. And when you're an awesome babe on the run you don't have time to keep digging into your purse for sordid little palettes.

I said, "Tomorrow we'll buy you lipstick."

One of the runners went to see if he could rustle up some lip colour for the show.

"*Dobry*," she said. "I will like to have this pink lips every day. Also Zveta will like to have."

Half an hour to curtain up and the Ursari haven't arrived. The stage manager's a bit tense.

I said, "I wouldn't worry. It was exactly the same at King's Lynn but they turned up in their own sweet time and they put on a great performance."

One of the stewards says, "I know for a fact they were in town last night. They got chucked out of Yates's Wine Lodge and Paradise Island."

Another ten minutes passed and the theatre was filling up nicely. Zveta seemed all right but I made her take a Xanax anyway. Boyko came round with a bouquet for Stanka, cellophane wrapped and taller than she is.

He said, "I saw a tape of the *Good Morning* show. Why'd you let that Lilova woman do all the talking?"

I said, "Because she's good."

He said, "They should all get a turn. My *baba* could say something. You've got an interpreter."

I said, "I've got Olga."

He says, "She no good? Fire her. You want me to deal with it? Say the word and she's on the next flight home."

But I couldn't do that to Olga. She's great value. What she does to the English language, you could pay top dollar and not get entertainment that good. And hellfire, *somebody* has to graduate bottom of the class.

I said, "How many seats are you filling tonight?"

"First two rows of the Grand Tier," he said.

I said, "Where do you find all those guys?"

He said, "I know a lot of people."

150

I said, "Are you an agent for Slav walk-ons?"

He laughed.

"Not Slavs," he said. "Balkans, if you don't mind. Catch you later."

I thought, "Whatever."

Then the Ursari came piling in, the same red shirts, and it was the darndest thing but when I looked them over I couldn't be absolutely sure which one had been my Friday night hook-up. There was one who gave me a real icky smile but he was an old lizard. It definitely wasn't him. The Tens did look at me but it was as if they never saw me before. I swear there wasn't a flicker. Which is weird but, like, totally cool with me.

It was a pretty good show. A bigger house than King's Lynn, but the audience was a bit muted. I blame the Ursari. Two rest days with nothing to do but get wasted had kind of reduced their wattage. But my girls were terrific. Zveta led them on like she'd done it a thousand times and they looked so kind of *authentic*, with their sewing in their hands for the sitting songs. Lubka found something extra too, especially when they sang "Trees of the Forest" and "Go Down". It's not that she'd been working on it. They never practise, never try out a new riff. As far as I can make out they'd no more think of talking about it than they'd discuss breathing.

I said, "You sounded great tonight. Did you have a shot of rakia before you went on?"

"*Ne*," she said. "Else it was Mother of God helped me, else it was this nice pink lips."

We just got back to the hotel when Mal phoned. He'd found my trench coat, nobody knew anything about Corcoran's leather recliner, and the only message I had was a voicemail about Mach 10's Far East tour.

I said, "I get the feeling you're throwing me crumbs. Tell me about my new office. Did you take a picture?"

He said, "I thought it'd be better if I told you about it first. Jessica was right, it is on the third floor."

I said, "And does it have good light?"

He said, "It has one of those overhead strippy kind of fittings."

I said, "I'm talking about windows, Mal. Does it have good windows?"

Silence.

I said, "Does it have any windows?"

He said, "We could get some of those light bulbs that mimic real daylight."

I said, "What else are you keeping from me? Am I sharing? Did they put me in with the floor polisher?"

He said, "It's not that bad. It's just not what you've been used to, but they're changing things for everybody. It's a different working environment concept."

Yeah. The Insultingly Small Windowless Closet Concept.

He says there's a new girl on Reception, someone they brought over from Starburst, not very friendly, and the Muffin Top has gone to Human Resources. He doesn't know if Hunt Madson moved in yet.

I said, "What about Sasha?"

"Who's Sasha?" he says.

I said, "Sasha's the airhead with grotesquely big chest puppies and a snake tattoo on her ankle. The one Dave Corcoran was screwing."

He still didn't know who I meant. I could wonder about Mal.

He said, "How did the show go?"

I said, "I don't remember. I don't care. All I know is, tomorrow morning I'll be on the first train to London and you better be on the first train to Stoke-on-Trent. I'll tell Olga you're in charge."

The girls have an interview with Radio Stoke's *What's On* at two-thirty followed by a photo session with the *Six Towns Sentinel* in a wildlife park where monkeys roam free.

He said, "Will you come back in time for the show?"

I said, "I don't know, Mal. Depends how many crimes of violence I end up committing. They might not let me post bail."

I went downstairs to buy cigarettes and as I get out of the elevator I hear something, down the far end of the hall. It's Jerry, wearing nothing but a towelling robe, and he's tap-tap-tapping on Olga's bedroom door.

Well I'll be.

So then I shower, pack my bag, order a cab for seven a.m. I'm flipping through the channels looking for a movie because there's no way I'm going to be able to sleep with all this Starburst shit going round in my head and I'm just thinking I'll blast a nice fat rail of primo nose candy and see what's on the pay channel when I hear somebody knocking on my door. Can't be

Jerry, he already scored. Too late for it to be Lubka, too polite for it to be my little Rom friend.

It's Boyko. Tie loosened, jacket slung over his shoulder and a bottle of Odessa champagne in an ice bucket. He has a dimple when he smiles, just on the one side.

He said, "You tired? Only I have a Bulgarian property you might like to check out."

CHAPTER
TWENTY-TWO

I have to say, since the day I quit Pittsburgh, guys have flocked to me like iron shavings to a magnet. I got off the bus at New York Port Authority, I didn't know where I'd be sleeping that night. All I knew was where the clubs were, where important things were happening. I found my way down to CBGB's, crossed Pete Belkin's sightline and the next thing is it's eleven a.m. and I'm in his penthouse wearing one of his shirts and drinking real cappuccino. Troy Hill to the Sherry-Netherland in one move.

Belkin was older than me, of course. I learned a lot from him. He was an ugly little stallion but he had the nose for trends, same as I do, and he knew everybody in the business. Also, he wasn't the possesssive type. Quite the opposite. I should make a list some time, all those guys he recommended I connect with. I should see how many names I can remember.

"Life's an all-you-can-eat, Buzz" he used to say. "Enjoy!"

And he certainly did, till the first coronary.

Calling myself "Buzz" was his idea too.

He said. "An industrious honeypot named B.E.E. Wexler? Sting in the tail? Always on the go, always wired? It has to be Buzz."

I didn't make the transition to younger guys until I came to London. They don't always know they're younger because I look so fabulous, but I know and it works for me. By the time I left New York I'd really had it with guys who had like, bypass surgery scars and kids they had to drive to summer camp.

I never allowed any of my playmates to move in though, not till Dingaling. He was the one before Felix. I mean, I have a certain lifestyle. I have nice stuff. The younger generation can be messy. They don't always understand the value of things. But I reached a point, I couldn't get it on with Dingaling till I'd picked up his room. He'd lie there in his skuzzy sheets laughing at me, calling me "Mom".

He'd say, "I don't get it. What's your problem? You been touring with Feel the Steel. What you told me they don't even wipe their ass."

So I figured it'd be better if he stayed with me because I have maid service three times a week, and then when he moved on Felix just kind of slipped into the vacant space.

Boyko now, he's a whole new category. Twenty-seven, so he's in great shape, plus he made some money but didn't acquire any of the baggage yet. Single, self-supporting and buff. This could be a very good direction for me to go in. He's old enough to be his own man too.

He said, "I can't believe you buy into that Urban Music scene. It's so ugly. It's for kids."

He listens to Harry Connick Jnr. Also he doesn't ingest mind-altering substances.

He said, "My dad did steroids. I've seen what can happen."

I said, "Steroids are *body*-altering."

He said, "All the same as far as I'm concerned. You're fucking yourself up while you line somebody else's pockets."

Fine. All the more for me. Anyway the product I use is totally guaranteed pure. I get it from a doctor for Chrissake.

He's pink and smooth, like a freshly washed, six-foot baby, and he wears a cross on a chain. Bulgarian Orthodox. It's different to the crucifix Catholic girls wear. It doesn't have the little body on it.

I said, "Do you really believe in that Jesus stuff?"

He said, "Let's call it an each-way bet."

Great kisser. I wonder where he learned that?

He was gone when my alarm woke me. He'd snuck away and I hadn't heard a thing. There was just the ice bucket on the night table, with the empty champagne bottle turned upside down. And I was lying there thinking how this Grannies tour thing wasn't turning out half as bad as I'd feared what with the amazing sound they make and Lubka being such a sweet, sunny fruitloop, plus the free Olga and Jerry sideshow and now the Boyko bonus, when it hit me there was a horrible reason I had to be awake so early. I had to catch the seven fifty-seven to London Euston, with no First Class accommodation till Preston. I had to get to the office and see what damage that peckerhead Madson had done to my empire.

CHAPTER
TWENTY-THREE

As I walked in the door I had a bad feeling. It was like I'd been gone a year. There was a smell of sawdust and fresh paint and they'd installed this '50s-look reception desk, red leatherette and chrome, kind of neat. But there's a girl behind it I never saw before, asymmetric bob cut and a tongue stud.

She said, "Do you have an appointment?"

I said, "I'm Buzz Wexler. You're new."

She said, "Who are you here to see?"

I said, "I'm not here to see anyone. I'm head of Urban and New Trends. And you are?"

Her name's Ashlyn. They must have brought her over from Berwick Street so visitors can receive a warm Starburst welcome.

She said, "If you work here you should have photo ID."

I said, "Ashlyn, my name and my reputation are my ID. Now I'm going up to my office."

Next thing there's a kid the size of a meatlocker barring my way to the elevator.

He says, "Everything all right, Ashlyn?"

She said, "She says she works here but she's not on my list."

She's running her finger down this list of names. Twice she goes through it and even I can see, reading it upside down, my name's not there. I'm really dying to pee and that second espresso is making my heart flutter and the ape is just standing there, blocking the light.

I said, "I know you. I've seen you on the door at the Punch & Judy."

He said, "I work for Starburst now."

Like we have some valuable asset that needs guarding. Apart from my considerable talent. Like we're dealing in plutonium.

I said, "I really have to use the bathroom."

The Meatlocker says, "You can see our problem. If you're not staff you have to have a guest pass. For a guest pass you need an appointment. We can't let people just come in here and use the toilet."

I said, "So shall I like, just do it on the floor?"

Ashlyn said, "Is there somebody I can call? Somebody who'd know you?"

Somebody who'd *know* me! And she was so cool. I mean, she seriously had no idea who she was dealing with.

I said, "Okay, get me Hunt Madson, right now."

She said, "I'm afraid Mr Madson's out of the office. He's fully involved all day."

I read a book one time. There was this guy, lived along Central Park West or somewhere, and he went out to pick up the dry-cleaning, came back and his building was like, not his building any more. The doorman didn't know him and his name wasn't on any of the mail boxes. He couldn't even find himself in the phone book. What it was, he'd kind of time-travelled. It was a neat story. I don't remember what happened in the end.

And that was me. Barred from getting into my own goddam building by a pre-teen and an eighteen-inch collar Door Nazi. Omitted from the internal phone directory. A non-person.

I said, "My intern is Mal Cleaver."

She starts going down her list again.

I said, "But he's not in today. He's out of the office, assisting me."

She says, "Well isn't there anybody else? There must be somebody."

She's kind of oozing exasperation. It's like I'm some sad old coffin-dodger fumbling for coins at the supermarket checkout, holding up the line. Except there was no line. Ashlyn is not overworked. Her only role is to make a person's arrival at the threshold of Comet-Starburst as daunting as possible. Whereas when the Muffin Top was downstairs she used to perform all kinds of extra duties: she drew up the coffee spreadsheets and collected signatures on birthday cards. The Muffin Top!

I said, "The girl who used to be in the front office. She breathes through her mouth and her midriff bulges over the top of her jeans. Her name might be Jennifer."

She said, "I think you mean Jessica."

Jessica. Of course.

Five minutes and the Muffin Top appears.

"Hi, Beryl," she says. "Is Ashlyn giving you a hard time?"

She signs me in.

She said, "This is Buzz Wexler, Ashlyn. Third floor. You might get calls for Beryl Wexler sometimes. That's her real name."

The Meatlocker's rocking on his heels, looking out at the passing parade. He said, "She needs to get photo ID. You let people just walk in without ID and use the toilet, anything could happen."

It's a sobering thought.

I said, "You could get a little porta-potty. Have it out here where you can keep an eye on what people are doing. I'll suggest it to Madson."

We go up to the third floor and it's like a construction site. There are carpenters at work and everything is being rearranged in zones. Easy Listening. Movie and TV Tie-In. Spoken Word. I didn't even know we did Spoken Word. And as we walk along people pop their heads up over the panel walls, like synchronised prairie dogs.

I said, "I don't see Urban."

Muffin Top says, "Urban's not here. It's gone to Berwick Street."

I said, "Then no wonder I'm not in Ashlyn's phone book. I'm not up here at all. Why would I be up here?"

She looked at me and for one split second I saw this flicker of something I didn't like. Something close to pity.

She said, "But I don't think you're actually with Urban any more. I could be wrong, but I think you're with World Music now. Mal was in yesterday. Have you spoken to him?"

Did you ever have that thing where there's this loud, like, swooshing going on inside your ears, so every other sound seems very far away, even your own voice?

I said, "Who told you I'm not with Urban?"

She couldn't remember.

When things are in zones you don't get an actual office any more. You get a cubicle. Somebody had put my stuff in those plastic trays, like they have in airport security. Ten years of my life in two trays. There were a couple of old Post-Its that said Dorothy Luft called.

I said, "Who's in Dave Corcoran's old office?"

She didn't know.

I said, "Is Sasha still here?"

Sasha's gone to Berwick Street, to the Starburst outfit. *She's* in Urban Music. But doing what? Making vacation charts with her coloured pens?

I said, "Did she get a promotion?"

The Muffin Top thinks so.

She says, "Did you have a nice time in Bavaria?"

I said, "Did Sasha get my job? What's her title?"

She said, "I wouldn't really know. All the titles have kind of changed. I'm a Human Resources Administration Assistant now but I only started yesterday."

I said, "Close the door."

There was no door.

She says, "It's Starburst policy. It makes for better communications and greater accessibility."

* * *

Except when you're a senior executive with twenty years under your belt and you drop by to find out what's left of your career. Greater accessibility. I'll bet Madson has a door. If he gave Corcoran's little fuckbuddy my job he better hope Chubb made his door.

The Muffin Top says, "I think you should sit down. You don't look so good. I'll get a first-aider. I'll get you a glass of water."

I said, "I never touch the stuff."

Then my hearing came back A1 and I knew the main thing I had to do was get the fuck out of there, away from the smell of new carpet and treachery.

I called Corcoran's cell from the cab. He sounded rough.

I said, "Are you hammered?"

He said, "I'm asleep. It's seven a.m."

He's in Antigua.

I said, "What are you doing there?"

He said, "Considering my future. Trying to sleep late."

Starburst gave him a nice cheque and canned him.

I said, "You knew this was coming."

He said, "No I didn't. Nothing was certain. You know what it's like. There's a different rumour every week."

I said, "You set me up. You manoeuvred me off my own territory, sent me out of town with the Bulgarian State fucking Circus. It was a load of bull about that World Music girl being in hospital. You did it so

164

nobody'd be minding the Urban store and Sasha would just happen to be waiting in the wings."

"No," he's saying, trying to interrupt me. "No. That's not true. Holly *is* in hospital. And Sasha was starting to move over to Urban anyway. We already agreed that."

We agreed bupkis.

I said, "You fucked me over, Dave. You planned the whole fucking thing and I'm going to get you for this."

He said, "I planned what? Excuse me, but I'm the one got kicked to the kerb. You're still employed. So what did I get out of this cunning plan?"

I said, "You're sitting in Antigua spending your severance money and I get the World Music cubicle. You think you got the raw deal? How come it wasn't the other way round? Because you set it up, that's why. 'These Grannies are something special, Buzz. This has got your name on it, Buzz.' Well guess whose name is on the New Trends door now? Sasha Big Jugs. Your little playmate."

He said, "You know your trouble, Buzz? Paranoia. I think you're smoking too much dope. Okay, I was pointing you in the direction of World Music. It was a possible career move. I was suggesting you think about the future, that's all. You know, come that grey day when you wake up and you're fifty? So when Madson offers you World Music you could do a lot worse than accept. Nothing's forever, Buzz. You can't be forty-five and heading Urban and New Trends. It doesn't convince. Frankly, it's embarrassing. And I say that as an old friend."

I said, "I'm not forty-five. *You're* forty-five. I'm an incredibly youthful forty-two."

He said, "And as far as I'm aware you still have a job, should you choose the wise course of giving it a try. Just think about it. The party's over. It's cold outside, baby."

Not in Antigua, I'll bet.

He said, "Calm down, why don't you? You're always going off the deep end. One of these days you're going to get blood pressure."

Not me. Mad suits me. My engine runs on mad.

He said, "I wish you all the best, Buzz. Just don't go to bed angry."

I don't intend to, Dave. I'm going to stay up all night and think of ways to get even with devious double-crossing bastards like you.

I mean, this is so not right. I have more energy than Sasha and all those kids wired together. You couldn't run a flashlight off them. So what do I do? Hurry north, to Stoke-on-Trent, to rendezvous with the Gorni Goofballs? Do I doorstep Madson? Do I eat crow, crawl back past Ashlyn and find out what other gems World Music has in the lockbox? None of the above. First I called Dr G, told him the Mebaral just doesn't do it for me any more and, seeing I'm going through this like major life crisis, could he kindly find me something a little stronger? He says he has the very thing. Niravax. Then I called Howie Schlepper at Store Front, to set up a meet. The Rockwell Bar, three p.m. Topic for discussion: the future.

I don't remember getting home. I do remember I was on my way to pick up the new pills and I made this decision to do a kind of detox, like fruit and carrot juice and stuff for a few days, to get myself looking uber-gorgeous for Pittsburgh and the Urbies. And then I was coming out of Dr G's office and I suddenly thought what if Sasha muscles in on Spam Javelins and I don't even get a decent seat at the Urbies, and I felt so stressed I took a Niravax right there on the street. Then I met Howie. I definitely met Howie. And I think the net of it was he didn't have anything for me. He's kind of down-shifting. He can afford to. He lives with that bitch who starts celebrity real estate trends. She was behind the Wyoming ranch fad, and then some little town in Ireland that's suddenly gone A-list. Maybe I should get into that. I could.

So that was Howie, thanks for nothing. But I know I didn't overdo it. Two spicy melon martinis. Maybe three.

All I know is suddenly my cell's ringing. Mal.

He says, "Are you on the train?"

I said, "What day is it?"

It's still Tuesday. It's early evening and I'm in my own bed, when I probably should be some place else. But I have ringing in my ears plus my tongue feels like a used scouring pad and I have an overwhelming sense of hopelessness so I'm going to stay put.

He said, "Are you all right?"

I said, "I'll see you tomorrow. If I get through the night."

I know I slept some more. I don't know how long but when the phone went again it was dark outside. My cell's ringing and it's somewhere inside the bed. I'm trying to locate it and the ring tone's starting to sound really impatient, then me and the comforter both end up on the floor and I hear this chipmunk voice lasering into my brain.

It says, "Buzz Wexler? Hi, how are you today? This is Dabney Apple calling from the Urban Music Panel. Congratulations on being chosen as recipient of our 2004 Lifetime Achievement Award!"

CHAPTER
TWENTY-FOUR

Lifetime Achievement Award 2004. For once in his life Hunt Madson got something right.

Dabney said, "You will be in Seattle for the Urbies?"

Well obviously. Without Buzz Wexler there can *be* no Urbies. But getting a personal award is different. It's less than a month away and there's stuff I need to do. I'd have liked to schedule a thread lift, maybe get my teeth whitened. Then there's my acceptance speech to work on. She says oftentimes honourees don't make a speech. They just accept the trophy. It's an engraved crystal obelisk.

I said, "Dabney, they oftentimes don't make a speech because oftentimes they're dead. But I'll be saying something, you can be sure of that."

She said, "This is especially exciting for me because you'll be the first ever honouree of the female gender."

Dabney's in for a disappointment if she's hoping for one of those feminist whines from me. I never even knew that glass ceiling was up there till I heard the scrunch of broken glass under my boots.

So now I'm wide, wide awake. People to call. Madson; please leave a message. Dave Corcoran; voice mailbox full. Lisa and Toni; fuck Lisa and Toni. When do they ever call me? Dad; across the ocean in Troy Hill a 1960s ivory dial phone rings out and rings out.

I got Dorothy, eventually.

I said, "I have some news."

"Let me guess," she said. "You're not coming."

So I tell her about the award and all she says is, "That's nice."

Nice? That's *nice*? She's so wrapped up in herself. Plus, she has no idea about Urban. Her idea of cutting edge'd be like, Boy George.

She said, "I hope it won't interfere with your visiting Father."

I said, "I will visit him. I already promised him breakfast at IHOP."

She said, "Well he never mentioned it to me. You'll need to remind him."

I said, "The reason I'm coming is my artists have a gig in Pittsburgh. Five women, all a certain age. They sing. It might be your kind of thing. I can comp you if you'd like a ticket."

She said, "Is it at the Mellon Bowl? I saw Garth Brooks there. Kenny and Janine got me tickets for Mother's Day."

I said, "It's at the Bulgarian Cultural Center. Thursday June 10."

"Oh no," she says, "Thursdays aren't good for me. But Janine might be interested. Depending."

I said, "Depending on what?"

"Well," she says, "things are a bit up and down for her right now. She had a disappointment in love."

170

I said, "You want me to talk to her about men, give her a few pointers?"

She said, "That's a joke. Forty-four and you still didn't find Mr Right."

Even my own sister can't get my age right.

I said, "I've had a hundred Mr Rights. Soon as they turn into Mr Over-rated I move on. And I'm not through yet, not by a long stretch. You can read all about them when I write the story of my life."

She said, "Thank you, I'll pass on that. And if you mention me or Father or Kenny and Janine kindly don't say our names or where we live. We're well thought of and we'd like to keep it that way."

I said, "You think Dad would like a ticket for the show?"

She said, "Why don't you ask him yourself?"

I said, "I will if I ever get through to him. I'm not convinced he knows who I am any more."

"Well bingo!" she says. "That was my point in the first place. He never sees you, so how can he be expected to remember you? He's old, Beryl. And he's out every day riding around with women we don't even know. One of them gets her hooks into him, we can wave goodbye to our inheritance."

Our inheritance.

I said, "Do you mean two and a half bedrooms and a back porch that's been falling to pieces the past twenty years?"

She said, "I mean our childhood home."

She's so cranky these days. I'd have expected she'd be through the change by now.

Mal said, "You sound a lot better. I was worried about you before."

He was so sweet. He said he was very proud to be working for the winner of such a prestigious award and he already feels he's learned a lot from me. "An awful lot" were his actual words. He said he'd get Lubka to tell the others about Lifetime Achievement. Apparently the Burnley show had a nice review in the *Lancashire Telegraph* and he'd asked Olga to translate it for the girls but he was pretty sure she missed out the bit about them *making a refreshing change from the plastic perfection of the old Soviet-style choirs.*

I said, "How did the radio interview go?"

He said, "Brilliant. Lubka asked all the questions. She wanted to know how much the presenter paid for her blouse, had she ever been to Bulgaria, would she like to come, and did she happen to know whether Ronald Reagan still receives visitors? They ran it three times because people phoned in wanting to hear it again."

I said, "And the photo session at the monkey park?"

"Terrifying," he said.

I said, "Did they attack you?"

He said, "I meant it was terrifying for the monkeys."

I said, "And how's Stoke-on-Trent?"

"So-so," he said. "It's a funny place. It's not your average, dumpy town centre. More like several dumpy outcrops in a cluster formation. The Victoria Hall's a really nice venue but it was only just over half full.

Boyko didn't send anyone tonight. It made quite a difference."

I said, "Are the girls upset?"

He said, "About the empty seats? No. I don't think they noticed. Anyway, they're taking away happy memories of Stoke. They've discovered TK Maxx."

He says TK Maxx is a store where you can buy a whole outfit, shoes, bag and everything for fifty pounds, and Lubka did. She wants to wear it for her next TV appearance, Thursday. *The Titch Marsh Show*. She says she's bored with the embroidered apron look. This is how it starts. I've seen it so often. Somebody in the group starts flexing their muscles, the next thing you know you've got five wannabe soloists and the party's over.

He said, "We have to be at the TV studio by twelve-thirty tomorrow. Jerry says he'll get us to the hotel by eleven-thirty. Shall we meet you there?"

We're staying at a place called the Cleveland Acropolis. I never heard of it.

I said, "Notting Hill, right?"

He said, "Kind of east a bit."

The address looks Notting Hill-ish so it could be okay. It could be one of those boutique hotels. 300-count linens, splits of fizz in the icebox, john designed by Alessi. I'd say the winner of Lifetime Achievement is owed a little pampering.

I said, "You know, my bands always stay at the Lanesborough when they're in London."

He said, "World Music works from a different list. I think they like to use places more appropriate to the artists."

Yeah? Like what? Four-star teepees? World Music may be heading for some big changes.

God, I was feeling so up-up-up. I was fit for anything. I got dressed, went down to the gym for an hour, bought a cold Chardonnay from the All-Hours and the set dinner for two from Wing Po with a side of deep fried wontons. The fortune cookies said GO WHERE THERE IS NO PATH, which is absolutely my motto and always has been, and BIG THING WILL COME YOUR WAY, which shortly and weirdly came true because Hunt Madson called me.

"Lifetime Achievement!" he says. "How'd you like that! Congratulations! And didn't I tell you it was on the cards?"

I said, "Hunt, live long enough even you have to get something right. I've been trying to reach you all day. We have to talk."

"Polo," he says. "I was at a polo game. We're looking at sponsorship for next year."

I said, "Well I went to the office this morning. At least I tried to. I'm in the middle of a tour, but I'd heard some alarming reports about furniture being moved. So I was on a train before daybreak practically and what do I find when I get to Dean Street? Grand fucking larceny is what I find. You've stolen my division. You've given it to Sasha, sent it off to Berwick Street without a word and you've moved me to a door-less niche in the back passage of World Music."

He said, "Come on, Buzz, Dave Corcoran talked to you about this, before you went on the road."

I said, "We talked about me, Head of Urban and New Trends, doing him the very great favour of filling in for a sick World Music rep. Five weeks on the road, in exceptional circumstances, end of story. *That's* what we talked about."

He said, "Then you came away with the wrong impression. As far as I'm concerned you *are* our revamped World Music division. It's not an area Starburst ever developed so if we retain it, it makes sense to give it to somebody from Comet. One of the survivors. And that's you, Buzz. You're definitely a survivor. How are the Hungarians?"

I said, "When we get to Seattle you and I are going to talk. We'll do it after I've received the industry's most prestigious award. That way you might bring a little respect to the table. And they're not Hungarians. They're Bulgarians. Know your artists, Hunt. Particularly the ones who just went from nine to seven in the World Music charts."

He laughed.

"Sure," he says, "great, terrific. We'll talk in Seattle. And I'm glad you're being a sport about the award, Buzz. About getting called from the substitutes' bench, so to speak. You know, there are some people who'd say 'Ed Rix sends it back to the kitchen, you think you can replate it and serve it to me? What kind of kick in the head is that?' But I'm glad you don't see it that way. It reflects well on you."

Ed Rix turned it down. So then they call me. The fuckers.

I handled it great, though. I know Madson. He's such a spoiler. He was hoping to flatten me but he just bowled his usual gutter ball.

I said, "Hunt, I don't like to speak ill of the dying but Ed Rix always was a phoney. Anybody know why he turned it down?"

He says, "The way I heard it, Ed described the Urbies as a mutual jerk-off session between a bunch of lowlifes who actually hate each others' guts. It could be the medication he's on."

Some people do see Lifetime Achievement as an end-of-the-line kind of award. Lou Frumkiss got one, he's dead. Alcohol-linked insult to the brain. Baz Napper's plane hit a mountain. Milo Vernon had a perforated appendix. Shit. Off the top of my head Spinks is the only survivor I can think of. They nominate you, maybe it brings bad luck. The Curse of the Urbies. Maybe I should call Dabney Apple, tell her on second thoughts, no thanks. Except. Seeing there's a plot to push me over the cliff, it's going to be a very useful asset. With an award like this I'm golden. GOL-DEN. I can go to Groove or Harmony and name my terms. If that's what I choose to do. Maybe I won't.

Maybe I'll just walk away, do something different. Dragging into the office every afternoon, I mean, who needs it? If you run your own operation you can please yourself. Take calls from bed. That'd be cool. Like, where is it written you have to be fully clothed and upright to make a deal? I do some of my best thinking in the tub.

I did it though. I got it. Lifetime Achievement. So shove that up your butt with a coconut, Sasha. All I have to do now is go to Seattle, ascend the podium, look awesome.

CHAPTER
TWENTY-FIVE

The Cleveland Acropolis is in West Paddington. It has a worn staircarpet, there's some kind of service chute six inches in front of my window and I can only open my closet door if I stand on the bed. Also, there is no bar. I told the girls not to unpack. I'm not staying in a flophouse.

Jerry said, "The thing is, Buzz, your ladies here, they don't expect five-star treatment. I mean, if you've got an artist like Celine Dion, fair enough. That's as it should be. But World Music artists, they don't expect it. Give you an example. I drove that calypso band when they were touring last year. They put them in a bed and breakfast on the Cromwell Road and they were very happy. Perfectly acceptable."

Perfectly acceptable. That's the British for you. You could smack them around and serve them toasted dog shit, they still wouldn't complain. And I don't ever recall giving that preening little douche permission to call me Buzz.

Mal's giving me a don't-beat-me look.

He says, "It is only for one night."

I said, "Oh well then, nothing to complain about. Tell you what, maybe we should all just go sleep under

Waterloo Bridge? Maybe we should just put a great big dent in World Music's cardboard box budget."

Then Floyd wants a word.

He said, "You remember I mentioned a bad smell, when we were in Burnley? Well, I had the whole van valeted while we were in Stoke and the smell went away. But now it's back. As a matter of fact it's worse. So really, that can only mean one thing."

We have a recurring artist-related hygiene situation. Been there before, ticked that box. I mean, when Angry Belgians toured Germany in '95 we had a pet ferret on the bus. I was on the Feel the Steel tour when Headbusta had temporary continence issues. If you're talking front-line tour bus action, I've seen it all.

He said, "Come and smell it for yourself if you don't believe me."

I said, "Mal, go sniff the van."

He said, "I already did. Floyd's right. It's kind of sour. I thought it might be those little leather slippers some of them wear, but it isn't."

They're both looking at me, like suddenly this is *my* problem.

I said, "You didn't search through their luggage?"

"I didn't think it was appropriate," he said. "They are ladies."

I said, "Olga, as soon as they're settled in their rooms I need you to help me check their bags. We're looking for a bad smell."

She said, "I am interpret. Is not my function."

I said, "I'm a senior record industry executive. Is not my function either."

I thought Dora was the most likely culprit, seeing how she wears almost her entire wardrobe every time we travel and she still hasn't totally overcome her fear of Western plumbing. She's okay with ordinary faucets now. Lubka did a lot of work with her on that. But she can't handle power showers. She just does a top and tail in the hand basin every morning, same as she would at home. Anyhow, the smell wasn't Dora. She'd just washed three pairs of bloomers and a singlet and she was sitting in her slip watching *This Old House*. Actually, she smelled of baby powder.

Stanka was relaxing too, chatting on her phone. *Her* room is big enough you can leave the closet door open and still walk around. Very fancy. Boyko must have gotten her the upgrade. She's padding around in her old lady slippers and this, like, totally retro, black and crimson ruffled nylon negligee. It gave me a horrible flashback to something Dad gave Mom for their anniversary one year. Only the problem with Stanka's is she's wearing it with a thick-knit cardigan.

She's beckoning us to come in. "*Edna minootka*," she's saying. "*Edna minootka. E muzhut mee!*"

I said to Olga, "Who's Edna Minootka?"

She laughed. Hey, let's get that down on paper. For the record, Olga Ilievska laughed.

She said, "*Edna minootka* is to say we will please wait one minute. She speaks now with her husband, Danil Stoyan."

Stanka's smiling, shaking her head, trying to put the cell onto speaker phone. She's saying, *"Da, da! E muzhut mee, Danil!"*

Then we hear this old guy shouting, *"Dobur den, gospozha Buzz, dobur den gospozha Ilievska! Kak steh?"*

Olga's doing simultaneous translation up close in my ear. "Greetings, Mrs Buzz, Mrs Ilievska. How ya doin'? etc."

They had high winds in Gorni last night apparently, so Stanka's husband has been on a rescue mission in the tomato patch all morning. His son owns a dozen hotels, his grandson has a fleet of Beamers and his wife's album is currently number seven in the World Music charts but Danil Stoyan remains a man of the earth. And for the record, Stanka's luggage smells of Pour Elle.

Zveta was running a big hot tub, bubbles right up to the rim, tumbler of booze on the vanity. She always looks so wary. You ask her something, you can see her trying to work out what answer you want. But she smells just fine. A blend of apricot rakia and magnolia-scented bath foam.

Kichka was still in her jacket and babushka but she had all her swag laid out on the bed. Sweet Jesus. The clothes hangers, I knew about. The hotel soaps and the shoeshine cloths, the single-serving marmalades, the teabags and the message pads, fair enough, that's what they're there for. The tampons and the condoms she had to have paid for. But the Travelodge fire exit notice? The toilet brush, the three TV remotes, the ten thousand sachets of Sweet "n" Lo and a little china dish of hard mints she must have lifted from the Radisson reception desk? Nothing that smelled cheesy though. Which left only Lubka.

You could smell it the moment she opened her door. Olga said something to her.

She's smiling. "*Da, da*. Come, I will show!"

So we follow her into the bathroom and she has this line of sheer, like, popsocks, strung over the bath and they're filled with some type of dairy product. I guess it used to be milk, only now it has lumps. It's dripping. And it smells.

Olga's muttering, "Is chiz" and Lubka's beaming.

"*Izvara*," she says. "Tomorrow we will eat."

Farmer's cheese.

I said, "Why are you doing this?"

She said, "Always I make for weekend. Very tasty."

You can take the girl out of Gorni but you'll never get all of Gorni out of the girl.

Olga says, "It does not give me surprise this people makes chiz in bathroom of de luxe hotel. In my opinions, better this people stay in their village."

I said, "Okay, Lubka, this has to go. This is a health hazard."

"Please?" she says. "What is hazard?"

Then Olga starts yelling, "*Stiga! Selyanka! Ujasna mirizma! E risk!*"

Lubka says, "Is not risk. Is good of health."

I said, "Then you better eat it before we leave here because Floyd will not allow a cheese factory in his van.

182

Anything you don't eat goes down the toilet and the popsocks go out with the trash."

"Ne," she said, "Is waste. I can wash this knees high. I will wear for next show."

I told Floyd. No more smells and as much farmer's cheese as he can eat for breakfast tomorrow. "Sorted", as they say in London.

"Great," he said. "Thanks a mill. The other thing is, on the drive down I had this funny feeling we were being followed. Not Vilk and Nosh. Somebody else."

I said, "Could it have been the Dairy Product Police?"

He said, "No. It was an unusual number of blokes driving in Raybans. Given the totally shite weather conditions. I wondered if we should mention it to Mr Big."

I don't think so. I suspect Boyko overestimates his position in the gangster food chain. Besides, I'm selling these girls as loveable old nutcases. The last thing we need is Boyko's personal SWAT team swarming all over the next venue.

CHAPTER
TWENTY-SIX

Mal and Olga took the girls to the TV Centre while I did a quick trawl at Benny Wu. He's having a closing out sale before he opens his new Bond Street store and I'm in this complete like, schizophrenic flap about my outfit for the Urbies. Floyd said he'd ride shotgun in the bus, see if we really did have anyone tailing us. I think Jerry was quite hoping we did so he could go into his Crouching Fatboy routine, vanquish all the bad guys and impress Olga.

I'm only an hour behind them but I get to the TV Centre and we have a crisis. Kichka's gone missing. Apparently she'd had a few stomach issues on the way to the studio, she went to the bathroom as soon as they got there and never came back. Security has an all-points alert out for her and the girls aren't due on the set for a while yet, but it's unsettled them. Dora's wringing her hands. Stanka's trying to get Boyko on the phone. Like, what's he going to do? Even Lubka looks worried.

I said, "What was wrong with Kichka? Did she eat any of that pantyhose cheese?"

"Ne," she says, "It can be it was cookies Dora did buy in Stoke-of-Trent. This cookies was not good. I have tasted. Then Dora has thrown away but Kichka does take all things from dustybin."

Then she brings out this package from Kichka's hold-all. Best Friend Gravy-Coated Treats, for smaller breeds.

She says, "Try. You will see. Is not so nice like Jaffy cakes."

I said, "Lubka, these are not for people. These are for dogs."

She said, "But is cookies. Dogs does not eat cookies."

She still doesn't believe me.

Kichka's been missing for nearly an hour. The production assistant says not to worry, an old lady in a folk costume won't get far without being noticed but, worst case scenario, will the others be okay to sing without her?

Lubka says, "Even four grannies is lost, one granny can sing. But we must find Kichka Nikolova, else she will be afraid. BBC is very big city."

The presenter came down to the green room to say Hi. A friendly guy. It turns out his name isn't Titch Marsh at all but Alan Titchmarsh. I advised him to change it. Titch Marsh sounds much snappier. He talks in a funny flat way too, kind of like they did in Burnley though he didn't like me saying so.

"Burnley!" he said. "Bloody Burnley! That's Lancashire. You're talking to a Yorkshireman."

Well, excuse me. I mean, they have so many far out accents in England. When I first came over I expected everybody to talk like Sid Vicious.

He said, "I hear one of the ladies has run off. I don't usually have that effect on women. Who have we got looking for her?"

According to the production assistant, just about everybody from the director-general down.

They were checking the restrooms again when they got a message from the front gate. A woman in an apron had been spotted, acting suspiciously on the Ring Road outside the building. Mal ran with one of the security guys, I followed, and Olga was huffing and puffing behind me, trying to keep up. It's Kichka, no question. She's bending over looking at something on the ground, and the wind is billowing her skirt so we can see her drawers. By the time we get to her she's down on her knees. She's trying to lever up a storm drain lid, and she's gesturing to Mal, she wants him to give her a hand.

It's a simple enough story. A woman retrieves dog biscuits thrown in a trash can by her friend. She eats them, develops a gut-ache and so receives an urgent call of nature. Emerging from the bathroom she takes a wrong turn, because, oh yes I forgot to say, she's in the labyrinthine headquarters of a major TV company where she is due to appear on a daytime magazine show within the hour. Way leads on to way, wrong turn to wrong turn. The woman finds herself outside the building. Does she turn back, mindful of her fellow performers and her appointment before the cameras? No. A keen walker, she trudges on, savouring a rare break in the soft summer rain. Her mind drifts to, well, who can say? A cucumber patch in her faraway homeland? Then something engages her attention, something lying directly in her path. Perhaps, without realising it, she was seeking it all along. They say we're all seeking something. To you, to me, what she's found is a sewer lid, but to the heroine of our story, a woman who has a crater in the road outside her house, it's an answered prayer. And as no one is standing guard over it with an Uzi she assumes it's free for the taking. It all seems perfectly reasonable to me.

Lubka's on the couch with Titch.

She says, "I like your furnitures. In Gorni we do not have so nice."

We should have warned him, with Lubka if you want to keep control of the interview you have to grab the reins and keep her on the bridle.

Titch says, "I know we're going to hear some marvellous singing from the Gorni Grannies. One of the reviews called it one hundred per cent proof woman-power. What do you say to that?"

Lubka says, "Woman power, what is?"

He said, "It's woman doing their own thing."

"*Da*," she said, "we have this custom. Mens tells us bring beer, cook dinner, stitch button. Only we wait till they go asleep or they watch footballs. Then ladies can sing and make jolly party, for their own selves. You have wife?"

He said, "Yes thank you, I do. Now Lubka, when we think of a country like Bulgaria we don't expect to hear about jolly parties and people enjoying themselves. I suppose we still think of factories and May Day parades. All a bit grim. So did you ladies sing during the Communist years too?"

She said, "If you were good comrade you can sing in State Choir. You can sing approved song "How We Live in Paradise". Else if you are anti-state element you can sing real song of Bulgaria. In house of my family we did sing this songs but very quiet, like mouses."

Olga was steaming.

"Big layer," she was hissing. "Lubka Lilova is big, big layer."

Titch said, "I know this is your first time out of Bulgaria. Tell us what you think of England."

She closes her eyes while she's thinking.

She says, "England is very nice place. Very nice peoples. I will say only you have too much noises, it can be of cars, else wagons, else loud music in shopping centre, but there is not singing. I will like to hear singing of English ladies when they go in fields, else when they make new apron but I did not. Where is kitchen of this house? Where is bedroom?"

He said, "I don't live here, you know? This is just a studio. As soon as this show's over they clear everything away and put something else in here."

"*Da?*" she says. "Why they take away? Is nice chair, nice table. I will like to live in this house."

Titch said, "Lubka, tell us what you're going to sing for us today."

She says, "We will like to sing "Mama Did Braid My Hair". Is song of Dora Gavrilova. Tomorrow she is at sixty-five years."

He said, "Happy birthday to Dora for tomorrow. Now when you say it's her song, do you mean she wrote it?"

"Ne," she said. "Is song she did sing to get husband. It was time of harvest and Grozdan Gavrilov have heard her voice. 'Acha!' he have said, 'here is strong worker. Is good plan I will marry her.' He had big land and he was already old man."

She's talking to this guy like she's known him all her life and he's trying to wind up, but stopping Lubka is like stopping an aircraft carrier.

He says, "I'd love to carry on chatting but they're telling us it's time for the song. You'll have to come back another time."

"Da," she says, "is time for song." And she gets to her feet. But she's still talking, back to the cameras.

"Now Grozdan Gavrilov is more old," she says. "He can be dead already, but he is not. Even he does not know what is the day. But in Gorni this does not matter. After song, you will show me where is bedroom, where is kitchen. I will like to meet your wife."

CHAPTER
TWENTY-SEVEN

I'd been looking forward to a little more Bulgarian action while we're in London. Boyko told Stanka he'll definitely be at the Crawley show. But he wasn't in town last night and just as well, as things turned out. I didn't get rid of Olga till nearly two a.m. Boy can she hold her liquor.

First we had a row about the latest TV performance. She seems to think this agency she works for will be checking out every move the Gorni Grannies make, monitoring daytime TV and asking themselves where is Olga Ilievska? Why wasn't she on that couch with Titch and Lubka?

She said, "How I can give satisfactions if you do not allow me to work?"

I said, "You *are* working. Every time I need to explain something to the girls you're working."

"Is not true," she said. "Always Lubka Lilova does interrupt. Always you allow her to make interview full with error of English language, also incorrect history of my country. Because of this perhaps I will be terminated. Perhaps I will be without celery and it will be your blame."

190

I told her she was a lousy interpreter. She said she had testaments from the World Darts Council and the International Confederation of Tobacco Workers. I said she had no sense of humour and no sense of theatre and I wasn't going to let her ruin Lubka's performance which, as a matter of fact, everybody loves.

She said, "Not only. Also, you wear too short skirt. How you can be high echelon business executive? You dress like fruit pastry."

And off she thundered. Half an hour later she came tapping at my door, a bottle of vodka in her hand.

"I am sorry of my words," she said. "I do not like there can be disunderstanding between us."

Me either.

She said, "Mal Cleaver did tell us of prestige award you have winned. It served you right that they did give this. How I am proud at your friendship! I will like to drink toast."

So she comes in, perches on my bed because there's no room for a chair in this fairy shoebox they put me in, and we smoke the Menthol Slim of peace. The second glass, she gives me the story of her life, from the day she started at Kozlodui School Number Five through to this afternoon when she went on the London Eye with Jerry and tried to have a discussion about The Future. Uh-oh.

It appears she's fallen for Jerry in a big way and now they only have five days left till we leave for the States she's wondering Where Things are Going. Not following you back to Bulgaria, Olga, you can bet your last lev.

I said, "I kind of knew. I saw him going to your room."

She said, "He came to bring gift of Abba CD. After chitchat and vodka toast we have made hot embrace and he did admire my melons. But I did tell him, we must attend in professional manner end of tower. When English tower is ended we can unloose our selfs. I will return after tower of United States, then we can be lovies. 'Olga', he did say, 'three weeks, who can say what will occur. We are not spring hens. Why we will not have our happiness this night?' So we did have our happiness."

I said, "Good. Enjoy. Have some more. You on the pill?"

She's not on the pill. She said problems like that are easy to sort out in Sofia. You can get a scrape done during your lunch break, practically.

I said, "Well this kind of thing happens on tours. You're all cooped up on the bus, eating every meal together, the chemistry starts to happen. You're staying in the same hotel, who's going to say no? It can be fun. But when the tour ends everybody's back on their marker. You understand? There is no future to talk about. I mean, doesn't Jerry have a wife and kids and stuff?"

She said, "He had wife. Two wifes. But now they are not married with him except for technical detail. Buzz, you can explain me 'technical detail'?"

Poor Olga.

I said, "Forget it. You're in Bulgaria, Jerry's here, how's that ever going to work? Have your bit of fun and move on. That's what I do. Maybe the driver we get in Chicago'll be cute. You seeing somebody back home?"

She said, "Always I have been professional person. Always I travel there and here, I did not have time for boyfriend. Now my work is not so much. It can be I will have free times with opportunity of personal relationship. But Jerry Driver does not like to speak of this."

She was close to tears.

She said, "I worry of my career. How I will pay my apartment? How I will pay gasoline for my car? Is difficult time in my country. Is many problems."

I said, "Is that so? But you're always telling me you have all things necessary for happiness in Bulgaria."

She went to the door. For one blissful moment I thought I'd offended her again and she was leaving, but she was just checking nobody was out in the hallway eavesdropping. All clear. But she kept things down to a whisper anyhow.

She said, "I will be frankly with you, Buzz. I do not like this new Bulgaria. Under Chairman Zhivkov all things was better. All people did work, all comrades did enjoy song and laughter. We have made glorious achievement of Five Year Plan in four years. We have received reward, it can be of nice apartment, else shopping coupon. Only anti-state elements did not. Now is different. Now freemarket persons come with big hurry, take all best things, examples, gasoline company, apartment at Vitosha Mountain. When we complain they do laugh at our faces. They say, 'If we are thiffs, tell to police'. But we cannot. Reason, police is their friends. It can be these thiffs will rob my Bulgaria till no thing does remain."

I said, "You're starting to sound like Lubka. Are you talking about people like the Stoyans?"

She said, "Lubka Lilova is dangerous non-educated person. She did not learn correct facts of socialism. But she has knowledge of Gyorgi Stoyan and Boyko Stoyan. She can understand what is this family."

I nearly told her about me and Boyko getting it on. I'd just have loved to see her face. But it wasn't the moment. I just said, "Boyko seems all right to me. Okay, he likes showing off his toys but he works hard, creates jobs, treats his grandmother like a queen."

She said, "Still I will not entrust him."

She topped up our glasses.

She said, "Buzz, tell me your opinions of Jerry Driver. How I can make him love me?"

Oh boy. Fortunately she didn't really want me to give her any advice. She just wanted to talk. How sad it was, Jerry going home to an empty house. What an English gentleman he was yet at the same time physically passionate and not so English at all. I guess it was the Bulgarian melons unleashed that side of him. How she never felt like this about anyone before and she'd be very happy to start a new life, create a proper home for Jerry, do a little part-time interpreting. Yeah. And not have to worry about the price of gasoline because Jerry'd be bringing home the pork knuckles.

Then the tears started. Three vodkas, it happens.

How suddenly she feels lonely and tired and she doesn't want to grow old, all alone in a studio apartment in a country run by people like Gyorgi Stoyan. I mean, it doesn't sound so bad to me. Get a good decorator in, a studio can be okay.

I said, "You won't be alone. You've got friends and stuff. Family. You have sisters and brothers?"

She says, "I had sister. Now I do not."

So she helps herself to one of my flabby Cleveland Acropolis pillows, makes herself comfortable and tells me her tragic tale.

Born 1961, same year as me, in some town up north, near the border with Romania. Mom and Dad were welders, both dead now. Dad worked at the nuclear power plant, got a Hero of Soviet Labour award in 1965. And then there was Olga and her sister. The sister was older by twelve years, just like me and Dorothy. She wouldn't say her sister's name. She doesn't even say "my sister". She calls her "the sister".

She just said, "The sister did ruin all things."

I said, "Well I have a sister too and we don't get on, but you know what? We don't need to. We're grown up. We go our ways."

She said, "The sister was anti-state element. In 1968 she did make many agitations against Soviet assistance in normalisation of Czechoslovakia. One day at meeting of *chavdari*, group leader did tell to all children what the sister has done. 'What shall we do with this girl what has anti-state family member?' she have asked them. 'Send her away,' they have replied. '*Chavdari* is not for persons of anti-state family.' Then they have sent me away. They did shamed me, Buzz. Even they did take my *chavdari* scarf. It was forbidden to keep."

195

Chavdari was a kind of youth club for grade school communists. Evidently they like to start them young. She's really sobbing by now. Some people get like that in drink.

I said, "But Olga, that's more than thirty years ago. So they didn't want you in the *chavdari*. Fuck them. I got thrown out of Presbyterian Bible Study. Fuck them too. You got to let this stuff go. Move on."

She says, "You do not understand. If I cannot be *chavdari*, I cannot be *Pioneer*. I cannot make advancement in my education. Thus at age of sixteen I have gone away from my family. I have made new name, different than sister what has ruined all things."

I said, "That's fine. You got to look after number one in this world. Your sister made her choice, you made yours. So be it. Anyway, sixteen is the right time to strike out on your own. I did and look at me."

She was sniffling and snuffling, "They did take my scarf. It was beautiful blue. I made secret scarf but it was not comfort to me. It was not correct blue of *chavdari*."

She was shit-faced. I mean, she couldn't even work out how to open the door. I had to take her to her room.

After that I took a Niravax and I think I called Dad, to tell him about the award. I think he said, "No thank you, I already gave."

So this morning I'm trying to surface and every time I get like, about an inch from daylight, something pulls me under. Then the phone goes. Mal.

196

He says, "I just wondered if you're nearly ready?"

He says we have to check out by twelve. He says everyone else is downstairs and Floyd's waiting for my bags.

I said, "Mal, I'm not in a good place right now."

He says, "Yes, but we'll be in a different hotel tonight."

He says we'll be at the Ramada, at Gatwick airport.

I said, "We're flying? Remind me, where are we flying?"

He says we're not flying anywhere but it's eleven-thirty and do I need an aspirin? Then I saw all Olga's balled up Kleenex and the empty glasses and the vodka bottle and it all came back to me. There were five Bulgarian funsters downstairs who had to get to some venue in Crawley for a sound check.

CHAPTER
TWENTY-EIGHT

Holy fuckshit. What. A. Day. I mean, you go on the
road with Knifey-Spooney, you expect sorrow. Get
through a week with Lime Twist and you haven't
needed to consult with the legal department, you are
blessed. Five old ladies from Small Potatoesville, what's
the worst thing can happen? One of them takes a heart
attack? Nothing so simple.

Tonight's gig was at a theatre called The Hawth. A
nice little venue, holds about nine hundred and ticket
sales took off big time after Titch Marsh's TV show.
The Tutrakan boys showed up for a run-through. The
Ursari had been sighted. Dressing rooms allocated. So
far, so good.

Mal said he'd take the girls to a mall in Croydon, to
help them relax before the show. I had a Bloody Mary
lunch, hair of the dog that bit me, and went for a lie
down. Four o'clock my phone goes. Mal doesn't want
to worry me but Kichka's missing again.

I said, "Mal, I am so not worried. These malls have
security cameras. They'll find her. And if she has any
stolen goods in her bag, tell them she's insane."

He said, "They've been looking for half an hour. I
think she must have wandered outside."

I said, "I presume Vilk and Nosh are looking for her too? They know what she looks like."

"Well," he said, "the thing is, they went to get a sandwich and they haven't come back yet."

He wanted to call the police. I told him to stay put, give it a while. The second I get off the phone from Mal, Boyko calls me. First thing he says, "I hope you didn't call the police? I'll handle this."

I said, "Whoa! One minute. How did you even hear about this?"

He's shouting, "Did you call the police? Did you?"

I said, "Nobody called the police. Why are you getting so excited?"

He said, "They got my gran, you stupid cow. This is Bulgarian business. *I'll* deal with it, Bulgarian way. No police."

I said, "Who got your gran? Nobody got her. Stanka's at the mall with Mal and the rest of the gang. Kichka's the one who's missing and not for the first time. And don't call me a stupid cow."

Silence.

"Kichka Nikolova?" he says. "You're sure about that?"

I said, "She went walkabout. She did it yesterday, she'll probably do it tomorrow. She's nuts. Not a case for the police."

He said, "I got a message. I got a demand."

I said, "Not for Stanka. Ask Mal. Ask Vilk and Nosh. They're there."

He said, "They're out of range."

I said, "Keep trying. They're only in Subway getting Melts."

More silence.

He said, "Fucking Subway! Anything happens to my *baba*, they're dead."

Floyd drove me down to the shopping centre. We got there just ahead of Boyko. He has two *bortsi* with him, real inconspicuous-looking guys in mirrored shades and black wife-beaters. Still no sightings of Kichka. Security are sweeping the mall again, Olga and Vilk have gone out into Wellesley Road, Jerry and Nosh are checking North End.

Mal said, "I really, really think we should call the police."

Boyko said, "And I really, really think you should stop peeing your pants and leave this to me. It's personal."

First thing he does is tell his gumbas to take Stanka to his car.

I said, "Why? She's safe. She's fine."

He said, "She's safe when I decide. She's safe when my dad's people pick her up from the airport. Till then, she doesn't leave my sight."

I said, "She has a show tonight."

"No," he said. "No show. She's going home, first flight tomorrow."

I said, "She's under contract."

"Fuck the contract," he said. "It's a crap show anyway. There's a good reason that singing's dying out. It's called progress."

I said, "They're billed as the Gorni Five."

He said, "Not my problem. Tell them she's sick."

I said, "We're not even half way through the tour."

"Tough," he said. "Replace her. Fucking racket they make you could replace her with something out of the monkey house. You're so worried, *you* go on in her place. You're old enough."

He started to move away.

I said, "And what does that mean?"

"Born Pittsburgh, Pennsylvania, 1961," he said. "*That's* what that means. Beryl."

The ass-wipe looked at my passport. He must have gone through my pocketbook.

He's walking away.

Mal says, "Excuse me, but while you two are arguing Kichka's still missing."

Boyko turned, but he's still walking away, backwards.

He said, "Don't worry, junior, she'll be back. I told them they got the wrong lady. They're fuckwits. You don't need the police. You get the police involved, cause me any inconvenience, you'll be sorry."

Lubka starts jumping up and down. She says, "Boyko Stoyan is idiot *mutra*. We will call police, Mal. English police is good. Buzz will say yes."

Well Buzz had another little matter to clear up first. I went after him.

I said, "What do you mean, going through my purse, looking at my documents?"

He said, "I like to know what I'm dealing with."

I said, "You mean *after* you get laid?"

He's got a smirk on his face, his hands up, touch-me-not.

He said, "You really want to know? OK, you had me fooled. Okay, you were a pretty good lay. You just don't look so good when you're asleep. I have to say, when you're asleep you look like what you are. Know what I'm saying? You think I go with old women? I don't. Not twice."

He gets to his car and the passenger window rolls down. She's ash blonde, about eighteen, bee-stung lips and silver earrings. Behind her I can just make out Stanka between the two heavies.

I said, "If you're taking Stanka away you can take your other two gorillas as well. We don't want your garbage."

He's getting behind the wheel.

He says, "Don't worry, you won't see that pair again. I always clean up after myself. Window up, darling."

And he was gone. Actually, I think there's something truly pathetic about a guy who can't handle a fully-loaded awesome babe, just because of the date on her birth certificate. And actually, now I think about it, there's something quite ugly about khaki-coloured eyes.

Olga came back from searching minus Vilk. He'd received a message on his phone, turned white and disappeared. Jerry came back without Nosh, ditto. No goodbyes. If you're working for a guy like Boyko Stoyan and you get recalled because you fell asleep on the job, I guess your whole life passes before you.

Mal gave me a long cool look.

He said, "I called the police."

I said, "You don't think that was just a little bit premature? You don't think you should have waited for me to make that decision?"

"No," he said. "As a matter of fact, I don't."

We didn't speak again till we got back to the hotel.

I said, "Look, you had your own way, you wasted half an hour talking to the police and no doubt dropped Boyko in the doodoo, like I care. So why do I get the impression you're mad at me? Are you going to tell me what I did?"

He said, "You mean apart from drinking too much and popping pills and over-sleeping and being more interested in running after Boyko Stoyan than finding Kichka? Absolutely nothing."

I said, "You need to lighten up a little. And I did not run after Boyko. We had some unfinished business, that's all."

He said, "I don't want to know."

I said, "And shithead though he is, I think he's right about Kichka. Now they know they got the wrong granny they'll let her go. What else are they going to do with her? Who's going to pay to get Kichka back? Her sons don't have a cent. If they've got any sense they'll say 'keep her'. She's demented."

He said, "She's not the only one."

I said, "Call Serena at One World. Tell her we have a slight glitch."

Lubka wanted to speak to me alone.

She said, "If Stanka Stoyanova goes away and Kichka does not arrive Gorni Five is Gorni Three. But suddenly did come in my head jolly good plan. You can sing. Same you did in mikrobus. You can stand close with Zveta, sing straight, no problem. You have good voice."

I said, "Lubka, I cannot sing. People are paying money to see this show. They've seen the posters, some of them have bought the CD. They're expecting five grannies, not three grannies and an all-American chick."

She said, "You think only United State has pretty ladies? Also in Bulgaria we have. Plenty pretty ladies."

I said, "I didn't mean it like that. It's just that you have a particular look. I can't wear all that droopy peasant stuff."

She said, "For sure you can wear. I will borrow you this things. Now we will find Zveta and Dora. We will sing song to wake up you voice."

She's messing around tying this red cotton babushka round my head, trying to give me the authentic Bulgarian look. As if.

She said, "Buzz, I did hear you shout with Boyko Stoyan. Is good thing. Nobody ever did shout with him. For Stanka he is big *momchentse* but if he is my boy I will smack his bottoms."

I said, "I really don't think I can go on. I can't do this."

"*Da*," she says, "you can do. Is show businesses. Even police does not find Kichka this night, still we can be Gorni Four."

I said, "Are you worried about her?"

"Some worried," she said. "I made prays to Mother of God but it can be she did not hear me. In Bulgaria we are close to heaven. In Crawley we are not so close. But I think they will not hurt old lady."

Mal's still pissed with me but he brought his gran backstage to meet everyone. She'd had her hair done for the occasion.

She said, "I'd just like to say how thrilled we are, me and Mal's father. This is a wonderful opportunity for him. Going to America and meeting all these artistes. Much better than when he was selling those bread rolls. He's been to college, you know?"

I kind of had the feeling she'd practised saying it all, in front of a mirror, to be sure of getting it right. Mal was squirming like a nightcrawler on a hook.

She said, "And I think it's very sporting of you to go on in place of the missing lady too. Very game. And you really look the part."

But I didn't go on in place of the missing lady. At seven-fifteen Kichka Nikolova was deposited on the circle in front of the Hawth Theatre. According to the steward who witnessed the event a black Mercedes with tinted windows slowed, barely to a halt, a door opened, an old lady was bundled out and the car drove away at speed. Kichka appeared unharmed and was under the impression she'd been the guest of Bulgarian friends whose name she couldn't remember. She told Lubka they gave her coffee and cake. No one in the audience would have guessed that the old lady with the braided hair and the emery paper voice had just walked away from a bungled kidnapping. She went to it like a true pro.

And going through her bag for clues as to where she'd been taken we found a reel of duct tape, a replica Beretta handgun, two prepaid phone cards and half a pack of Individual Bakewell Tarts. So that'll larn 'em.

CHAPTER
TWENTY-NINE

In two days has occurred many excited events. First at Whitgift Shopping Centre of Croydon Kichka Nikolova is disappeared. Low and high we did search her with assistance of shopping police but without result. Next has arrived Buzz Wexler, also Boyko Stoyan, grandson of Stanka Stoyanova. Why does Boyko Stoyan interest his self in this problem, I have asked myself? Quickly I have understood. Enemies of Boyko Stoyan, in believe of making hostage his grand mother, have snitched away Kichka Nikolova in error. Then big argue has commenced. In opinions of Mal Cleaver, also Lubka Lilova what does always interfere, we must report to police. In opinions of Boyko Stoyan we must not. For secret reason he does not wish English police to enquire in his affair. Then guards of Boyko Stoyan did take away Stanka Stoyanova. Even nothing was her blame, Boyko Stoyan says she must return immediately to her home.

"But what of contract?" did cry Buzz Wexler.

"Fug contract," replied Boyko Stoyan.

Next Buzz did chased behind him to his limousine with big shouts. Some I did not understand. My Jerry says it was shouts of personal nature. He does not admire Buzz Wexler for her behaviours. Example, in one moment she can be gay, then in twinking of eye she can be angry. Howandsoever I have become to like her. She can be kind friend.

At Cleveland Acropolis hotel we did talk with ourselves of many things. Of lovies, of education, of career. I am certifiable of Plovdiv Institute, she have attended University of Life but without achievement of diploma. I do not know where is this institution. In our lifes are many similars.

1. Both we are born 1961, both we live alonely.
2. Each we have taken new name to begin new life.
3. Each we did attain highmost level of our profession but of the future we have worries because always the world does change.

Buzz did say, "Olga, you must not always be interpret. You can change. You can be any damn thing you wish."

But I do not know what damn thing I will be. Perhaps we have drunk too many vodka. Before I did never speak with other persons of private subject. In Bulgaria it is not our custom. But I believe there was not danger to speak with Buzz Wexler because she quickly forgets all things.

At shopping centre then have arrived police, one male, one women, without weapon and Mal Cleaver has made report of displaced granny Kichka Nikolova. Then police official did say, "When we will find this lady it can be problem because we do not speak her language. Instantly we will require your aids, Ms Ilievska."

I have replied, "I will come now to headquarter to be alert. It is my roll."

Howandsoever they believed this was not necessary.

Next Buzz Wexler did lament, "Instead five songsters only remain three. Wow is me!"

Here was danger that music tower will be liquidated. Then Lubka Lilova has made plan that Buzz Wexler can take place of Stanka Stoyanova else Kichka Nikolova, that she can wear cloths of Gorni granny and sing songs of gone-by time.

"How can this be?" I have asked. "Buzz Wexler does not know our language. Instead I will do this. To safeguard our celeries I will adorn my own self as peasant and sing songs of primitive era."

Lubka Lilova cried, "You will not! Better Buzz Wexler sings without words that Soviet puppydog sings without energichno."

But how can Buzz Wexler have this energichno when she does not understand words?

Lubka Lilova then did say, "I will tell you, Olga Ilievksa. Is because Buzz Wexler has heart soft as feather bed. When she listens our songs, tears come in her eye. You have heart hard as button."

This argument did not interest me. Lubka Lilova is non-educated pheasant. Then with good fortune suddenly has appeared Kichka Nikolova without assist of police else payment of ransom.

"Where were you gone?" we have asked her.

"How can I know?" she did reply. "I was not in this place before. I made pleasant visit with four Sofiantsi. They brought me in deluxe automobile to their apartment. They gave me to eat and drink and now I am returned to sing in spectacle."

Thus has been resolved problem. Before start of show manager has made announcement, this night Stanka Stoyanova will not appear for reason of disposition. I am not sorry for departure of Stanka Stoyanova. She was all right old lady but with her is departed ugly lifeguards. This is good.

Now we are arrived in city of Portsmouth-Southsea, nervous centre of English navels. Today we will make cultural tower in Dockyard of Lordnelson and Mary Rose, also we will go in birthplace of Charles Dicken, world-known author of Pigwig Paper and Tale of Two City. After time of repose, Balkanalia! spectacle will take place at King's Theatre. This is deluxe theatre of highest level. In this theatre have appeared world-known stars, examples Rex Harrison and Sean Connery. Also famous comedy duo, Spike Milligan and Dame Thorndyke.

Yesterday we have gone in Clarence Pier for photo opportunity with leading British newspaper, *Winchester Clarion*. Clarence Pier is place of traditional British merrymaking. Here is Golden Horseshoe Arcade with machines what take money but give no product. Only it makes noise and flashy lights. With this machines five quids is soon disappeared. We do not have such machines in Bulgaria.

For photographs we did go in Waltzer carousel. I will explain. It has many chairs. When carousel begins, chair spins, also floor of carousel. This is too much spins after lunch of ham sandvichi and lemonsoda. Lubka Lilova and Zveta Borisova have enjoyed but so long I live I will not ride in Waltzer carousel again. Even it does not spin it can be dangerous. Thus Kichka Nikolova did fall and injure her angle so that quickly we must take her in hospital for X-ray and bangdage.

Furthermore result of Waltzer carousel, Dora Gavrilova have made pipi in panties. Lubka Lilova says is no problem, hotel will wash. Howandsoever this can be problem because Dora Gavrilova wears all panties in one day. Now all are wet how can she go there and here?

Buzz Wexler have said, "Olga, the sun does shine. She does not have need of panties."

But for sure Dora Gavrilova must not go in Charles Dicken Birthplace without undergarment. It will give out bad name of Bulgaria so even Bulgarians of good education shall be tinted.

Last evening with Mal Cleaver, Floyd Baggages and my Jerry we have enjoyed traditional repast of fishandships. Kichka Nikolova did not attend because she must rest her angle. Also Buzz Wexler because she is fatigued. Even she does not wish to go in Charles Dicken House.

"Why shall we do this?" she did ask. "Better we go in Cascades Shopping Centre. There Gorni Grannies can have pleasant time."

But Charles Dicken is great writer of toiling masses under capitalist joke. Certainly we must go in his house and give umbrage to him. Buzz Wexler is American person, perhaps she does not understand this.

Lubka Lilova has said, "I know this Charles Dicken. I have seen movie Tale of Two City, star Dirk Boregarde. I have seen with satellite dish. I will like to meet this Dirk Boregarde."

I do not believe this can be possible. Why shall star of screen wish to meet non-educated songster? Also, Buzz Wexler did say for sure Dirk Boregarde has already deceased to be. I am glad of this. Lubka Lilova thinks now she makes music tower she can meet any person, example American Imperialist War-Monger, Ronald Reagan. She believes grannies of Gorni will be most famous Bulgarian people of whole world. Soon she will receive cold douche. This is colloquial expression. From my Jerry I learn many things.

Now I understand he could not speak of our future when we ride on London Eyes, reason, sensation of nausea. But he have reinsured me, he wishes I will be always in his side. Together we can enjoy pleasures of rich Bulgarian inheritage.

Already inside my mind I make preparation for vacation with my Jerry. I will show him characteristical villages, examples Koprivshtitsa, Zheravna. I will take him in historical city of Plovdiv where he can thrill to atmospheric streets. Perhaps we will hick in forests of Mount Vitosha and sleep in kumpink tents. How I am happy with this pleasant man!

CHAPTER
THIRTY

Portsmouth is a Navy town, looks kind of down on its luck, but there are some cute sailor boys on the street and the King's Theatre is a darling little venue, red and gold, like a chocolate box. Fourteen hundred seats and we've sold eleven hundred and change. The local press is *very* excited to be featuring us. Damned right.

The first thing the girls wanted to see was the ocean because this time it's the real thing with like, boats and waves with white caps on and everything. None of them dared stand anywhere near the water's edge but every time the sea crashed against the wall they jumped back and screamed. Then the photographer said he had a great idea for a picture: a ride called The Waltzer, on Clarence Pier. Sounded good to me.

Mal said, "I don't want to be a killjoy but have you ever seen the Waltzer?"

He's worried somebody might have a heart attack.

I said, "You *are* a killjoy, Mal."

He said, "We're down to four. We can't afford any more casualties."

I said, "That's one way of looking at it. But something like a heart attack can be terrific publicity. I do have some experience in these things. When Black

Jello did their Mid-West tour in '94 it was a total washout until Tav OD'd on methadone. Topeka had cancelled, Omaha had cancelled. They couldn't have filled a church hall in Whiskerville before the Tav incident. After that it was a sell-out."

He said, "A tip worth remembering."

We get to Clarence Pier and Lubka spots this kid's carousel, like giant tea cups with little seats inside. And the photographer says okay, we'll give that a try, so Lubka and Zveta start to climb aboard and the ride operator comes running out, waving his arms.

He says, "They can't go on there. That ride is for children only."

I said, "You don't even need to press the starter. It's only for a photo. For the *Winchester Clarion*."

"All the more reason," he says. "I can't afford publicity like that. You'll get me shut down. It's against regulations."

Olga says, "In Bulgaria we will not have this regulation."

So we decide to go with Plan A.

Olga says, "What is purpose of Waltzer?"

I said, "Adrenalin. It gives sad people with empty lives a thrill."

She said, "Then I will try. For cultural experience."

We got some great pictures. Lubka, all smiles, in her pink cowboy hat and her black fishnets. Dora screaming, showing her gums and her big white, dimpled knees. Kichka and Mal, huddled together like a pair of pixies in windbreakers. Zveta looking a little

214

spacey, but happy and really quite pretty. As Floyd remarked, a couple of weeks out of Gorni has taken years off all of them.

Just so long as it didn't dump them on me.

So a good photo session, but everything comes with a price tag. As they came down off the ride Zveta threw up all over my new Kate Spade sneaks and Kichka lost her balance, looked to me like she could have busted her ankle. Mal said it was probably only sprained but she should go to the emergency room, get it checked anyhow.

Well I totally don't do hospitals.

I said, "You're the Ambulance Cadet. You go. And take Olga with you. She complains about being underworked. This'll make her feel important."

He was right, her ankle wasn't broken. They kept her waiting on a gurney for a couple of hours, then they strapped her up and recommended renting a wheelchair for a couple of days. I never saw Kichka so happy. When Mal wheeled her through the hotel lobby it was like the arrival of the Queen of fucking Sheba.

He said, "I got her some crutches as well but I think she'd better do tomorrow's show sitting. If one of the Ursari boys gets carried away he could knock her flying."

Lubka says, "With Kichka in wheels chair we will look like Three and Half Grannies. But is okay. If Buzz will sing with us we can be Four and Half."

But Buzz doesn't feel like singing. Actually, Buzz doesn't really feel like doing anything. Maybe I have a summer flu coming on. Mal and Jerry were planning this fish and chip dinner but I couldn't face it. It's an English thing. Just fried fish and potatoes but they go crazy for it.

I said, "I'll pass. I think I'll just get room service."

He said, "Are you all right?"

I said, "I'm tired, Mal. I'm so tired I can't tell you."

He said, "Yeah, you get an early night. I'll take care of everything."

I said, "Did you ever drive your car when the gas tank light was on red and you just kept driving anyway, to see what happened?"

He said, "No. I'm the kind of person who never lets the tank go below half full. Would you like me to bring you a battered sausage and a cold beer?"

He can be so sweet.

I looked in on Kichka before I turned in for the night. The hospital said to give her an aspirin if her ankle started to hurt, but she was looking just fine. The TV was blasting and she was hopping around on her good leg, laying out the day's booty on her bed: sterile gauze, assorted sizes; non-allergenic adhesive tape, two reels; tweezers, small; antiseptic towelettes, one pack; the doofer they put in your mouth if they have to do CPR, one sealed unit; latex exam gloves, lots; latex exam glove dispenser, stainless steel, formerly wall-mounted, one. Not bad. I guess they must have kept the defibrillator well hidden.

Yesterday I had the low-grade blaahs but today has been a whole other story. Today has been a deeply okay kind of day. I slept till nine, ate two eggs sunnyside with wholegrain toast, got a wash and blow-dry and then met the girls for their last-chance English shopping. Lubka had seen stuff she liked in a store called BHS when they were in Croydon, then Kichka went missing and everyone was in a flap. She didn't get the chance to buy anything. But Mal said BHS have a store in the mall here too and as Lubka felt she might have found her style, I wanted to be with her. It can be an exciting moment, I know. I remember the time I tried on my first Benny Wu. It was like coming home.

Mal said, "I think I should warn you, there's nothing Benny Wu about BHS."

But that's okay. I woke up this morning with my Fuck Hunt Madson, Fuck Boyko Stoyan, Lifetime Achievement Winner's smiley face on. When you've reached the top you can afford to be generous with the less fortunate. Lubka's like a butterfly struggling to break out of her dull old Gorni chrysalis. Well, maybe more like a moth than a butterfly, but she still needs help, and who better to give it than me? I struggled that struggle years ago. And if she insisted on shopping in the Mother of the Bride section today, who was I to contradict her? When she gets back to Gorni and tries hoeing potatoes in ankle-length jersey, she'll realise her mistake. It doesn't matter. Through mistakes we grow.

She wanted to wear her new dress and jacket for tonight's show but I had to draw the line.

I said, "It's one thing to freelance below the knee, the audience finds that charming. But they expect to see you in your skirts and aprons. They want a taste of traditional Gorni."

"Pah!" she said. "Perhaps in United States we will not be olderly songsters no more."

She has this idea, once we get to Chicago she's going to persuade Zveta's daughter Rosa to fill the gap Stanka has left. I've warned her not to get her hopes too high. Rosa is rumoured to be very busy making movies. But Lubka's got this into her head since she saw the new line-up for the Scandinavian leg of Balkanalia! While we play the U.S., a foxy looking group from Macedonia will be joining Tutrakan and the Ursari. Balkan folk songs with added mascara.

She said, "This movies of Rosa Borisova is made up story of her daddy. Dimitar Borisov is idiot. He drinks glass of beer, he goes asleep, he dreams. Where is this movies? I do not see them in my TV. For sure Rosa Borisova will like to sing with us, go in famous theatre, nice hotel. For next Comet record Dora Gavrilova and Kichka Nikolova can stay in their house, take care their vegetable. Only we will be Zveta Borisova, Lubka Lilova and Rosa Borisova. We will be this thing what you say. Foxy. We will be Foxy Bulgarian Songsters."

I knew tonight's show would be fabulous. I could taste it. When the Tutrakan Trio play, the audience is very quiet, kind of tranquillised. And when the Ursari get going people are up and out of their seats. But when my girls sing there's pure love washing in over the footlights. You can tell people just want to wrap them up and take them home.

We've had women hanging round the stage door every town we've played, some of them hoping to hook up with the Ursari boys, I'm sure. But tonight it was the Grannies they all wanted to meet. It's the first time they've been asked for autographs.

Lubka said, "What shall we write?"

I said, "Write your names."

She said, "But what is for?"

I said, "It's because you're famous. These people are your fans."

So they're writing out their names, concentrating so hard, like it's a test in school.

Любка Лилова

Цвета Борисова

Kichka wouldn't sign. She thought it was some kind of scam.

I said, "How did you ever get her signature on the recording contract?"

Lubka said, "Do not ask me this question."

Dora was willing to sign but she was apparently never much of a student so Lubka wrote her name for her.

Дора Гаврилова

One of the fans said, "Tell them we really hope they'll come back."

Lubka said, "For sure we will come."

I said, "What is it exactly you like about them?"

She said, "I don't know. They make you smile just to look at them, but then some of the songs make you want to cry. Funny really."

Her friend said, "I know what it is. It's because when they're up on that stage they don't care whether we're there or not. I reckon if you locked them in Parkhurst and threw the key away, they'd still sing. You can just tell."

We're piling into the bus when the formerly cute Ursari kid sidles over. He still has my business card, except it looks like a dog chewed it. He's giving me the come-on. Looking for an encore I guess, it being the last night of the tour.

No, no, my friend. I once mistook you for a Ten, but now I find you're barely a Seven. Besides, call me fastidious, but when a guy feels the need to hawk onto the sidewalk, he better do it before he propositions me, or after. Definitely not during.

Mal had four bottles of chilled Spumante waiting for us back at the hotel. Everyone was bubbling and happy. Lubka's ready to conquer America, Dora's two weeks nearer to being reunited with her sheep, Zveta's excited about seeing her daughter, Kichka's imagining all the lovely money she's going to get. Only Olga seemed distracted.

I said, "What's wrong? Is it Jerry? Do you want one of my chill pills?"

She said, "Buzz, I must tell you a thing."

I said, "Tell."

She said, "You will not like."

I said, "Try me."

She said, "I cannot go with you in United State. I will remain here with my Jerry. He did ask me if I will go with him in his home to be his lovered one. And I did tell him yes. Now you will be angry."

I said, "I'm not angry."

She said, "But where will you find high-level interpret in this short time?"

I said, "Don't worry. It's true it'll be very hard to find someone to match your standard, but somehow we'll get by. I'm only concerned that you're doing the right thing? You've only known Jerry for two weeks."

"*Da*," she said, "But he is English gentleman. He has good job, also house of three bedroom in Harpenden. Is good opportunity for me."

He wears white socks, Olga. He picks his nose hairs while he's driving and he doesn't even know he's doing it. He has goldfish named Agnethe, Bjorn, Benny and Anni-Frid.

I said, "Okay. If you're happy."

She said, "Thank you, Buzz. Except when I win Komsomol medal of student excellence I never was so happy as this. With my Jerry I will throw precautions to wind."

I hope she doesn't do that. Not till all those little Olga eggs are past their Hatch-by date.

We ordered more fizz and Dora went to fetch what was left of her peach rakia. And the singing started. Mal did "We Are Family", Jerry did "Take a Chance on Me", Olga gave us many verses of "We Will Build Bright Futures". Then Lubka started us with "Golden Apple". I hummed the straight voice with Zveta, and for "Trees in the Forest" and for "Go Down", and I hardly made a mistake. It felt so great. Shit, it felt as good as an ice cold Vodka Yuzu and a l-o-o-o-ng l-o-o-o-ng line of top quality sniff. Almost.

Lubka said, "Now Buzz Wexler will sing American song."

I said, "Now Buzz Wexler won't."

But they were all drumming on the table tops. So I gave them a song:

By the Big White Candy Mountain, everything looks clear and bright.
You can pack away your troubles and stay up all the night.
Oh let me go where there's plenty of snow,
Where the rains don't fall and the winds don't blow,
Where you're always wired and you never feel tired
By that Big White Candy Mountain.

Then, for some unaccountable reason I ate two servings of smoked salmon sandwiches and four enormous Gorni sour piggles and I was so tired I went to bed without purging. Must be losing my grip.

CHAPTER
THIRTY-ONE

When Kichka arrived ten days ago she had one large suitcase and a shopping bag. Today she had two bags to check, a carry-on and a backpack, and the new luggage is practically the only thing she actually bought. All the extra stuff is stolen goods. I mean, Lubka had to buy another bag too but that's because she's developing a taste for diva-wear. She was down at the breakfast buffet this morning in a white feathered fascinator.

I said, "Are you travelling in that?"

"*Da,*" she says. "So I will be elegant for arrival at United State of America. In bag it will be squished."

Olga came with us to Heathrow to say goodbye. Now the big love story is out in the open she just can't keep her hands off Jerry. I had to send them away to buy gum and magazines, before I hurled.

Check-in is going really slowly and then I realise Mal's joined the wrong line.

I said, "This is coach. Business Class is the other desk."

He didn't move.

I said, "We're not flying Business, are we?"

He was kind of braced. I could see him calculating how bad a time I was about to give him.

I said, "Do you know the last time I flew coach? I don't think you even were born. But here's the thing, Mal. This morning I took one of my new Niravax capsules. Which means I'm in an ultra, ultra fluffy frame of mind. It means they can put me in cargo and I won't complain, so long as there's drinks service."

A nervous little smile.

I said, "And just to show you I really, really mean it about being in a good mood, let me guess where we're sleeping tonight and then be totally okay about it. Not the Four Seasons, of course. And probably not even the Park-Hyatt. I'm going to go out on a limb here and say tonight we'll be staying at a Howard Johnson."

Not a Howard Johnson.

I said, "Am I close?"

There's nothing to read in his face because Mal knows nothing about Chicago hotels.

I said, "Just tell me we're not at Fat Johnny's Last Resort. That's the only small thing I ask."

BudgetLodge. He kind of squeaked it out.

He has the passports clutched in his hand and when I try to look through them he gives me all of them except his own. I guessed what it was. Either a bad photo or a bad name. Turned out it was both. Mal's full name is Limahl Herbert Silas Cleaver.

I said, "Hey! That's great. You have three dumb names, same as me! We're tied."

"Limahl" was because his mom liked Kajagoogoo. "Herbert" was for his dad, "Silas" was for his grandad. A lot of thought must have gone into that. An act of gratuitous psychological cruelty visited on a helpless child. But I didn't feel I could say too much. Mal's mom died of an asthma attack when he was two, so she's now ascended to a pedestal well above criticism-level. And Mal actually likes his dad.

I said, "You want to see mine?"

He said, "I know your name's Beryl."

Correct. "Beryl" because my folks were pitiless sadists without a lick of taste. "Eunice" after my mom. And "Ermengild" for my grandmother, who, incidentally, always went as Gilda and probably would have killed stone dead with one glare anybody who dared call her by the full E name.

He said, "I won't ever tell anybody."

I said, "And your secret is safe with me."

Of course my passport photo is unusually excellent so I do have the advantage over him there.

London to Chicago non-stop is nine hours. Zveta was supposed to be sitting next to me but Lubka insisted on changing.

She said, "I will not sit with Dora and Kichka. Only they talk of their fruits garden, of their hanimal. I will sit with you."

She had this copy of *Celebrity!* magazine, studying the red carpet shots at some arthouse movie awards ceremony.

She said, "I have question. In Sofia I have heard soon they will make Walk of Fame. In your opinions they will give me star?"

I said, "Maybe for the group. Maybe a little constellation, for the five of you. Unless you're planning to go solo?"

"Ne," she said, "I will not be solo. Star can be for all Grannies. Only Stanka Stoyanova shall not get because she have runned away to her home."

I said, "Stanka didn't have any choice. What about your Aunt Mara? She sang when they made the recording but Dora's here doing the tour. How are you going to work that one out?"

She thought for a minute. Then she said, "Aunt Mara will not wish to be in Walk of Fame. Aunt Mara does not wish any things for herself."

Mara is Lubka's mother's sister. She's very old, she was married to Vasil Petkov and she's been a widow longer than I've been alive. No kids. Lubka's all she has in the world. Her husband was sent to a camp and just never came back.

Lubka said, "I did not remember Vasil Petkov. I was little child. He was Party member. They say he was very good communist, but one day his brain have waked up. It was time of Second Five Year Plan. Soviet puppydog Zhivkov said Second Five Year Plan must be finish in three years and one half. If you say this is not possible, suddenly they will give you vacation in Lovech Camp. It was called place of re-education. Else you change your minds, else bye-bye. It was very bad place. There was many deads."

Exit Vasil. It reminded me of Dad's old joke about communists.

226

"All those who voted for our Illustrious Leader may now put down their hands. And move away from the wall."

By the time this happened Lubka's dad was already off the scene, sounds like he was a pillar of the liquor industry. So Mara moved in with Lubka and her mom and they both got jobs in a salami factory, same place Lubka ended up working when she left school. And that's how Lubka learned to sing, listening to Mara and her mom. All those songs about corn fields and roosters and pine trees but they were sitting in Sofia in a concrete high-rise called *Nadezhda*. Which means Hope.

She was quiet for a while, following the photo captions with her finger, saying the letter sounds to work out the names. She still finds the different alphabet difficult.

I said, "Apart from watching movies every night, how did you come to learn English?"

"Wife of boss," she said. "At salami factory."

She worked there till it closed down in 1990.

She said, "Boss was Mr Banev. He had English wife, very nice person of good education. Some time they wished to go in concerto else in cinema I did sit on their babies. Two boy, one girl. Some time also they made big party for business delegate. Then I did clean house, else help in kitchen. Only we did speak English. So I did learn. Now I have dish I can listen English every night."

I said, "Your English is very good. Better than Olga's."

She laughed. She said, "You are not wrong."

I said, "Did your husband work in the salami factory too?"

"Ne," she said, "Lazar Lilov did work in metals factory. I did meet him on trolleybus. Oh, he was most handsome man. Same like David Nivens."

Lazar wasn't a Party member, though.

She said, "Even I eat grass I will not have communist husband. But in our time, it was not so bad like in days of Vasil Petkov. There was not camps. Camps was finish. Except you are highmost official, in our time it was not advantage to be member of Communist Party. All shops was empty."

In 1991 they decided to go to Gorni to reclaim the old family houses and the land. Mara went with them. Lubka said it was that or starve. Zhivkov was out of office by then. He'd resigned in '89 but things got worse before they got better.

She said, "There was not bread. There was not milk. So we returned in Gorni. We did not know how we can grow food. Always we had lived in city. But Mara did teach us. First you must get pig. Pig is good as machine to dig land. Better. With pig, after he cleans you field you can make him in sausage. First we have growed potato, cabbage, egg of chicken. Already there was apple tree, nut tree, mushroom in forest. Next year we have growed tomats, spinaches, cheese of goat. Still we grow this things, except cheese of goat. After Lazar is dead I will not have goat."

I said, "Why? Did the goat cheese kill Lazar?"

"Ne," she says, "infeksia did kill Lazar. He made cut of his toe, very, very bad. He made with big knife, when he cutted grasses. Perhaps knife was not clean. Soon he was dead."

He was only forty-nine.

She said, "He was most good husband. When he is died it was two years I did not sing. Then Aunt Mara have said, Lubkochka, is too long time. Else you sing, else soon you will be in grave with Lazar Lilov. So I did sing. Aunt Mara always is right. But I will not have goat no more. Is crazy animal what will eat you whole house."

She keeps turning the pages of her magazine back to the same photo. It's some D-list nonebrity, with fat creases in her neck tan and a totally sad pair of bronze gladiator sandals. But the thing that's drawing Lubka is the dress. It's a mint-green night-mare of marabou-edged chiffon. It's like a swirl of sundae topping that got extruded from an aerosol can and garnished with feathers, and it has these sleeves that look like a pair of sprouting pineapples.

She said, "How much, this dress?"

I said, "Nobody buys those gowns. They just borrow them."

She looks at me in total, like, dumbstruck amazement. Every time she turns her head the long feather on her fascinator nearly pokes out my eye.

She said, "How many days you can borrow?"

I explained about how the awards gown game works. Hottest property gets first dibs.

She said, "When you get Achievements award perhaps you can borrow this gown? How beautiful you will look. Where it will be, this party? I will come with you."

I said, "The Urbies aren't like that. Urbie winners don't wear pastels."

Of course, if I'd known for sure I was getting Lifetime I could probably have cut a very good deal with Rubber Queen, but I've never gone around looking for favours. Buzz Wexler doesn't live in anyone's pocket.

Mal came by on his way to the john. Lubka showed him the photo.

She said, "You think I will look nice in this gown?"

He said, "I think you'd look better in blue."

I said, "We might have a candidate here for a makeover feature. Women's page, one of the U.S. dailies? What do you think?"

He said, "I think it'd be like putting your dog in a Santa costume. And then circulating his photo to all the other dogs."

Lubka said, "Why will English people give costume to dog? Why does English buy special cookie for dogs? Is crazy country. I like, but is crazy."

I said, "If you had a gown like that, where would you wear it?"

She said, "I will wear insides my own house. At night time, when there is nice movie, I will put lipstick and highbrows like Bette Davis and fishingnet knees high. I can be elegant for my own self."

Sometimes I could love that woman.

★ ★ ★

So we land at O'Hare. Flight's on time, Immigration fast-tracks us because Kichka's in the wheelchair, luggage is all accounted for and we have a reception committee waiting in Arrivals. There's Wally, driver of our air-conditioned twelve-berth sleeper bus. He looks kind of Indian but he's not wearing a turban or anything. And we have Rosa Borisova, nineteen-year-old daughter of Zveta, accompanied by a guy who appears to be her pimp. Rosa is a looker. She has the same blue-black hair as Zveta, same long neck. Zveta cried when she saw her. Or maybe it was the sight of the gum-chewing dipstick she was with that made her cry.

Rosa said, "This is Neno. He's my fiancé. Mama says you need a singer."

"Manager," Neno says. "I'm her manager. How much are you paying?" He's a mean-looking little punk.

I said, "And what kind of managing do you do for Rosa?"

"Modelling work," he says.

Not catwalk, you can be sure. Not with DD-cup bazookas.

Rosa says, "I do glamour modelling. And I've done film work."

I said, "Can you sing? "Trees in the Forest" and all that traditional stuff?"

She said, "Yeah, I can do that. What do we wear?"

Neno said, "Leave it to me, okay? We have to agree the money first."

I said, "I can't talk to you about money. This is supposed to be a promotional tour and right now only

231

three of the original artists are here. Rosa'd be replacing Stanka. Maybe Stanka'll be willing to come to an arrangement with Rosa, but that's not up to me. As far as I'm concerned the tour goes ahead whether Rosa's on board or not."

Rosa says, "I am on board. I want to go sing with Mama."

And Neno says, "Not if I don't agree to it, you won't. That's why you need a manager, make sure you don't get ripped off. What you gonna do, work for nothing?"

Lubka's whispering something to Rosa.

Neno said, "You speak to this Stanka, see what she's offering. You can let me know."

I said, "I have a better plan. Stanka has a manager too. You speak to him. Boyko Stoyan. I'll give you his number. You two kind of speak the same language."

Lubka said, "Even Rosa does not sing in show, she will come with us now in hotel, have cup of coffee. Is too long time she does not see her Mama."

We're outside the terminal building waiting for Wally to swing around with the bus and Mal notices two guys are hauling the Stars and Stripes down to half-staff.

He said, "Does that mean something?"

The skycap says, "Sure does. The President died."

I said, "You're kidding? When did that happen? Did somebody shoot him?"

He said, "I ain't talking about President Bush. I'm talking about President Ronald Reagan. Gone to his rest. It's a sad day for this country. It's a sad, sad day for the world."

232

CHAPTER
THIRTY-TWO

How bad are things? Well, the carpets in this place must have been here since around 1960, and the El is only five floors down from my window, going to be rattling by all night, but the AC is working and the coffee shop is a really classy joint. They wipe the necks of the ketchup dispensers and everything. There's also encouraging news from tonight's venue. The Claudia Cassidy seats three hundred and we have advance sales of two hundred and change. But the rest is gloom. Fort Wayne Lutherans only sold seven tickets so they're cancelling and Lima Memorial Hall double booked us with a meeting of the Ohio Blue Star Mothers and the booking secretary doesn't know what to do because, well, it *is* the Blue Star Mothers.

I said, "Then we might as well fly straight from here to Reno."

Mal says, "But we've got the Pittsburgh booking. The Pittsburgh people say they've had a lot of interest."

Everyone's so goddamn determined to make me go to Pittsburgh.

He said, "I know you're upset about Fort Wayne cancelling and everything, but I still think we should go."

I said, "I'm not upset about Fort Wayne. I don't even know where it is."

He said, "It's in Indiana. I think we should go because we have the bus, and what we can do is stop in some of the towns, as we go through, and the Grannies can sing. They can sing anywhere, out in the street if they have to, and it'll be great publicity. Like a road show. And it is on our way to Pittsburgh."

I said, "But are we sure Pittsburgh's going to happen? Did they sell any tickets?"

He says it's not actually a ticketed event.

I said, "You know what that means, Mal? A Thursday night, no money has changed hands, it'll be raining, there'll be an episode of *Survivor* nobody wants to miss, and it'll be a case of 'fuck the Bulgarians'."

He says, "Well they sounded really keen. And it'd be better than sitting around here all week. Chicago's not really a Grannies kind of place, is it? I don't think they like the tall buildings."

I called Dad.

I said, "This is your daughter."

He said, "Well Dorothy's sat right here threatening me with sheltered living so you must be the other one. Can't fool me."

I said, "You remember my name?"

He said, "Don't you start. She just asked me do I know what year it is. Dadburnit, I ain't telling. There's one of them hanging calendars back of the kitchen door if she's so keen to know."

I can hear Dorothy in the background shouting, "That calendar is 2001."

I said, "Ronald Reagan died."

"I know it," he says. "Ninety-three years old. Date of birth, February 6th, 1911. You hear that, Dorothy?"

She's yelling, "And he had Alzheimer's."

He says, "Fortieth President of the Union and the greatest, bar Abe Lincoln and George Washington himself."

I said, "That's a pretty sweeping statement."

"Well," he says. "And maybe Teddy Roosevelt."

Dorothy comes on the line.

I said, "I'm in Chicago."

She said, "That's no help to me. You know the latest? He has a fifty-pound bag of shortening in the shower stall."

He's shouting, "Well I can't keep it on the porch. If the sun gets on it it's liable to turn rancid."

She says, "And if he can't get in the shower he won't be keeping himself clean."

He's saying, "I am clean. You get to a stage in life you don't sweat any more. It's a scientific fact. I read it in *Reader's Digest*. Smell my armpit."

I said, "Dorothy, can we cut to the chase here? I told him I'd see him Thursday or Friday. Does he know, does he remember, did he write it down? Is there any point at all?"

"Yes," she said, "of course there's a point. You can see him one last time before I kill him."

Lubka won't move from in front of the TV. Everything's about Ronald Reagan. She wanted to light a candle for him but BudgetLodge don't have, won't allow candles. Kichka's ankle is swollen from the flight, Dora's missing having Stanka around and I'm suffering a post-Niravax rebound. I'm tired but I can't sleep. I'm hungry all the time but as soon as I look at food I could gag. Dr G did say I might have to experiment a little.

I said, "Lubka, here's what I think. Everybody's exhausted and tomorrow's another big day, so why don't you all get something to eat from the carry-out while Mal and I go discuss a few things?"

"*Da*," she says, "is good plan. Tonight I must help Zveta Borisova. We must speak with Rosa on telephone, take her far from this Neno. He is bad type. Rosa must come in Grannies Tour, have jolly nice time. It can be she will meet nice husband instead this *kriminalen*."

Mal keeps saying, "What if Kichka wanders again? Do you think it's okay to leave them?"

But Kichka's on the fifth floor, with a sprained ankle. And she'd never get into an elevator on her own because she thinks some kind of black magic makes it go up and down. Besides, I could use a break. What I need right now is the chinkety-plink of an ice cold cranberry vodka, followed by a full slab of barbecued baby back ribs. With fries.

So we're sitting in Houlihan's and Mal's giving me the third degree about my pharmaceuticals.

I said, "I only took a dexxie. It's to give me a little energy boost, get me through the evening. I have been up twenty hours."

He said, "We all have. Why don't you just go to bed?"

He doesn't understand. I know what I'm doing. I've been taking this stuff for years.

He said, "I worry about you."

So sweet.

I said, "Why? I'm the grownup."

He said, "Well for one thing, if anything happens to you, I'll be out of a job."

Not so sweet.

I said, "Anyway, everybody takes *something*."

"I don't," he says.

Well I know he's a cry-baby about smoking. He goes crazy if I point my cigarette anywhere near him. And he only drinks beer. He says he doesn't like the taste of anything else. As if the *taste* is what it's about. But I cannot believe he never tried a little wonderstuff on a Saturday night. Who does he think he's kidding?

I said, "You're not Christian Scientist are you?"

He thinks he's Church of England.

I said, "Mal, if you ever reach the level I'm at, you'll need something too, for the stress. Do you have any idea the pressure I'm under?"

"No," he said, "not really. If you mean about losing Stanka, we got through Crawley and Portsmouth all right without her."

No, losing Stanka was nothing. If Rosa comes in it'll be an improvement.

He said, "Is it your other bands?"

I said, "It's a million things."

What am I going to say? How do I begin to explain my life to this child? Okay, Mal:

1. I got evicted from my office, fucked over by Hunt Madson and offered an award they salvaged from Ed Rix's trash can.

2. I may be the only sane member of the Wexler family left alive.

3. My last lid-lift isn't wearing well.

And 100. When I go to bed I can't sleep, when I get to sleep I can't wake up, I'm maxed out on my cards, my apartment depresses me, I hate weekends, and the last two times I got laid I didn't feel a thing. Neck up, neck down, nothing.

He said, "I *am* trying to help. Only at the moment I can't see anything else that needs doing. And if you don't tell me, I'm not a mind reader."

I said, "Don't worry. I always get like, bipolar, when I know I have to go visit my folks."

He said, "And not only then."

He ordered the Club sandwich.

He said, "Well you may be dreading it but I'm really looking forward to meeting your dad. We all are. Lubka can't imagine somebody like you coming from an ordinary family. She thinks you're the last word in glamour."

It's true, I am. And it's a kind of miracle. Growing up in Troy Hill, who were my role models? Not Grandma Wexler. She had a turkey-gobble neck and thin hair. And in my lifetime Grandma Shorsky never left her bed. She just lay around eating Cracker Barrel cheese and reading *True Crime* magazine. She must have weighed 200 pounds at the end. And Mom? Well, I guess she did think of herself as glamorous but then she suffered from a number of delusions.

Encouraged by Dad she believed men preferred women with saddlebags and flubbery rolls of goosh. Fortunately for her this meshed with her understanding of dietetics. The Shorskies believed butter to be as essential to life as oxygen itself. We probably averaged a stick a day. I remember particularly her liverwurst and potato chip omelette which was drowned in it. If you wanted a low-fat healthful eating option in our house the Lemon Jell-O Tuna Ring was about your only hope.

The gospel according to Dorothy is that Mom was a wonderful, attentive, homemaking mother but she's remembering a different person. Eunice Wexler, the early years. My memories go back to when I was around four, so I'm sure I'd still have passed for cute, but even then I had the definite impression I'd done something to annoy her. Like, existing. She was forty-two when she caught for me and in those days there wasn't much you could do about a thing like that. I guess it'd be a cold shower, when you first found out. But hell, it wasn't like I interrupted her career.

If I had a kid I'd buy clothes for her all the time. Every weekend we'd be down at the mall. Not my mom. Everything was Dorothy's old shit, turned up or let out, "revamped" as Mom called it. I curse the name of Isaac Merrit Singer. My first day at Allegheny Middle School, she made me wear a poodle skirt that was practically obsolete when Dorothy wore it in 1959. The summer of '74 I was the only teen in the civilised world who didn't have a pair of bell-bottom pants.

Even Shirley Hooten got taken to Gimbel's a couple of times a year and God knows, Mrs Hooten could be cheap.

I said, "Mal, when I was twelve years old I made a mental note of the location of the Greyhound bus station. When I was sixteen I spent my birthday money on a one-way ticket to New York. Everything I am is in *spite* of my family."

He said, "You mean, if they'd been different you wouldn't have left home when you did?"

Kind of a question is that? Possibly. If they'd been very, *very* different.

He said, "But then *you'd* be different. If you hadn't run away to New York and met the people you met, you wouldn't be who you are now, would you? And you wouldn't be getting a Lifetime Achievement Award from the Urban Music Panel."

I said, "What's your point?"

He says, "Well, you could argue, you are what you are *because* of your family. So maybe you should actually be grateful to them. Maybe that's why you're so hostile about them. Because you don't like saying thank you."

I said, "Is this what they teach you at St John Ambulance? Psycho-analysis? What do you think of Rosa?"

"She seems nice," he said. "She's pretty. I hope she does come with us. But only if she dumps the boyfriend."

I said, "Why? Are you interested?"

He said, "Do you mean interested as in *interested*?"

I said, "Well are you?"

"Wrong reading," he said.

I said, "Well I can be forgiven. You never seem interested in anyone."

Nothing.

He said, "All I meant was, Neno looks like trouble. I bet he carries a gun. What is it with these Bulgarians and security? The ones I met when I went bird-watching weren't like that. It must be something that gets into them when they leave the country. Like Boyko. Carrying on as though the butterflies are waiting to jump him."

I said, "Which in Stanka's case was true. Or Kichka's, as it turned out."

He said, "About you and Boyko —"

I said, "Yes?"

"Nothing," he said. "Forget it."

He went to the men's room.

The waitress says, "Nice kid. I got one about his age myself."

I said, "Is that right?"

"Yeah," she says. "Isn't it great when you can take them out and they don't need a booster seat any more? A few more years and he'll be picking up the check."

CHAPTER
THIRTY-THREE

Rosa was a great addition to the line-up for the Chicago show. She's quiet, like her mom, but there's fire in her when she sings. She has cleavage too and instead of a babushka she wears a kind of bandanna decorated with silk roses. Lubka says it's not exactly traditional headgear for girls from Gorni but she's willing to let it pass. She knows a winner when she sees one. The only drawback was, to get Rosa we had to accept Neno, the non-optional slimeball in the pimped-up Honda Civic.

Rosa does a lot of bikini work, car shows mainly, but she has made one movie. She said it was set in Afghanistan and she played an army doctor, which sounded strangely mainstream, but then she explained. In between battles and emergency procedures she had to like strip off the surgical scrubs and get it on with two nurses, one guy, one gal. I don't think it'll be playing at the Multiplex.

I said, "You're a bright girl, nice looking. Do you think this is the way to go, career-wise?"

She said, "Neno says it could lead to something."

I said, "He doesn't make you do stuff you don't want to do?"

"Not really," she said. "I don't mind. And the money's pretty good."

I said, "You got your own bank account, right?"

She said, "Neno looks after the money side. He makes sure people don't rip me off."

It's funny how things turn out. Lubka tried insults and I'm pretty sure Kichka tried some kind of incantation but it was the Ohio State Highway Patrol that relieved us of Neno. Even on a good day he's the kind of guy who drives angry and this afternoon he was extra mad because when the girls sang in Van Wert Rosa attracted intense but non-paying interest from the boys at the firehouse. I don't think Neno would have minded anybody admiring Rosa's frontage, as long as money changed hands. We were just entering Lima when Wally suddenly stopped the bus.

He said, "Your friend just got pulled over. I guess we better wait?"

Lubka said, "Is police did stop him? What he did do?"

Wally said, "Easier to tell you what he didn't do. Worst driving I ever saw. I hope they throw the book at him. Oh, he's making a run for it. No, they got him. Now he's really in trouble."

Lubka said, "He will go in prison? Is jolly good idea. Wally, please to open door. I will get down, bring Rosa to this bus. She must not go in prison."

She'd got her hair in jumbo rollers but she didn't care. She was off, trundling along the kerb, waving her arms at the patrolman. For a big woman Lubka can really move. By the time I caught up to her she's got Rosa's door open and she's shouting, "Get from this car, Rosa Borisova. Come in bus with your mama, else this crazy makes you killed."

Neno said, "Rosa, stay where you are."

So far they'd got Driving with a Suspended Licence, Driving Without Liability Insurance, Failure to Yield to a Funeral Procession and Attempting to Flee.

Lubka said, "Listen at me, Rositska. You are beautiful girl. You are good singer. Why you will stay with this *gloopak?* You come in bus. We have nice times. Is true, Buzz?"

I said, "Lubka's right. And wouldn't you like more time with your mom?"

She was hesitating, you could tell.

Neno said, "You go with them, we're finished."

Then she saw Zveta climb down from the bus and just stand there, arms open wide. That did it. She was out of the car. Neno was yelling after us, calling Lubka names. Rosa was crying, Zveta was crying, Dora and Kichka were shaking their fists at Neno through the rear window of the bus.

I said, "Can the girl come with us? She has a singing engagement in Pittsburgh tomorrow night."

The patrolman said, "You better take her. This guy won't be driving her."

A big cheer went up when we got back into the bus. Just Mal looked a bit uptight.

I said, "Problem?"

"No," he said, "no problem. Apart from the fact that we're now likely to be pursued by a raving psychopath who knows every detail of our travel itinerary."

Lubka said, "I have question. He did call me fatoldfugger. What is?"

I've spoken with Dad every day since we got here, to try to get it clear in his mind when he'll be seeing me. I tell him which one-horse towns we've been driving through and he keeps me up to date on Ronald Reagan's movements.

I say, "I'm in Indiana. A town called Warsaw."

He says, "Warsaw, Indiana! That's where Tilly's knee implant was manufactured."

I say, "Who's Tilly?"

"A friend," he says. "I mind her dog kibble."

I say, "Are you dating?"

He says, "I believe they make Co-Co Wheats there too, but I'd have to check on that. It could be Froot Loops. They took him from the funeral home this morning. He's reposing at the Presidential Library till Wednesday. There'll be thousands wanting to see him."

I say, "We were just in Marion, Ohio."

Dad says, "Popcorn Capital of the World! You're getting around."

I say, "My ladies are promoting their album. They just sang at a home for seniors."

He says, "That makes no sense. Folks in a seniors' home, their money's all spoke for. They tell you to be careful with your money, so you can enjoy your old age. Then you get old and start enjoying it they tell you

you're pixilated and you'd best hand it over and go in a seniors' home. They get you every way to Sunday. He's on his way to Washington, by the by. They just put the casket aboard the transport, flying him out of Point Mugu. I watched it on the TV. I tell you another interesting fact about Marion, Ohio. President Warren G. Harding is buried there."

I tell him, "Okay, Dad, we just left Akron."

He says, "Akron! Home of the World of Rubber museum. The President's at the Rotonda now, so folk can pay their respects. They flew him in to Andrews Base Wednesday, drove him into town, then they put the casket on a trailer, pulled him the rest of the way with black horses, real beauties. He'll have enjoyed that."

I saw a newspaper picture of Nancy, waiting by the limo while they were moving the casket from the hearse to the gun carriage. She looked terrific. I'd love to get the name of the surgeon who works on her.

I said, "I'm surprised you didn't go up to Washington yourself, to pay your respects."

He said, "I would of, but I can't wait on line three hours, not with these bagdarn water pills."

I said, "What about the show, Thursday night? Are you coming to that? They have bathrooms."

He said, "I don't know. I might. Is Dorothy coming?"

I said, "No. She has a Girl Scout bake sale or something vital to the well-being of the nation. Janine might come. You could come with her. I'll spring for a cab if Janine doesn't drive you."

246

He said, "I wouldn't ride with Janine. She's not safe out. I'll drive myself. Where's it at?"

I said, "It's in West Homestead. At the Bulgarian Cultural Center."

He said, "I've been at the Polish Club many a time but I don't think I know any Bulgarians."

I said, "Well you're about to meet some. As a matter of fact, one of these girls is a very big fan of Ronald Reagan. She thinks he changed the world."

"A right-thinking person," he says. "I'll come. Now there's something I have to ask you. What's this new name you like to go under?"

I said, "It's Buzz. Something I have to ask you. Why did you ever call me Beryl?"

He said, "I don't recall. It's a long time ago. I think Mommy chose it. It's a rock, you know? It's a gem stone. You could wear it on a pendant. Beryl is the state mineral of New Hampshire."

I said, "The only gem I'm interested in wearing on a pendant is a diamond. Which state is that?"

He said, "You got me there. It might be Delaware. Land of Tax-Free Shopping!"

There's nothing wrong with his mind. At least, not in the way Dorothy means.

CHAPTER
THIRTY-FOUR

I was telling Rosa about the Urbies and my award and everything. She loved my Hector Munro, but she just about fainted with envy when I showed her my Rubber Queen dress. So I put it on to show her and it was a bit of a struggle because these sleeper compartments get sweaty even with the air con. Also, when you're on the road you so easily put on weight. In the office I can go all day on cigarettes and coffee and maybe a mango smoothie. If I have to do lunch I just get the egg white omelette. But these girls love the All You Can Eat and before you know it you've eaten about three thousand calories worth of ranch dressing.

Rosa thought I looked fabulous, anyway. Like she said, I am in great shape for my age and it could be the Niravax making me like, retain fluid.

I said, "It'll look better than this for the actual ceremony. I'll probably do the Cabbage Soup diet for a few days before Seattle."

So I'm back in the sleeping compartment, where there's hardly room to breathe let alone bend and stretch, and it doesn't matter what I do or which way I try it, I can't get the fucking dress off. But it's a well-known fact that panic makes you swell so I lay down on the bed and tried to think calm thoughts. Which isn't so easy when you just discovered you blew up like a freakin' life raft and you only have ten days to get yourself back to a state of omygod fabulousness and then your intern comes along, interrupting you with non-urgent information.

He said, "I've got some good news I thought you'd like to hear."

I said, "Tell me through the door."

He said, "Local press in Youngstown. They're going to do a photo story. Are you all right?"

I said, "Of course I'm all right. I'm just getting changed."

Why wouldn't I be all right?

He said, "Sorry. I thought you sounded a bit not all right."

I said, "Well I'm not. Just tell Rosa I'd like to see her for a minute."

She took her time coming.

She said, "Maybe if we cut the strap? You could wear it strapless."

I said, "Do you have any idea what this cost? There'll be no cutting. Single strap is the look. I don't care if you have to bury me in it."

I suppose humiliating experiences always feel like they go on for hours. I was butt naked underneath and even with a dusting of Dora's talcum powder it took a long, long time to ease the dress up and over my head.

Rosa said, "You mind if I say something?"

I said, "I know, I know. I've got fluid retention. Don't worry. First place we stop tomorrow I'm going to buy every stick of celery they have. And radishes."

"Yeah," she said. "Radishes is good. You mind if I say another thing? Only I just wondered, don't be offended, right, but is there any way you could be pregnant?"

Which of course I absolutely could not because I get a depo-Provera shot five times a year. In fact I'd have had the one that was scheduled for May 14th if only I'd had an intern to remind me about it, if I hadn't had Dorothy hounding me with phone calls and that lying bastard Corcoran scheming to get me out of town and completely taking my eye off the ball. But even so, I should still have been okay because I'll bet that hormone stuff stays in your system longer than they say it does.

I said, "No, I'm sure I can't be. Why?"

She said, "Well, I've had bit of personal experience. And I couldn't help notice you got veins showing on your tits. Really noticeable, you know? Like roads on a map. But perhaps yours are like that all the time. Everybody's different."

Well there's just no way. Read my lips, Jose. But somebody puts an idea in your mind and even though it's beyond crazy it can start to bug you.

Lubka was up front in the living area, singing. I knew she wouldn't mind me going into her quarters. Nothing bothers Lubka. I knew she'd understand I didn't want to go into a big explanation in front of Mal and Wally.

250

Anyway, she probably didn't even remember buying that stupid pregnancy test at Quids In.

Instructions for use. As movement of the motor home vehicle permits, pee into a clean, dry dixie cup. Remove the test stick from its foil wrapper. Remove the plastic cap from the test stick. Place the absorbent tip of the test stick in the urine for five seconds. One and two and three and four and five and . . . Replace the cap. Lay the test stick on a flat surface with the indicator window facing up, light a cigarette and await the delivery of the verdict. One pink line, acquitted. Two pink lines, life without parole unless you get a little procedure organised pdq.

Foreperson of the jury, how do you find Beryl Eunice Ermengild Wexler?

We find her knocked up.

Well hang on. The reason they sell off those test kits for a pound is they're old stock. The chemicals deteriorate and then they give a positive result, give you a scare. There are all kinds of explanations why my Rubber Queen tube dress shrank a size and my face suddenly looks like Mom's.

Why is it, when you need to speak to a person privately suddenly everybody's hanging around them. It took me ages to get Rosa alone.

I said, "Do me a favour? Tomorrow, when we get to Youngstown, go buy one of those tests from the drug store? And whatever you do, don't tell anyone it's for me."

"Sure," she said. "Best thing. Put your mind at rest."

★ ★ ★

A night can seem very long when you have to wait for a friend to go to an Acme Pharmacy and buy you a pregnancy test that won't lie. You have time to think about how completely unacceptable the situation would be, and where'd be the best place to get things fixed, just supposing. Before Seattle, that's for sure. There's no way I'm going up to collect Lifetime Achievement looking like an unopened liver sausage.

Lifetime Achievement is the final award. The smell of fear and bile'll be subsiding. There'll just be a whiff of Madson's carbon emissions if Banana Bubbles beat Spam Javelins. Which they won't.

Lights down, drum roll, serious voice.

"Each year The Urban Music Panel presents just one of its prestigious Lifetime Achievement awards. This year's honouree has shaped urban music over a staggering twenty-five year period. She started in 1978, assisting the late, great Pete Belkin in the promotion of ground-breaking bands like The Finger."

Screw that. I don't want them bringing up Belkin's name. There are going to be kids there who weren't even born when Belkin expired. Besides, it's *my* night. Mal has to call Dabney Apple. Tell her under no circumstances do they mention Pete Belkin. Not that he wasn't a fabulous guy. He was aces. We had the best times. And the whole drink issue, the stuff the papers wrote about him after his mishap, they might have done themselves a favour and asked somebody who was actually in possession of the facts. I mean some people are missing, like, an enzyme or something. They can't process alcohol, same as some people can't do shellfish. It's metabolism, that's all. And oftentimes people don't realise they have this missing link problem. Till it's too late.

Then they'll say something like, "Working as an independent and through labels like Pure Vinyl and Comet Cutting Edge, tonight's honouree has been a mentor, a rainmaker and a visionary. From her discovery of Post-Nasal Drip in Queens, New York in 1980 to her creation of tonight's Best Industrial winners, she has been an innovator. From the early days of Crustgrind to today's emerging Post-Thrash scene, her energy and her intuition have made her a legend in her own lifetime. Ladies and gentlemen, the recipient of UMP's 2004 Lifetime Achievement Award and four weeks pregnant with the spawn of a passing Bulgarian, Buzz Wexler!"

No, no, no. The way to put this completely out of my mind is to take another Niravax. And fuck the side effects because

1. I'm not pregnant and

2. Even if by some weird flukey chance I am, I soon won't be.

CHAPTER
THIRTY-FIVE

Let's just say three tests have now shown up positive for the totally creepy reason that my body thinks I conceived. Which hypothetical jerk-off could be the cause of this? Could Felix have left me a little parting gift? Or Boyko Stoyan? Or a nameless wham-bam Ursari boy who smelled of stale sweat? No. Delete all. This is not in the game plan. In the unlikely event I ever decide to have a kid the donor daddy is going to be a six foot *summa cum laude* WASP. I mean, it's not like I'd have to live with the guy or anything.

Maybe I'm getting The Change early. That'd be cool. That's nothing to worry about. Look at Cher. I'll get HRT instead of contraceptive shots. Kill the baby idea once and for all and buy that time-share on St Barth. I didn't get any hot flashes so far, and my tits look more like rocks than empty change purses but, like Rosa said, every woman is different.

I could skip Pittsburgh or Reno and just fly to New York. I could see that obgyn in Murray Hill. He fixed me up before. Or I could leave it till we get to LA. Take a couple of days out before the Mendocino gig. There'd be less explaining to do. And in the meanwhile, everything might come good. I think it will. If I eat the radishes and quit taking the Niravax. I could wake up tomorrow five pounds lighter.

We had a date with the Youngstown *Vindicator*. The girls stood outside the Giant Eagle store and sang "The Maple Tree" and "A Silver Spindle". Quite a crowd gathered, wanted to know what we were giving away. The photographer said barring a major automobile accident it'd make the front page. It should do. Dora and Kichka were in their standard Balkan crone-wear. The Borisovas provided the glamour element because, under the influence of Rosa, Zveta has started wearing a wired bra and glittery eyelash bling. And in the center was Lubka in her *What Would Reagan Do?* trucker's hat and matching sweatshirt. All she needs to get now is the tote bag and she'll have the full ensemble.

We barely filled two hundred seats at the Oakland Center. A polite audience but nothing caught fire. Like one of the stewards said, with Ronald Reagan lying in state it's not a good week to be gigging in a red state. We were out of the theatre by quarter of ten. Lubka wanted to go to a steak house but suddenly I just had to have cold sesame noodles and shrimp with snow peas or *die* so we went to the Main Moon. Where the Gorni funsters prodded at a chicken-beef-pork combo platter till they were sure everything on it was dead, then drowned it in soy sauce and ate every last mouthful, and Kichka pocketed six pairs of vacuum sealed chopsticks.

I was totally okay till they brought the orange slices and we started reading the fortune cookies.

Mal said, "Uh-oh. I think Olga's found her new career."

AVOID UNNECESSARY GAMBOLS.

RELAX. NO MAN IS FLOORLESS.

YOU DESERVE ADMIRATION OF YOUR PEARS.

Which would have been more appropriate for Rosa than for Dora but Rosa was quite happy with SOON YOU WILL GET NEW CLOTHS.

Lubka's was SPEAK NO EVIL, HEAR NO ELVIS

She said, "I do not understand this cookies."

Kichka wouldn't let Mal open hers. It'll go home with her to Gorni. Hundreds of years from now archaeologists will find it, still sealed.

Mal said, "Go on then, Buzz. You're the last one."

Fortune cookies are so uncool. I mean, who can even be bothered? You know, it could have said something like YOUR LUCKY COLOUR IS BLUE and most likely I'd still have flipped for a minute. I think I'm becoming MSG intolerant. A lot of people are. You can get chest pains, dizziness, flushed skin. You can even break down into uncontrollable shakes and snotty, embarrassing weeping just because your fortune cookie message says YOU ARE FULL UP OF PRECIOUS TREASURE.

Rosa whispered something to Zveta, Zveta whispered something to Lubka and Mal said, "I'll go and take care of the bill then, shall I?"

They were all looking at me. Kichka even stopped counting her chopsticks.

Lubka said, "This cookie I understand."

I said, "I'm tired."

She said, "How you can be tired? Dora Gavrilova is olderly lady, she is not tired. Wally is not tired, even he drived bus many hours. What work you did today? None work."

I said, "I don't feel so good, that's all."

"*Da*," she said. "Is because you have start of baby. Is nothing. Soon you will be hundreds per cent."

Sweet Jesus. I should have known I couldn't trust Rosa to keep her mouth shut.

I said, "Rosa had no right to say anything. Allow *me* to know if I'm pregnant. And I'm pretty sure I'm not."

Lubka said, "But I say you are. Already I did see this in your face. Only it was mystery, did you get secret boyfriend, else did you go to special doctor, like you have told me at ocean of Hunstanton, to buy baby in bottle? In United State of America all things is possible."

We're staying at a Best Western just off the Interstate. Another night sleeping under nightmare swirls of tangerine.

Lubka said, "Before you go in sleep I will come in your room."

I said, "I'm really, really tired."

"Still I will come," she said.

She brought what was left of her plum rakia. I figured the best thing was to just tell her everything and short-circuit the interrogation.

I said, "First of all, do not discuss this with anyone."

She said, "I will not."

I said, "That includes Mal."

"Even Mal, I will not," she says.

I said, "Okay then, yes, it seems like I may be pregnant, and no, I don't know who the father is."

She said, "Who is father, you can know in future, when you see face."

I said, "I'm not going to see any face, Lubka. I'm getting rid of it, as soon as we reach civilisation."

She said, "Getting rid? What is?"

I said, "Don't act the innocent with me. You have abortions in Bulgaria. Olga told me it's as easy as getting new heel tips."

"*Da*," she said. "*Abort*. We have. We learn this from Soviet Union, how to kill without no question asked. Why you will kill this baby?"

Because it doesn't fit in with my life plans right now. Because every child should be a wanted child. And this one isn't.

She said, "You don't want this baby? Give to me."

I said, "Look, don't lay this on me. I know you had a child, I know you had some kind of tragedy in your life but that's nothing to do with my situation."

She said, "I did not have tragedy. I had babygirl. It was gift from God."

I knew I shouldn't have let her in the room. With Lubka there's always the danger she's going to call God to take the stand.

I said, "Well, whatever. But if she was a gift from God it was pretty mean of him to give it to you and then take it back."

She shrugged.

She said, "When God gave to me I did not ask 'oh, why you give me such nice gift?' If He taked back, so what can I say?"

Her baby's name was Iordana, like the river Jordan, because Lubka's Aunt Mara christened her in a little trickle of a river, somewhere in the outskirts of Sofia.

I said, "Why your Aunt Mara? And why in the river?"

She said, "Because there was not church, there was not priest. It was bad time in my country. *Krishtenye* was forbidden."

Baptism. Dorothy's two were both christened and Kenny's kids. I think I'm godmother to one of them. I definitely remember ordering something from Tiffany's.

I said, "Does it count, without a priest?"

She seemed to think it did. No priests around, what are you going to do?

She said, "Only she asks Holy Spirit will come. Even she made *krishtenye* for me when I was baby. In kitchen bowl."

I said, "Why didn't she do you in the river?"

"Was too cold," she said. "I am born in December."

Iordana died when she was five. Sounds like it could have been whooping cough. She showed me a photo she keeps in her billfold, black and white and really dog-eared: Lazar and a little girl with a ribbon in her hair. I could get a decent print made for her.

I said, "I'm really sorry about what happened to you, Lubka, but this is me we're talking about now and I'm not ready to have a kid."

"When you will be ready?" she said. "In few years you cannot make babies no more."

I said, "And maybe I'm not meant for motherhood. I have a career. I enjoy a certain lifestyle."

She said, "You make baby without name of daddy, is not lifestyle. Lifestyle is nice sofa and vacation in Rivieras of France."

I said, "I had a boyfriend. It could be his. But he's gone."

She said, "He can come back. You must tell him of this baby."

I said, "He won't come back because I don't want him back. And anyway, it might not be his."

I didn't feel like giving her the full case history. When you're telling another person stuff like that it can sound too complicated. It can make things seem a bit squalid.

I said, "You're not going to like this."

She said, "You say you will get rid this baby. Already I do not like."

I said, "The thing is, I slept with Boyko."

She went so still, it was like she stopped breathing.

I said, "You understand now? It was just once, it didn't mean anything and if I am pregnant I'll soon have everything tidied up."

Silence.

I said, "You have to realise, age differences mean nothing here. And neither does sleeping with a guy. It's just, like, a leisure activity. You might go see a show or get dinner or get laid. Or all three. Women's bodies are their own. We have choices. And my choice is to get a D&C and resume my life."

She said, "It can be child of Boyko Stoyan?"

I said, "Yes. It can be. So now you see why I have to do what I have to do? He's just a flash musclehead and I never want to see him again as long as I live."

She said, "It can be baby of son of son of Danil Stoyan and Stanka Stoyanova. But Stanka is at seventy-five years. She is too olderly to take this baby. If you will not keep, you must give to me. I will rise him up so he is not big idiot like Boyko Stoyan."

Well, excuse me, but if I ever have a kid *she* is going to be a girl.

I said, "I can't give you my baby."

"Why?" she said. "You think I will not be good mama? If you do not want, why you cannot give to your Lubka?"

Because that's a whole different ball game, Lubka and you damn well know it. Because right now it's not anything. Right now it's just a blobby piece of gunk. Because once it's turned into a little cutie in size zero Oshkosh pee-jays you can't send it away two thousand miles to live in a house with an outdoor john. Not when it could have its own en-suite in a Docklands sub-penthouse and go to an A-list kindergarten.

I said, "I'm sorry but I can't explain. We're from different worlds. And I'm very, very tired."

She said, "I understand. We will drink health of baby. Then you will go asleep."

I said, "No rakia for me, thanks."

She said, "But is of plums. Is very good. Has more nice taste than peaches rakia of Kichka Nikolova."

261

I said, "I know. I tasted it before. I just don't feel like drinking."

So then she's laughing, rubbing my knees, squeezing my arms.

"Oh Buzz," she says. "But always you like to drink. For sure this is good sign. I put with little water. Is good for blood, good for baby."

I said, "Not in America it isn't. Not in England. If you're pregnant you don't drink alcohol. No sushi, no oysters, no Roquefort."

She said, "Is crazy countries. Even my country is not so crazy as this."

I did eat some of her sour pickles though. Man, they are so good. They make them after the first heavy frost. Cornichons, cauliflower, any tomatoes that are still green on the vine. Everything goes into brine and vinegar.

She said, "I have question. If you will flush gift of God in WC tomorrow why he cannot have nice drink of rakia tonight?"

I said, "Because maybe I won't flush it down the WC, as you so crudely put it. I have options, that's all. And anyway it's not a he. It's a she."

"Da," she said, "It can be you are right. But she is Bulgarian baby. Still I think she can have rakia before you send her back to God."

I'm not letting her play headgames with me. If I don't feel like drinking, that's my affair and Lubka Lilova can read into it any darned thing she likes.

CHAPTER
THIRTY-SIX

Rosa wanted to know where we were staying. Good question. Those cheapskates in World Music had booked us into some two-star across from the Pirates' stadium, but I soon fixed that. I called Madson.

I said, "Hunt, did you ever bring a band to Pittsburgh?"

He didn't think he ever did.

I said, "Well, I did. I was here with Strep Throat in '97 and let me tell you something. The William Penn Omni is where you stay. Otherwise, what does it say? That Starburst are too cheap to do the right thing by their artists?"

"Strep Throat?" he says. "Hell, Buzz, they were big. Didn't they play the football stadium?"

They did. God, that was a great tour. The fans had the hotel under siege. When we needed to leave the building we had to have a decoy limo out front and then slip out through a service door.

I said, "They were big. But they only became seriously big because I made it happen. I gave them the star treatment, got the buzz going. Buzz by name, buzz by trade. And now I'm doing what I can for these girls. They have great attitude, Hunt. We're up against it

263

here. The whole damned country pulled the shutters down till after Reagan's funeral. They've sung in every flyblown mall between here and Chicago. We even slept a night in bunk beds on the tour bus, like we're freakin' girl scouts. Would you do it? You wouldn't. I'm booking us into the Omni and I don't want any grief with my Visa card."

He said, "I don't know, Buzz. You'd better speak to Finance."

I said, "No, you're the big kahuna, *you* speak to Finance. Tell them Buzz Wexler's artists do not stay at the Why-Pay-More?"

He said, "Pittsburgh's your home town, right?"

I said, "So what? I'd be saying the same thing if we were in Poughkeepsie. Flying coach, staying at Budget Lodge, it's so not fair on the Grannies. They're old ladies."

He said, "Very affecting, all this concern for some old ladies. I tell you what, I'm going to okay this place you want to stay, but it's a one-off. Don't expect to do it any other place. The rest of the tour you follow the script. You're with Starburst now, Buzz. You'll find us a much leaner operation that Comet."

I said, "Is that so? Where'll you be staying for the Urbies, the Seattle Y?"

He said, "I guess the eyes of Pittsburgh are upon you, hunh? Local girl gets major music industry award. I'll bet you have interviews lined up like a taxiway at JFK."

As a matter of fact I'm choosing not to grant interviews. Pittsburgh had its chance with me. They

264

blew it. I was here in '96 with Hex Dump, they couldn't even get my name right. I came back the following year with Strep Throat, they didn't even mention my Pittsburgh connection. So be it. Last thing I need is people trying to reconnect.

"Hi, this is Barb Brinkelman. Did you used to be Beryl Wexler?"

Yes, Barb, that was me. Except *you* always called me The Chunker.

"Hi Buzz, remember me? Dee Dee Hendel, Allegheny High?"

Of course, Dee Dee. I have perfect recall of everyone who ever mocked my homemade dungarees. Sure, *now* you want to be my friends. Now I'm the famous, fabulous, award-winning Buzz Wexler. Well you're too late, losers. The show left town.

We're coming in across the Vanport Bridge, along the Penn Lincoln Parkway and then into town through the Liberty Tube.

Mal says, "You're in a better mood than I expected."

He's right. I'm Code One veering to Code Two. I haven't thrown up for five hours and my tits feel more like large pebbles than actual boulders. I think the radishes are working. I knew it was all a false alarm.

He said, "When do we get to meet your family?"

I said, "We're not the Carnegies, you know? My dad said he'll come to the gig but more than likely he'll get confused and go to the Polish Center. And my sister's girl Janine might put in an appearance but on the whole I think she won't. Which is fine by me."

265

The Cultural Center told Mal we can expect a full house because as well as the Grannies, their resident dance ensemble will be performing, plus they just put up a new exhibit of historical Bulgarian legwear which a lot of people are eager to see, *plus* they'll be serving traditional snacks after the show, which always brings in a good crowd.

I said, "Lubka, I think tonight of all nights you should leave off the cowboy hat and the fishnets. You're going to be among your own people."

"*Da*," she said, "You are right. Tonight all we will wear apron and kerchief and *kindouri* slippers."

She was quiet for a minute, then she whispered, "Underneath I will wear wire undycup brassiere but none other person will know this."

We check in at the Omni and I give them two hours to shake out their aprons and rest up before the show. I'd hardly had time to shower and do another bogus, bullshit, lying bastard pregnancy test, and Mal was on the phone.

"Two things," he says. "You know you said we should relax and enjoy ourselves because everything's paid for? I was wondering what the 'everything' covers exactly?"

I said, "Not the caviar taster-platter."

He said, "Okay. Only the beauty salon just called me. They want to know if it's all right to put three pedicures on the account."

Lubka, Dora and Zveta.

I said, "Do you remember a time when they were scared to use an elevator? Do you remember when they thought they'd be charged for the use of a shower cap?"

He said, "It's Lubka. They'll do anything now if she goes first."

It's true. They'd still be in a huddle, still be scared of magic-eye doors and automatic flushes if they didn't have Lubka running ahead of them, trying out everything like a kid in a candy store.

I said, "Of course they can get their feet done. What's the second thing?"

He said, "Well, you know Rosa said hell would freeze before she'd go back with Neno?"

Shit. I should have seen it coming. She was texting like crazy all the way in along Route 60, silly smile on her face. Neno's followed her here, in a Lincoln stretch driven by a friend called Einstein.

I said, "Was there a scene? Did he threaten her?"

"Yes," he said. "He threatened her with a dozen long-stemmed roses and a big sparkly ring."

I said, "Don't tell me she's leaving."

She's not leaving. She's going to complete the tour with us because Neno's really sorry he didn't treat her right and he's going to make amends and give her his full support. And the cow jumped over the moon.

I flicked through some magazines, tried to watch some TV. Everything is babies. Liv Tyler's planning to use chlorine-free diapers. Erykah Badu and The D.O.C are having a home birth. Summer Phoenix just had a baby. So did Heidi Klum. Geena Davis had twins for Chrissake. It's a freakin' conspiracy.

Then my cell's ringing.

"Aunty Beryl?" she says.

My niece, Janine.

She says, "I'm sposably coming to see your band tonight. Is there anything I oughta know?"

I said, "Yes, Janine. Never, ever again call me Aunty Beryl."

We're in Pittsburgh about like, five minutes and happiness starts breaking out. Lubka and Zveta had their toenails painted Summer Lovin' Coral. Rosa has a hickie the size of Rhode Island on her neck. Dora chatted with her sheep for the first time since we left the UK, and Kichka's kind of hypnotised by the chandeliers in the lobby. I can see she's scheming how to get one in her luggage but I'm mellow. Let her scheme. Even Kichka can't pull a stunt like that. But the weirdest thing is Mal. Suddenly Mr Argyle-Vest "n" Chinos is wearing his shirt collar popped up. Little things can make a difference. If he'd only upgrade those chain-store shades he wears he'd have minor dude potential.

I said, "You're looking somewhat slick. Did you take a walk around the lot? Did something catch your eye?"

He said, "I have no idea what you mean."

Lubka says, "I have question. How I can go to grave of Ronald Reagan?"

I said, "He's not in it yet. The funeral's tomorrow."

"*Da*," she said. "This I understand. But after funerals, next day we can go."

I said, "Not possible. Saturday we're flying to Reno. Wrong direction."

I thought they'd bury him in Arlington National Cemetery but Mal says they're taking him back to California, burying him in the grounds of the Presidential Library.

Lubka says, "*Da*, California. We are going in California. So we can visit this grave, no problem. We can sing him nice song."

Of course she has no concept of distances in the U.S. It's understandable. You could fit the whole land mass of Bulgaria into Pennsylvania.

Mal says, "Are you thinking what I'm thinking?"

Almost certainly not. I was thinking where can I get a jar of sour pickles right now, without attracting attention? I was thinking should I get Reduced Sodium? And I was thinking can I wear the Hector Munro pants suit to the Urbies or will the sheen on it make me look even more like a Goodyear Tyre blimp?

I said, "I'm listening."

He said, "Seeing as we have a free day before we go to Mendocino and seeing as the *Los Angeles Garment and Citizen* will need a photo for the feature they're running, why not kill two birds? Among the first to visit the late President's grave, The Gorni Grannies! Topical but unusual."

And possibly just corny enough to fly.

CHAPTER
THIRTY-SEVEN

Rosa wanted her mom to ride with her in the limo to the venue but Zveta's still looking at Neno through narrowed eyes. She recognises an ass-wipe when she sees one. So Lubka offered she'd go. She said it was to make sure Rosa didn't come to any harm but I think she just wanted to ride in a white Lincoln Super Stretch.

We get to Eighth Avenue and there's a reception party waiting to greet us. Even though it's drip-dropping rain there are a dozen of them lined up outside the Cultural Center, all ages. Bright shining American faces, but they're all saying *dobry doshlee*. All bar one. The little silver-haired guy in the oversized check jacket is just smiling warily and shaking everybody by the hand. Until it's my turn.

"Beryl?" he says. "Is that you?"

For some reason my father is part of the Bulgarian — Macedonian Cultural Center welcoming committee.

I said, "Don't tell me. Have I been Bulgarian all my life without even knowing it?"

"Well," he says, "I'll tell you what happened. I was here good and early because you never know if you'll find a place to park, and then I went inside to get the lie of the land. I told them you'd invited me and that lady in the mauve blouse said if I stuck with her she'd make sure I got a good seat. Then somebody said the stars of the show were arriving and we should all come outside and I thought it'd seem rude if I didn't. So here I am."

I said, "You look well."

"I am," he said. "Never better. You don't. You look like you could do with a good night's sleep."

I said, "Janine said she's coming to see the show. I don't think I'll know her."

Dad says, "You'll know her. She'll be the one comes in late and starts rustling in her bag. She's always searching for that Vicks thing she sticks up her nose."

I introduced Mal.

Dad said, "I shall be in trouble now. I called her Beryl. I forgot to remember she doesn't go as that any more. What is it they call her now?"

Mal said, "Buzz. Just think of her initials. B.E.E."

"That's it," he said. "B.E.E. Very clever. I shall remember that. I don't have anything against a person changing their name. John Wayne did it. Course, he went from a comical name to a good solid name. Beryl's gone the other way. None of my affair though, she's old enough to please herself. I reckon she must be forty. The other one, Dorothy, she's fifty-four. You wouldn't think I had a daughter of fifty-four, would you? I'm doing pretty good for eighty-two. Marilyn Monroe, she changed her name too. I don't recall what she was before."

There were children's paintings on the walls and a display of old leather sandals and thick socks, like the ones Dora makes, and the main hall had tables down either side, thumb-tacked with paper cloths. It reminded me of a church social.

Dad said, "This recital, is it just these three ladies?"

Mal said, "No, there are two more of them. They'll be here any minute. And there's going to be dancing as well."

Dad said, "It's a long way to come."

Mal said, "From Bulgaria? Yes, it is a long way but they're very energetic."

Dad said, "I meant from Troy Hill. Must be nine mile. Then you've still got to get home. I don't go out a lot after dark. The type of artist Bee brings to town — you'll note I've got her new name committed to memory now — they're not usually up my alley. They tend to be very way out. But she said this would be a bit different so I thought I'd better show willing. I'd have brought my friend Tilly along as well but anything Bee's thought up you can't be sure how suitable it's going to be and Tilly said she'd just as soon stay in anyway. They're showing *Bedtime for Bonzo*."

Mal said, "Well I think you'll enjoy the show. There's going to be food too."

Dad said, "Will that be before the singing starts?"

I said, "It'll be after the show. Bulgarian snacks. Didn't you eat before you came?"

He said, "I'm not hungry. I don't have but a bowl of oatmeal this time of night. More than that and I get acid reflux. I just hope things won't drag on too late, that's all. I got to be up in the morning. I got a big day."

272

Darn tootin! There's a state funeral happening tomorrow and Ted Wexler has nobody to help him manage it apart from the U.S. Army, the Marine Corps, the Air Force, the Navy, the Department of Homeland Security and the Coast Guard.

The show's opening with a display of Bulgarian dancing and the junior dancers are running round, getting over-excited. They wear these adorable little red flared skirts, white stockings and black ballerinas. The boys are in knee pants, red or black, with vests to match. The older girls are in layered shifts, embroidered aprons, black and white, and red babushki. It's a similar style to the stuff the Grannies wear but these girls all have waistlines and straight, white teeth.

Mal said, "I'd have expected Rosa and Lubka to be here by now."

I said, "Dollars to donuts they got lost. Einstein is surely called Einstein for a good reason. Call Rosa's cell phone."

He said, "I did. No answer. But I don't suppose there's any reason to worry."

The place is filling up. A guy in a fancy vest has started playing the accordion. Mal keeps trying Rosa's number and not getting her.

I said, "Don't stress. They'll be here. Maybe they got a flat tyre."

He'll learn. Artists going walkabout, bands going missing, it's all in a day's work. One time Gilgamesh had a gig in Hanover and two of them were missing.

Turned out they'd gone on a bender and ended up in the wrong town. They were wandering around Hamburg looking for the venue.

Mal went out to the street door. No sign of them.

I said, "You're not suggesting anything sinister could have happened? Like, Neno's revenge?"

He said. "No. Well, maybe. You must admit they should be here by now."

Two abductions in one tour. That would be beyond wild.

I said, "Don't forget, it isn't just Rosa. The ultimate kidnap deterrent is riding with her in that car. Would you mess with Lubka?"

He said, "I see what you mean. But I think I'd still better warn the girls they might have to go on as a threesome. With Zveta leading, I suppose?"

I said, "You know, if it comes to it, there are probably old-timers in the audience who could sing."

He said, "You're developing a very take-it-as-it-comes Bulgarian attitude all of a sudden."

They dance in lines, mainly. Sometimes one or two of them step out and do a little piece in the spotlight, but it's all very orderly, very polite. Dances of the Rhodope region, dances of the Pirin region. There's no gypsy sweat flying, no Tens with leather-clad hinies. I'm sure Olga would have approved.

So I'd given myself till seven forty-five before I'd start worrying, it's seven-fifty and I'm just wondering how much longer we can leave it till we report the disappearance of a glamour model and an Amazon, last

274

seen in the company of two Balkan muscle-brains when, bah-boom, the doors at the back of the hall burst open and in walk Lubka and Rosa, arms full of cut flowers, and behind them, Neno and Einstein, laden with bags from Filene's Basement and the Yarn Barn. Everything stops. Everybody's on their feet, applauding them. All they needed was "The Entry of the Gladiators".

No kidnap, no flat tyre. They just stopped off to do a little shopping on the way. Also they gave somebody a ride. Lubka noticed an old lady carrying grocery bags in the rain and insisted they stop, to offer her a ride home.

I said, "You mean she accepted?"

A ten-seater pimp-mobile pulls up and a guy with one eyebrow says "hop in"? I mean, would you?

Rosa says, "It wasn't far but then we got lost after we dropped her."

Neno said, "We didn't get lost. That old woman told us wrong."

Sounded like they ended up practically in Bethel Park.

They're making this slow progress through the hall, shaking hands with everyone. I know the next thing is likely to be Show and Tell with the shopping bags if we don't nip the situation in the bud.

Mal said, "The show started without you."

Lubka never notices when she's being chastised.

I said, "Onto the stage, Lubka. Everybody's waiting to hear you sing."

"*Da*," she said. "We will sing. But where is your Mr Dad? He is arrived? First I must say him hello."

My dad's not a big guy and with Lubka's bosom billowing over him he seemed to disappear inside his jacket. She kissed him on both cheeks.

She said, "How I am pleased I meet you. Your Buzz is very kind friend with us. She is like American sister."

Dad's smiling but warily, like a boa constrictor just threw its first coil around him and he's working out what his next move should be. Social kissing never really caught on in Troy Hill.

Mal's saying, "Lubka, to the stage. Now."

"*Dobry*," she said, "I go."

On the way past she whispers to me loud enough a deaf man could have heard it in McCandless, "I bought wools for nikting. Very nice. We can make baby suit."

And Mal made far too good a job of pretending not to hear.

So they get to the stage, put down their pocketbooks and begin. "A Golden Apple", "Beautiful Nedelya", "The End is Far Away". They're just starting "Trees in the Forest", the quiet bit where Lubka sings the first line alone then Rosa and Zveta kind of slide in, then Dora and Kichka, and the collision brings a stupid lump to your throat, when the doors bang open again and I hear a familiar voice say, "Oh, it started. Sorry!"

Dad leans over to me. He says, "Didn't I tell you? Ask Janine to go to the foot of the stairs and she'll go by way of Altoona."

276

Janine must be about thirty. I lose track. To me she doesn't look much different than when she was seventeen, still wearing the same dopey bangs, still got sinus issues. Anybody else, I'd call that a coke-nose but not Janine. She's her mother's daughter and Dorothy thinks you're on a slippery slope if you take Midol once a month. I guess Janine's kind of stuck. It was always assumed she'd be married by the time she was twenty so she always took jobs that'd see her through till her guy came along. Trouble is she's still waiting. When I think of what I'd achieved by the time I was thirty. I'd shaped the whole grunge aesthetic pretty much single-handed. I was the youngest ever VP at Way Out Front. I had my own loft.

She's scarfing down the cream cheese strudel, after the show.

She says, "I like the pastries better than the singing. What did you think, Grandad?"

Dad says, "Well they're not so tuneful as Patsy Kline and of course you can't tell what they're singing, but I'd still call it a good effort. And we didn't have to pay to get in. Me and Tilly went to the Lawrenceville Polish Fayre last year, it was five bucks to get in and another ten for a kielbasa sandwich and a beer. And that was for Seniors. Also, you got to bear in mind, Janine, these people aren't long out from under the iron heel of Communism. They still have to catch up to our ways."

She said, "Mom warned me I wouldn't like it but she said it'd be punk an 'at. You changed your job then, Aunty Beryl? You gone ethnic?"

I said, "How's your love life, Janine?"

"Complicated," she said. "Who's the guy in the leather bomber?"

I said, "That's Neno. He's in the movie business. Would you like to meet him?"

Lubka's joined us, flung a meaty arm around Dad's shoulder.

She said, "Mr Dad, I will like to say how I am sad of death of Ronald Reagan."

Dad said, "Thank you. But he wasn't a well man for a long time, you know? He lost his mind. They say there's nothing much you can do if that's what's on the cards for you. I've got a mini-trampoline myself. Ten minutes a day. I don't know if it helps. Tilly, that's my friend, she worries it's not properly stabilised but I haven't had any mishaps so far. I'll take my chances. I'd as soon die of a broken neck. Tilly, now she's into Sudoku. I don't know whether you'd have come across that in your part of the world? It's supposed to be beneficial for the brain. So is eating fish. That's why I buy a lot of tuna. Only now they say you've got to be careful because of the mercury in it. Bagdarned if you know what to believe. Too late for the Gipper, anyhow. Ninety-three's a good age though. You can't complain if you get to ninety-three."

Lubka's studying his lips, like that's going to help you follow the traffic flow on the ten-lane highway of Dad's mind.

Lubka said, "Mr Dad speaks English but I did not understand."

I said, "It's a knack. Just smile."

278

Dad keeps saying, "Well, I'd best be making a move."
But he doesn't.

I said, "I guess you'd like a rain check against that breakfast we were meant to get at IHOP? You going to be glued to the TV all day tomorrow?"

He said, "Yes. Ten-thirty they'll be bringing the casket from the Capitol building. I'll want to be in my seat well before that. I tell you what, if you and your ladies would like to join me, you'd be very welcome."

Lubka said, "He asks us to go in his house?"

I said, "Dad, you don't have room. There's seven of us, and that's not including drivers."

He said, "I can count. Two of you'll have to sit on lawn chairs, is all."

Lubka says, "Thank you, Mr Dad, we will like to come."

That's great. That's just what I need. Four hours, cooped up with the Sisterhood of the Bulgarian Headscarf in front of Dad's steam-powered TV.

Janine says, "Not often you invite cupney, Grandad. Mom'll be very surprised."

Dad says, "Then I'll thank you not to tell her."

CHAPTER
THIRTY-EIGHT

Mal says, "Erm."

Usually the sign he's going to tell me something I don't want to hear.

He said, "About going to your dad's house today?"

I said, "You really don't have to come."

He said, "You're sure?"

I said, "You got other plans?"

"Kind of," he says.

I said, "Okay. If I can come with you we'll say no more about it."

I get the nervous smile.

He said, "I thought it'd be nice to see something of the city."

I said, "You don't have to tell me where you're going. I'll just have Einstein tail you. You got a date?"

He blushed. He *does* have a date.

I thought it might be one of those Bulgarian folk dancers. There were some eminently cute candidates there, whatever your preference. But no, no. It's a Polish barserve from the Palm Court Lounge. Name? He's not telling. But he has black hair and green eyes and they're taking the Duquesne cable car ride. Holy fucking shit.

I said, "Mal, we're leaving tomorrow. Don't go getting involved. I don't want you running out on me like Olga."

He said, "Can I ask you something?"

I said, "Eat an apple a day. Don't cross against the light. Use a Trojan."

He said, "It's just that I get the feeling there's something going on I don't know about. Little things Lubka keeps saying? About babies? Is Rosa pregnant?"

Shit, I don't want this going out on CNN. I don't want to have to *explain*, specially not to a kid like Mal.

I said, "I hope not. Last thing the world needs is another Neno. On a more important point, if things go well enough for the question of dinner to arise, I suggest somewhere South Side. Café Allegro'd be good. Get the grilled calamari."

He said, "Anything else?"

I said, "Yes. Go shave again. Properly this time."

One down. And Wally's going to get some cold beers and watch TV. Two down. Then Rosa tells me she's persuaded her mom to go out to the South Hills Mall in Einstein's limo. Which just leaves Lubka, Kichka and Dora for Dad's Reagan wake. The good, the mad and the relatively harmless.

I said, "Lubka, don't you dare say a word about knitting yarn or baby suits in front of my dad. You understand? Not. A. Word."

She said, "But Mr Dad will be *dyado* of this baby. If we tell him it can be big celebrate."

I said, "No. No big celebrate. I'm still thinking about this. I still have choices."

That's what we marched for. A Woman's Right to Choose. Well Lisa and Toni did. I don't do marches but I was with them in spirit.

She said, "Why Mal Cleaver does not come with us to house of Mr Dad?"

I said, "He's going out with a new friend."

She said, "With friend what works in hotel bar? Is good plan. Mal is too much in bus with olderly ladies. This boys can get fresh hairs together. Perhaps they will go in parks, play with balls."

We get to Pittview and it's barely ten twenty-five, which is some achievement considering I've thrown up twice and my hairdryer kept cutting out, but Dad's pacing up and down out front. He's wearing a suit and a black tie.

He said, "You're late. I knew you would be. What is it with you people? I never was late in my life."

The moment of going in is what I always dread most, stepping across the threshold and smelling that smell. I guess it's the feeling that the black hole of Wexler gravity is going to recapture me and I'll never be able to get out again. It helped having the girls with me. To people like Dora I'm the Invincible Woman.

Dad has a new TV and a couple of new fireside chairs since the last time I was there. The best cups and saucers were set out on the dining table, and a plate of cookies and a box of man-sized Kleenex. The kitchen still smelled of frying but there was Cona coffee on the stove and an air-freshener in the john.

I said, "You see the one with the coiled braids? That's Kichka. Watch your teaspoons."

Lubka says, "You have very beautiful home, Mr Dad. Very elegant."

Tells you all you need to know about Gorni.

Dad says, "Well unless any of you ladies needs to powder your nose I'll ask you to be seated. The President is on his way to the cathedral."

The service isn't due to start till eleven-thirty but Dad likes to pretend we're actually there. You're shown to your seat and there you stay. He doesn't like people to go out for a pee or a smoke in case the casket arrives while they're gone. There was some big TV funeral when I was a kid, Winston Churchill or somebody. Mom gave me a colouring book to keep me quiet but I remember Dad going crazy because Dorothy was messing around on the sofa with Les Luft when she should have been following the ceremony.

He said, "Bee, I've made a few sandwiches for after. And then my friend Tilly kindly offered she'll swing by in her church bus. We can take these ladies to Wal-mart, show them the wonders of American consumer choice."

I said, "I keep hearing Tilly's name. Is she a special friend?"

He said, "Yes, she is. She's the wife of my very good friend Mitch."

I said, "Do you still have all of Mom's polka outfits upstairs?"

"No," he said. "I had to let them go. It was a wrench but I needed the space for my dry goods. Tilly took them. Now hush up. Here comes the motorcade."

We saw the whole thing, soup to nuts. There was a light
rain falling. Nancy stood under a big black umbrella
while they slid the casket out of the vehicle and the pall
bearers got into position. I love the way those marines
slink their hips and swing their arms when they're slow
marching. That is so cool. The Reagan family were all
there, even Patti. She could use a good hair cut. You get
to a certain age you need to keep things above the
jawline. Patti used to be, like, a revolutionary or
something. She didn't even speak to her folks for the
longest time. Now she says she had to run away before
she could go home. I read it in yesterday's paper and it
made me cry. The least little thing does it to me these
days.

Everybody was at the service. I mean *everybody*.
Kissinger, Margaret Thatcher, Prince Charles, Gorbachev.

Dad says, "Look at old Gorby. There's a man
that's come down in the world. Did you read what
he said? It's in the paper this morning. He said
Ronald Reagan was a good man but he didn't force
the Soviets to change anything because they'd
already decided to change anyhow. See, that's a
communist for you. They'll argue black is white. You
spend all your life telling lies, in the end I don't
suppose you even realise you're doing it. Well I don't
care what prizes they give Gorby now. Ronnie had
his measure."

Lubka said, "You are right, Mr Dad. Mikhail
Gorbachev was clever as fox. Even he keeps hands in
pockets still he did make Todor Zhivkov go quickly

284

away. He did not give him push. He did not give him help. Only after he is gone, oh, Chairman Zhivkov, bye-bye, have nice vacation in your dacha."

Then Dad's nearly out of his chair, fit to be tied because he's noticed that the Clintons are sitting up front with the Bushes and the Cheneys.

"Dogbarnit," he says, "what's that pair doing there? How come they're in front row seats? Talk about lowering the tone."

I said, "Well he *was* President."

He says, "He was, and if you ask me they should have run him out of town. They could of too. And look at the face on her. That's a face would make a grizzly think twice."

Still, Bill's cute.

When they saw the casket wrapped in the flag a big discussion broke out between Dora and Lubka.

Lubka said, "Why we cannot see his face?"

It seems in Bulgaria they leave the coffin lid off. Gruesome.

I said, "Why would you want to see his face? His picture's all over the papers."

"Ne," she said, "Is different. We must see face of deads to say goodbye. Body is holy. Is not to hide in parcel like old coat. It remembers us we can die too."

Well I'll stick with a good old all-American lid on, thanks all the same. I don't share the name of my surgeon with anyone and wouldn't want people peering in at me, trying to identify whose work they're looking at.

285

She said, "When Zhivkov is dead it was jolly good thing we see his face. So we can be sure he did not come alive and jump out of box."

The girls all stood up while the coffin was being carried into the cathedral and while it was carried out. It's kind of dumb but they made me feel I ought to stand too. Dad liked that. He'd have suited the military. World War Two they failed him, 4F with a shadow on his lung, and sent him to a munitions factory in Moon Township. He doesn't talk about it. He probably feels bad he didn't get into uniform on grounds of ill health and now here he is, still bouncing around on a trampoline, going on eighty-three.

They tolled the Bourdon Bell forty times as they were loading the casket into the hearse. Then they played "Hail to the Chief" and Dorothy and Janine arrived. Last time I saw Dorothy was when I was over with Strep Throat. I guess the next time I'll see her'll be when we bury Dad. She has her own key so she just lets herself in even if she knows he's home. I wonder how old you are when people start presuming to do that?

Dad says, "What are you doing here? You ought to be at home watching history."

Dorothy said, "I told you, I'm registering my disapproval. If the Reagans want a big funeral they shouldn't expect the working man to pay for it. Anyway, I felt I had to come. Janine said you were inviting the whole world and his wife last night. I might have known Beryl couldn't make a nice quiet visit on her own, like a normal daughter."

He said, "You bettern't call her Beryl. She's Bee now. As in B.E.E."

I said, "I didn't expect to see you, Dorothy. I thought you were going to take a break."

She said, "Chance would be a fine thing. How can I relax when he gets up to things like this? Inviting strangers in. When Kenny and Joli offer to bring the kids over he says he doesn't have room, and yet I see he's feeding these people."

Knackwurst sandwiches and iced tea. I so can't face knackwurst right now.

Dad says, "None of your bagdarn who I invite."

I said, "Anyway, you should be happy. They've made a big dint in his gallon jar of deli mustard."

Lubka's on her feet, eager to shake Dorothy's hand.

"How you do do!" she says. "We are very happy to know all family of Buzz. Mr Dad is very kind with us. We have seen all funerals of Ronald Reagan. Three hours we watch and electric was not broken even one time."

I said, "They get a lot of power outages in Bulgaria."

Janine said, "That's in Yurp, right? It must be terrible over there. Are they very underprivileged?"

Dorothy said, "Of course they are. That's why they swarm over here, taking our jobs. And that's why I have no wish to travel."

Dorothy's idea of travel is the Poconos. Her idea of a resort is Lake Wallenpaupack. Ten days of tossing horseshoes with the grandkids, toasting marshmallows and listening to Kenny's oft-told tales of dangerous convicts he's guarded.

I said, "Did Ehrhardt's give you a loyal-guest medal yet?"

"Nothing wrong with Erhardt's," she said. "Good wholesome food and beautiful lake views. And the electric never goes off. When are you leaving?"

Tomorrow's Reno.

She's clearing the plates and glasses and we haven't even finished. There's an Entenmann's crumb coffee cake still to eat. But Lubka's helping her, struggling to keep things light and friendly. It takes a lot to make Lubka feel uncomfortable but Dorothy's managed it.

Lubka says, "Next we will go to shops with Mr Dad. In big Wallsmarket store."

Dorothy said, "And I suppose Tilly just happens to be driving you."

I said, "Do you have a problem with Tilly?"

"Yes," she said, "as a matter of fact I do."

I said, "Dad told me she's married to his good friend Mitch."

"Oh yes?" she says. "And did he mention where his good friend Mitch is these days? Ridgelawn, Beryl. That's where. Two rows over from Mom. And Tilly's dog kibble is the reason Father's car stands in the street turning to rust."

Dad drives a 1985 Oldsmobile. It kind of doesn't owe him anything. But Dorothy was in full flood.

She said, "And I'll bet he didn't tell you about Mom's polka skirts either."

I said, "I know Tilly took them off his hands. About time too, if you ask me."

She said, "And what do you think she did with them? Ask him. Go on. Ask him."

Dad's in the kitchen, rinsing coffee cups.

"Cut them up for dog bed covers," she said. "All those hours of work, all that beautiful hand sewing. Bed covers for horrible smelly schnauzers."

So Dad shouts through to say Tilly's schnauzers don't smell and Dorothy says fine, why doesn't he just go ahead and dance on Mom's grave. And then it all boiled over, suddenly, like milk in a pan. Dorothy said it was absolutely typical that I'd come swanning in, brought a crowd of foreigners with me and couldn't even sit quietly with him for a few hours instead of encouraging him to go off buying things he doesn't need. I said I couldn't see any harm in going to the mall for an hour. She said I only couldn't see harm in it because I don't want to have to take responsibility for a parent with deteriorating mental powers. I said there's nothing wrong with his mental powers. Dad said Bee's right about that, thirteen twelves are a hundred and fifty-six. Dorothy said why did he always side with me when she was the one looked after him year on year. He said he didn't need looking after and the only person he was siding with was himself. She said oh no you always favoured Beryl and Dad said oh no he didn't. So I said darned right he didn't because him and Mom never even wanted me. Then everything fell quiet, except for the TV.

Dad stood there with a teacloth in his hand. He looked like somebody hit him.

He said, "Don't say that, Beryl. Bee. Of course we wanted you. Why would you ever think we didn't?"

It just felt that way. I know how it felt.

Dorothy says, "Typical. She can't be here five minutes without she has to throw a tantrum and be the centre of attention."

I said, "I was an accident. I came along and threw a wrench in your polka nights. You had to pay a babysitter."

Dorothy said, "Oh no they didn't. They didn't pay me a dime."

I said, "You dressed me in ugly clothes. You made me fat."

He said, "It was your natural build."

I said, "You called Mom 'Sugar Plum' and you called Dorothy 'Princess' but never called me anything nice."

He said, "I'm sorry. I didn't realise."

Dorothy was staring at me.

She said, "Janine's right, there's something different about you. You look puffy. Did you go to one of those Botox parties?"

Lubka's standing next to me performing thought transference with a stupid Guess What? grin all over her face.

And Dorothy says, "Jiminy Christmas! I know what it is. You're pregnant!"

I said, "Did you ever try engaging your brain before you open your fucking mouth? How can you just come out with something like that? You haven't seen me in eight years and you say I look *different.* You say I look *pregnant,* right there in front of Dad."

"Well?" she said. "Are you?"

When you have an important decision to make there are many techniques you may find helpful. You can do a grid analysis or draw an option tree. You can flip a coin. Or you can try on different coloured Thinking Hats.

White Hat: I'm forty-two, I'm employed, and I have equity of three hundred thousand sterling in a piece of prime London real estate.

Yellow Hat: Kids are cute and funny and you can buy them great stuff.

Black Hat: Kids don't let you sleep. They mess up your state-of-the-art sound system with peanut butter.

Green Hat: Why not borrow an orphan one Sunday afternoon, take it to the zoo, see if parenthood feels right for you?

Red Hat: Even if it's the dumbest move I ever made, I WANT A BABY.

Then there's the Cornered Animal decision that comes bursting out when you find yourself face to face with a holier-than-thou sister who's been waiting all your life for you to commit the really, really big one.

I said, "Yes Dorothy, I'm pregnant. And you're going to love this. Are you listening, Janine? I don't know whose child it is. There are several possibilities and you wouldn't approve of any of them but it doesn't matter because I'm going to do this all on my own. So now you'll be glad I moved away. Now you're going to be relieved you don't have to explain me to the neighbours."

There was the sound of a diesel engine.

And Dad said, "I believe I hear Tilly's vehicle outside."

CHAPTER
THIRTY-NINE

When Lubka discovered the Quids In chain in Burnley she was very happy. When she saw the Big Bird store in Youngstown she was mightily impressed. But nothing could have prepared her for Wal-mart. We walked through those doors and saw all those canyons of stuff she grabbed my arm.

I said, "Big enough for you?"

"I like," she says. "Is good bargains?"

I said, "First, tell Kichka, if she takes anything without paying she'll go to jail. Please make sure she understands."

Lubka says, "She will not understand. Is better she remains in microbus."

But I couldn't allow that. If she decided to go walkabout like she did in London we'd never find her. They cover miles on foot, these Bulgarians. She probably wouldn't stop till she hit Lake Erie.

Tilly said, "Don't worry, I'll keep an eye on her. You walk with Ted. He'd like to have some time with you, I'm sure."

I said, "Are you and Dad an item?"

She said, "Would it bother you if we were?"

I said, "No. Not at all."

"Let me put it this way," she said. "We watch out for one another."

Dad's trying to explain the meaning of Layaway, with Lubka translating. Ten per cent deposit and the balance over six months. Then Lubka's straight off to the Plus-Size Apparel Department with Dora in tow. Tilly's linked her arm into Kichka's. The store's busy. The post-funeral rush.

Dad says, "Is there anything in particular you're looking for? Anything you can't get over there?"

A supermarket is a good place to talk. You can push a cart and not have to look at each other.

I said, "Tilly's nice."

He said, "I don't know why Dorothy gets so riled with me. I'm no trouble to her. You'd tell me if I was any trouble?"

I said, "You're not. She's just a miserable cow."

He threw a couple of pizzas in the cart.

He said, "That thing you said before? About me calling Dorothy princess?"

I said, "Forget it."

He said, "Well I just never knew that's how you felt, that's all. And I'm sorry. I suppose I always left that side of things to Mommy."

I said, "Do you think my face looks puffy?"

He said. "They say you should cut down on salt. They say it's bad for the heart. Then they say, if you get charleyhorse which I do, both legs, every night, it means you need extra salt. Dadgummit, I wish they'd make their minds up. When you ran off, was it because you thought you weren't wanted?"

294

I said, "Kind of."

He said, "I'm very sorry to hear that. I always thought you went because you were bored of Troy Hill."

One pack of Chips Ahoy, one pack of Oreo Cakesters.

I said, "All the years I was in New York, all the time I've been in London, you never visited me. Dorothy's always on my case, she says I neglect you, but those planes fly both ways. You knew I'd pay."

He said, "I suppose we never felt the urge. And you came back once in a while. Blew in and blew out again. To tell you the truth we didn't like the look of the types you'd gotten in with. That rock and roll business you're in. You must admit."

I said, "But you never met any of the *types* I'd gotten in with."

He said, "We didn't need to. Dorothy used to clip things out of the *National Examiner* I'd as soon not have read. Nothing wrong with these foreign ladies, mind. They're very pleasant. But to speak plainly, Beryl — Bee — there were times we thought you were going around with opium fiends."

I said, "I've won an award. The Urban Music Panel's Lifetime Achievement award. I'm going to Seattle for the presentation."

Roast Chicken-flavour Ready Rice, Four Cheeses Elbow Macaroni, Hungry Jack Waffle Mix. Say it, damn it. Say "Buzz, I'm so proud of you."

He said, "Tilly's son lives in Seattle. Capitol Hill, Seattle. Washington. State capital, Olympia. State fish, the steelhead trout."

I can see Lubka and Dora up ahead, with quite a lot of stuff in their cart.

He says, "Lifetime achievement, eh? That's something. That's more than most of us get, doesn't matter how long we live. And that'll be for what, selling more records than anybody else, something like that?"

It'll be for changing the face of music, Dad. For being a legend in my own fucking lifetime.

I said, "Yes. Something like that."

He said, "What'll it be, a shield with your name on it?"

I said, "It's an obelisk. Crystal."

"An obelisk can be nice," he says.

A six-pack of terry socks, newborn size.

He said, "You shouldn't listen to everything Dorothy says. I don't need checking up on. As a matter of fact, it can be an inconvenience, waiting in to be visited. Did you want to register at the Baby Registry while we're here?"

I said, "I guess you're pretty shocked at my news?"

He said, "There's not much shocks me nowadays. Tilly's boy, the one in Seattle, he lives with a man. He reckons they'll get married, if they ever bring it in. I suppose Tilly'd have to go to the marrying, if it ever came off. Won't matter to me. I'll be long gone."

One green frog bath toy organiser.

He said, "Then there was a piece in one of Dorothy's magazines about a woman who turned into a man. She even grew a beard. There was a photograph. So there's no sense in being shocked these days. You'll wear yourself out."

I said, "Well. I'm not turning into a man. And I'm not planning on marrying a woman. I'm not planning on marrying anyone."

He said, "I'll tell you another thing. When me and Mommy got married she was already in the family way and that was quite a scandal in 1946. If I hadn't done the right thing, which I always intended to do, Mommy would have been one of those fallen women. We used to keep our wedding anniversary in August but we only said that for Dorothy's sake. If she'd found out we weren't married till Christmas Eve I think it would have been an embarrasment to her. So now you know something she doesn't. Nowadays folks wouldn't bother, of course. Next thing, people'll be marrying lower forms of life."

I think some people already did.

One sterling silver tennis bracelet for a daughter who inadvertently never got called "Princess".

Lubka had picked out drawstring Capri pyjamas that were on sale, a black sateen camisole with matching boxers, three sequined tank tops and a Sponge Bob backpack. Also two pairs of wedge mules, one gold, one silver, and a pair of tartan rain boots. I feel we're moving close to Imelda Marcos territory with Lubka. Dora had chosen a ten-dollar skirt, a coffee mug decorated with sheep and a set of Billy-Bob teeth. The full-grill lightly stained model.

Lubka says, "Is closed up package. Dora can try, is correct size?"

I said, "Not the teeth. If you try them you buy them."

Tilly calls me on my cell. She says, "I could use some help."

It's Kichka. She wants to go to Layaway and put a deposit on a pack of Klondike ice-cream bars. From which she already started snacking.

Which amounts to grazing. Which is probably a federal offence. I checked her bag. There was nothing else in it except a few broken pretzels, and the Pine-Sol from Dad's bathroom so she was let off with a warning, on condition she leave the store immediately. She's a lucky woman. She could have gotten a life ban.

Tilly dropped us at the hotel.

Dad said, "It wasn't that you weren't wanted, Bee. You came as a bit of a surprise, that's all."

I said, "It doesn't matter. I'm forty-two. I got a kid of my own now."

"Yes," he said, "but I wouldn't like you to go away angry."

I said, "I'm not angry."

I absolutely wasn't. And I haven't had a Niravax in four days now.

We watched the edited highlights of the funeral so Lubka could have another good cry. It's funny, the bit that really got to me was when they were taking him back to California and the plane flew by some little town in Illinois where he grew up and as they flew over the pilot dipped a wing.

Nine o'clock the phone went.

He said, "This is your father. I just wanted to say it was a pleasure to meet your ladies. And it was very nice to see you. Especially going around with a steadier type of people."

I can hear Tilly's voice in the background.

He said, "And well done for winning the obelisk. I'll be telling everybody in the warehouse club about it, you can depend on it."

Tilly's still saying something to him.

Then he says, "Bagdarnit, Beryl, I'm proud of you. Bee, I mean. You take care how you go, now. You and that little baby."

I reached for a Kleenex but Lubka had already emptied the box.

CHAPTER
FORTY

I waited till we were in the air before I told Mal.

I said, "I have something to tell you."

He said, "Is the engine on fire?"

I said, "I'm serious."

"So am I," he said. "I hate big announcements. They're always something bad."

I said, "I'm pregnant."

He said, "What I meant was, they're *usually* something bad. Congratulations."

I said, "That's a very *piano* reaction, Mal Cleaver. You're supposed to be amazed."

He said, "Sorry."

I said, "You think I'm too old."

He said, "No. Are you that old? Actually, I'd kind of guessed."

He said it was mainly the way I seemed very preoccupied but at the same time spookily calm. Then he'd heard Lubka use the word *bremenna* a few times and after he'd looked it up and found out it meant "pregnant" he figured it definitely wasn't Dora or Kichka and it probably wasn't Lubka or Zveta, so it had to be me or Rosa.

He said, "Does it mean you won't be needing an intern for much longer?"

Quite the opposite, I'd have thought. I'm going to have a daunting amount of shopping to do.

I said, "I expect you're wondering who the father is?"

He said, "Don't feel you have to tell me."

I said, "It could be my ex's. Felix. But on the whole I think it isn't because there wasn't much going on in the sack, towards the end. Or it could be Boyko Stoyan's, which you probably already guessed. Or it could be the result of another one-night stand which I prefer not to go into right now. As a matter of fact, you're the only person I've even mentioned it to."

He said, "Thanks."

I said, "How was your date?"

"Good," he said. "Nice."

I said, "You get back late? I called your room about eleven but there was no reply."

"Quite late," he said.

I said, "I've shocked you."

"No," he said. "You haven't. Believe me."

I said, "So what do you think?"

He said, "About people having babies? I think it's a good plan for the future of the human race."

I said, "Not about *people*. Fuck *people*. I mean about me."

He said, "Do you really want to know?"

I said, "Of course I want to know. You're my right-hand man. You're involved in every aspect of my life. Your honest opinion."

He said, "Okay then. I think considering the amount of alcohol and pills and nicotine I've seen you inflicting on your body it's nothing short of a miracle."

And then he pretended to read the in-flight magazine. Censorious little smartypants.

Once I'd told Mal, the cat was officially out of the bag and everybody was allowed to pat my belly and smile in a deranged way. We had a two-hour layover at Phoenix and we whiled it away with Guess the Sex of Buzz's Baby. Dora's method is, she asks you to show her your hands. If you show them palms up, which I did, that means a girl. Zveta swears by the wedding ring on a chain method which involves lying stretched out on the floor and creates a lot of interest at an airport departure gate. Mal hid behind a newspaper. They said the ring swung in a circle, which means a boy, but it didn't look like a circle to me. Lubka says the fact I've finished off their entire supply of Gorni piggles in the past week tends to indicate a boy, however I've also got an insatiable desire for chocolate-covered Turkish delight, and sweet cravings point to a girl. Maybe it's twins. That would *so* piss Lisa.

We get to Reno and we're just about to go to the arena for a soundcheck when Dabney Apple calls.

"Buzz," she says, "so pleased I caught you. I just wanted to run through a few things."

The venue is the Seattle Center, same space as last year, and the sponsors are Bar None Amplifiers, Crucial Wheel Trims and Everybody Smile Dental Gum.

302

It doesn't sound very promising for the gift-bags.

I said, "The main thing I'd like to know is the colour of the runway carpet."

She said, "I'll have to get back to you on that. The event design guys are totally brilliant. I heard they're using black calla lilies, and metallic star confetti sprinkled on black tablecloths."

Star confetti on black tablecloths. Myomyomy. That is ground-breaking stuff.

She said, "Did you make your own limousine arrangements?"

I said, "I'll probably arrive with the Spam Javelin boys. Did you speak to their manager? You should speak to Bryan."

She said, "I can certainly do that. Did you speak with him recently?"

I said, "I'm on the road."

She said, "Okay. It's just that my understanding is that Spam Javelins won't be attending the awards."

I said, "They're nominated for Best Industrial."

"Yes," she said. "But they decided not to come. It's to make a statement about the environment. It's to draw people's attention to the importance of reducing carbon emissions."

I said, "Whose carbon emissions?"

She said, "Well, everybody's really."

I said, "Who told you this crap?"

"Your London office," she says. "Sasha, actually."

You know, I created that band. They say God made the world but I was the one who said "Let there be Spam Javelins". And they were. I lifted their pimply butts out of Saskafuckingtoon and I made them into the new face of Industrial. Without me they're just four little pricks with a drum machine and access to somebody's dad's car-wrecking yard. They're around Sasha Actually for five minutes and suddenly they're making major image decisions without so much as a call to me.

Sasha Actually's out of the office. But Madson's in.

He says, "Buzz darling, can it wait till I see you? I should have been in Hammersmith twenty minutes ago."

I said, "Spam Javelins."

"Yeah," he says, "how about that? Boycotting the Urbies. Uber-cool. I wish I'd thought of it myself. There's gonna be a lot of media interest. It was Sasha's idea. Very smart girl. She has a future."

Like I could give a rat's ass about Sasha's future.

I said, "The whole thing's so dumb, Hunt. Nobody in Javelins can even say 'carbon emissions'."

"So what?" he says. "It doesn't matter. Celebrity activism, it's the coming thing."

I said, "Are Banana Bubbles staying away?"

Of course they're not.

He said, "How'd the Bosnians go down in Pittsburgh?"

I said, "There's something I may as well tell you before you hear it from anyone else. I'm pregnant."

He said, "Not mine is it? Just kidding."

I said, "But you know me. Nothing slows me down. It'll be business as usual."

He said, "You mean you're keeping it? That is so. Wow. No, that's great. Duper. Absolutely terrific."

I said, "And they're Bulgarians, by the way. Not Bosnians."

"Gotcher," he said. "So I'll see you in Seattle. We should do dinner. Best Industrial winner picks up the check. Another year or two we could all be staying home. Virtual award ceremonies. You know, Kyoto Protocol and all that?"

I never heard of Kyoto Protocol. They must be one of Madson's new bands.

Dora gave me my first knitting lesson this afternoon.

You put the needle point through the stitch, wind the yarn around, pull the new loop through, slide the old loop off. Repeat. If you put the needle point through the back of the stitch it makes a different kind of pattern. I never knew that. Binding-off is the best though. You make two stitches, then you pull the first stitch over the second stitch. Gone. So then what was the second stitch becomes the first stitch, you make a new second stitch, pull the first stitch over it. Gone. You just keep going till there's only one stitch left. And then. You cut the yarn free from the skein and you carefully draw the loose end up through the last stitch. And that's that. Everything is neat and tight and fast.

The Pavilion at the Reno Livestock Events Center is an interesting venue. It has a climate-controlled one thousand-seat arena with mylar sheets laid over the dirt floor and a powerful smell of cow doodie. We've come in right on the heels of a Red Angus cattle show. The girls are sharing the bill with a Knife-Dance Troupe from the Republic of Georgia. Amazing the stuff they do. I just watched them rehearse. Sword fights, human towers. And when they jump those guys are amped. I mean, they are *airborne*. Great costumes too. Black pants and long red tunics with like, side vents, and loops all across the chest with rifle cartridges. They're probably just fake ones for decoration, but it's a neat look. Plus, they have these divine knee boots in soft black leather. I am so going to get a pair of those.

Rosa isn't happy because there's no dressing room. I guess when they have rodeos here they just perform in their street clothes. The Knife Dancers are quietly dressing in their trailers but the bus isn't good enough for Rosa. She says the light's no good for putting on make-up. This was never an issue before. Lubka started using lipstick after her first major TV appearance but she never got starry about it. Now Rosa's got this agenda, to glamify her Mom.

She got her a bunch of free samples from Macy's in Chicago. Started off they were just using a little eye colour but it's evolved into a kind of Cleopatra-the-morning-after look, heavy on the eyeliner. Now Rosa and Zveta are done up like prom Barbies, Lubka's experimenting a little and the other two still look like extras out of *Hansel and Gretel*.

Mal said, "Do you think we should say something? Do you think Rosa's going in the right direction, image-wise?"

With artists you have to know when to let them have their head. They could be losing their way, or they could be stumbling towards something exciting. You have to allow things to unfold. Things take off for weird reasons. When they recorded *Singing the Harvest* their average age was like, a hundred. Dora replaced Mara, nobody noticed. They still sounded great. Then Rosa replaced Stanka. I didn't hear any complaints about that either. Ticket sales are excellent. LA is nearly sold out and we're starting to attract a different kind of audience. We're getting more guy-guy couples.

I said, "I've been here so many times before, Mal. Trust me."

He said, "I just wouldn't like to think people are laughing at them."

I think Mal may be too sensitive for this business. Let's face it, freak shows sell. People don't go to the circus to see a Homecoming Queen. With this combination of raw country voices and Rosa and Zveta's new post-Soviet hooker image, who knows, we could be tilting excitingly close to cult status.

Mal said, "I think I owe you an apology. I wasn't very nice when you told me about the baby."

Told it how it was, Mal. I can take it.

I said, "Did you notice, I'm not drinking? Except a glass of wine last night."

Two glasses, he says, but wine doesn't count. Else how did the French thrive to become such an annoying race? And I'm practically, hardly smoking.

He said, "I can see you're trying. It's hard to imagine you as the baby type. I suppose you'll get a nanny?"

I said, "But I'll bring the baby to the office sometimes. That could be fun."

He can push her round Golden Square in her stroller while I take important meetings.

"It could be," he said. "As long as your intern doesn't have to change its nappy."

A diaper service. That's another thing I need him to find out about.

He said, "Did you tell Boyko?"

I don't have any intention of telling Boyko. I'm running this show.

I said, "Trust me, he doesn't want to know, doesn't need to know. Boyko was just one of those things."

He said, "But some day the baby'll want to know about its father."

We'll cross that bridge when we get there. Father Not Known, it adds a dash of mystery. It leaves room for the imagination to play.

He said, "It's not as though you absolutely don't know. It's not like you were knocked down in a dark alley. You told me two of the people it could be so it's not exactly a closely guarded secret."

I said, "It's hazy. And as far as I'm concerned it can stay that way."

He said, "When it grows up . . ."

I said, "Please don't call it It. Call it She."

He said, "When she grows up, if I ever hear her wondering who her Dad was, I shall tell her what I know."

Which isn't much, Mal, let's face it.

I said, "You mean you're planning on still being around when she's old enough to ask questions like that?"

"Why not?" he said.

Now that is awesome.

I said, "I have these friends, Lisa and Toni. They're expecting twins but they got them from an agency because they're lesbians. So what are they going to tell their kids? Daddy was vial number 739, Caucasian, college graduate, Blood Group O. Personally I'd prefer to imagine it was some exotic passing stranger."

He said, "I know who my Mum was. I've got pictures of her. But I still wonder about her. I still like to hear my Dad and my gran tell stories about her. It must be terrible if you can't even do that. If all you've got is an empty frame. Or a vial number."

I said, "I'll think about it."

I really will.

I love this knitting shit. It's like, so Zen. Once you've got the hang of it it's really hard to stop. You just want to keep going and hope Dora has plenty more yarn. All these years Dorothy's been knitting blocks and stitching them into afghans for the poor and needy, I thought she was doing, like, good works. Turns out it's better than Valium.

CHAPTER
FORTY-ONE

I haven't been in LA since 2001. Angry Belgians were playing Pomona and we stayed downtown, at the Sheraton. That was some weekend. Anything we wanted, it was there almost before we asked for it. Cristal champagne, cases of Jack D, a pair of somewhat cute masseurs on call. Plus a big white candy mountain. I don't remember who supplied us but two lines of that shit and I swear I had bionic vision.

Scrolling through your LA address book when you've been away for a while can be a very depressing experience. People change their number, they don't let you know. They may have their reasons. Other people check out, take up permanent residence at Forest Lawn. Nothing you can do about that. I found Spinks though.

I said, "Hey, is that the Lifetime Achievement Survivors Club?"

"Fucking Nora," he said, "is that you, Wexler?"

Spinks is a London boy. We were kind of ships that passed. I went to London, he came to New York, ended up in California. Said he couldn't take the winters any more. Also he was more Crossover Thrash, which evolved into Classic Thrashcore and then later on

Goregrind and Terminal. We never trod on each other's toes. He's probably best remembered for discovering Sticky Viscera. And for getting Lifetime, of course.

I said, "You want to do lunch?"

"Lunch?" he says. "Remind me, what's lunch?"

I arranged to meet him at Roy's on Figueroa. It's kind of Hawaiian Fusion. He was nearly an hour late and when he did show up I wouldn't have known him. He is in *bad* shape. Hair's mainly gone, what's left is in a weedy little ponytail. His teeth are on the way out. I got the sashimi sampler, all he wanted was red wine.

I said, "I guess you heard I'm getting Lifetime Achievement?"

"Yeah," he said. "No. Well, I'm not in that loop any more."

He's doing more movie-related stuff now, consulting, trend-watching, liaising. Anything a producer needs to know about urban music, Spinks is the one they call.

I said, "They call you much?"

He said he has a few irons in the pipeline but things are generally quiet right now.

I said, "Tell me about when they presented you with the Urbie."

He says, "You've got me there. Remind me. Was that in Philly?"

It was Seattle 2001. The year my Bhangra Boys took Best Hip-Hop.

I said, "How did it feel, going up there? You looked so cool. Like, oh, Lifetime Achievement, okay, I guess I'll accept."

He roared. He shouldn't do that. His mouth needs work.

I said, "You between dentists?"

He tells me he got divorced again. That was number four. The bitch took him for everything.

I said, "After you got Lifetime, was it really like, overwhelming, the press interest?"

Intense, he reckoned. He couldn't remember which magazines interviewed him or which shows he went on but he has a fairly definite recollection it was intense. How could it not be?

I said, "I'll probably do a book. They've been after me for years to write my story."

He said, "Yeah, I could have done a book. Stuff I've seen, people I've worked with, you couldn't make it up."

I said, "Remember Liam and the dog muzzle?"

He said, "That's what I mean. You create a band, you live with them, you wipe up their messes, you've got the skinny. Stuff we know, you could blow the whole industry sky high. The fan in the street'd pay to find out that shit. I had a lot of interest, I can tell you. But then I thought, fuck it. You know? Why bother?"

I said, "I think it'd be nice, to get it all down on paper. Get it on record."

"On record," he says. "That's what I was going to call it."

He gave the big hello to a couple of suits who came in but neither of them took any notice. I'm afraid poor old Spinks is washed up.

He says, "So you're back on the road, hunh? That's what they do to you. They take the best years of your life. They wring the pips out of you and then they spit you out."

Not Buzz Wexler, my friend.

I said, "I am back on the road, but you know what? I'm here because I want to be. The Mark Taper Forum, tomorrow night at eight. Be there, Spinks, and be prepared to be amazed. When I heard these girls I told Dave Corcoran I wanted them, no arguments. Nobody else could see it but I knew they were something special. But that's me. I know when something's time has come. In this business you have to follow your instincts. Sometimes you have to take that little side alley, looks like it leads nowhere. Sometimes you have to say yes."

"True," he says. "Very true. You got any gear on you?"

I said, "Are you nuts? I just flew in from Reno. You can't carry stuff around any more. You practically can't even bring a razor blade on the plane. You have to buy when you arrive. When your work involves a lot of travel it can be a pain."

He says, "Who're you buying from?"

I said, "I'm not. I'm pregnant."

"Not mine is it?" he said. Silly old fool.

I said, "I can let you have a couple of dexxies."

"Naah," he says. "That's girl's stuff. I'm all right. It's just I'm between deliveries. Last supplier fucked me over. They always do. Everybody fucks you over in the end."

A very bitter guy, Spinks. He doesn't have his obelisk any more either. He sold it on eBay. Now *that* is sad. I spotted him a hundred.

He said, "You sorted? Your little bit of bother? I can get you a number if you're not fixed up."

I said, "I am fixed up, thanks anyway."

I've been gone three hours at the absolute outside, I get back to the hotel and I find a battlefield. Zveta's crying, Dora's crying, Kichka's braids have come unpinned and she has spittle on her chin, like a rabid dog. Lubka's got her arms folded and a face like thunder.

I said, "What happened?"

Mal looks like he took a direct hit.

He says, "Things got a bit out of hand."

I've seen this happen with bands so often when they're on tour. They're cooped up together for weeks. Personalities grate. The pebble in the shoe starts to feel like a rock.

It seems Kichka lit the fuse. She called Rosa a painted whore of Babylon. Zveta called Kichka a thief. Dora said Kichka couldn't help what she was and they should leave God to judge her, Kichka said it was proven long ago that God doesn't exist, Dora said He most certainly did and Kichka said a woman who believed her sheep was listening to her on the telephone when more than likely Grozdan Gavrilov had it butchered into cutlets the minute she was on her way to the airport, would believe anything. Then Lubka told Kichka she was an evil old witch and nobody wanted her in the Grannies any more.

314

I said, "You followed all this with your phrase book?"

"No," he said. "Lubka translated. That Dr Robertshaw was right, wasn't she? She said fame would spoil them."

I said, "It's just tour-bus fever. I can't remember getting through any tour without war breaking out."

He said, "I wondered if we could try calling Stanka. If she's in Gorni she could go round to Dora's house and confirm the sheep is all right. At least that'd put Dora's mind at rest."

I said, "Sure. You have Stanka's number?"

"No," he said, "I thought you might have it."

I don't.

He said, "But you could probably get it from Boyko. If you have his number? If it wouldn't be a problem?"

I said, "Don't look at me like that. Yes, I probably do have his number and no it wouldn't be a problem to call him. It was fun. No expectations. Yadda yadda. In the meanwhile, Lubka, you have to take the lead here. Tell Kichka you didn't mean what you said."

She said, "I will not."

I said, "You have a show tonight, you have a show Saturday. After that you can do what the hell you like. Right now it's your job to keep the Gorni Grannies on the road. I'm looking to you to lead from the front."

She wriggled for a minute. Then she said something to Kichka. Kichka scratched her chin, laughed, said something back. Lubka's right. She does look like an old witch.

I said, "Are you friends again?"

"Pfft," she says. "I will never be friend of Kichka Nikolova what has mouth big as Trigrad Gorge. But for good healths of Buzz Wexler we will not fight. Is not nice for baby. Only when we return in Gorni for sure she will make juju doll of Lubka and I will put insect in her spinaches."

There was a lot of background noise. It was late in England. I guess he was in one of the restaurants.

He said, "What do you want?"

I said, "Hi Boyko, how are you?"

He said, "I recommend you don't start pestering me."

I was so calm, like you wouldn't believe.

I said, "Keep your pants on. Are we grown-ups or what?"

He said, "I told you, I'm not interested."

I said, "Well I was going to ask you if you'd call Stanka, see if she'd do Dora Gavrilova a small favour, but now it comes to it I'm just going to tell you what a peckerfaced brag-ass grandma's boy you are and leave it at that."

CHAPTER
FORTY-TWO

It was the most perfect morning. We drove out along the Golden State Freeway through Glendale and Burbank. You swing west onto the San Fernando Valley after Pacoima and you can see the Simi Hills up ahead. There was a lot of traffic heading to the Reagan Library and it was building up to a hot day. I felt kind of hemmed in by clammy polyester. Lubka had told everyone to dress up in honour of the occasion. It was a big day for her.

She said, "Perhaps we will see Mrs Nancy."

I said, "I don't think so. She's been in the limelight all week. She'll be glad to throw on an old mu-mu and stay home with her memories."

Pete Belkin used to say Reagan was a mass murderer, a gibbering fool and an enemy of the working man. I don't remember exactly what he based that on. Pete didn't have a lot of contact with working men, except for that cute Cuban boy who walked his dachshunds. People say these things, they don't always stand up to close examination. Like they say we're a police state since 9/11, but all those people scrabbling to get a Green Card don't seem to think so. Lubka doesn't think we're a police state and she should know. She grew up in one.

She wanted to go straight to the grave but there was a big crowd. I figured if we waited till nearer lunchtime people would be heading for the coffee shop. We went to the museum first. They have a replica of the Oval Office and a display of some of Nancy's gowns. I assigned Rosa and Zveta to Kichka-watch. If she tried pocketing some presidential treasure, I didn't like to think.

I lost Lubka for a while. She was in the screening theatre watching newsreel footage of John Hinckley Jnr's shooting spree.

She said, "Is movie?"

I said, "No. It's real. Some people got hurt but nobody was killed."

She'd never heard about the Hinckley shooting.

I said, "I guess you didn't have TV in those days?"

Nineteen eighty-one. I was living with Belkin then, down in the Village.

She said, "Even we did not have food. In year of 1981 I was thin as Buzz Wexler. Why this person did shot Ronald Reagan?"

I said, "He was crazy. He wanted to impress a girl. You ever see an actress called Jodie Foster? You ever see a film called *Silence of the Lambs*?"

She's not sure. I tell her the story.

"*Da*," she says. "I have seen. But I did not see ending because there came big storm. Then I was too much frightened to go in my bed. I did not like this movie. I like movie *Scent of Lady*. Al Pacino."

I said, "Forget Al Pacino. He's nothing to do with this. Jodie Foster was the girl who played the FBI agent in *Silence of the Lambs* and the guy who shot Ronald Reagan had this thing about her. He was in love with her. And that's why he did it. So she'd notice him."

"Ne," she says. "I do not understand. Is American idea."

The burial site is behind the Presidential Library. Boy, that is one ugly grave. It looks like a gun emplacement. But I did like the inscription:

I know in my heart that man is good, that what is right will always eventually triumph and that there is a purpose and worth to each and every life.

I went through it, word by word, and Lubka translated it for the others.

Then she crossed herself.

I said, "What does that mean exactly, when you do that?"

She said, "Is to say, when you make pray you make with minds, also with heart, also with shoulder."

I said, "You pray with your shoulder?"

"Ne," she said, "is wrong word. When you have strong body what is word? Strength. You make pray with all you strengths."

I said, "Do you really believe in that stuff? God and everything?"

She said, "Most time I believe. Only when flies does eat my cabbage, I do not. Else when storm breaks my electric and I cannot see end of Al Pacino movie. Why you do not believe?"

I don't know. I never had time to like, go into it. I believe in what I know. I believe in Buzz Wexler.

She said, "I have question. If there is not God, why there is world, why there is stars? Why there is not nothing?"

Mal said it was a very fair question and he didn't have an answer.

She said, "If you do not believe God, who can you tell thank you when flies does not eat you cabbages?"

At the Reagan Library you're right at the top of a hill. Mal was convinced he could see the ocean, beyond the Santa Monica mountains.

Lubka says, "It can be we are first Bulgarians what visit this place."

I said, "Yes it can be."

She said, "You will sing with us."

I'd been hoping she'd ask me.

She said, "Same like before. No words. Attention only to sing straight."

I said, "Shall I follow Zveta?"

She said, "Ne, you must follow with me. Today Rosa will begin and Zveta will sing crooked."

I said, "But you always sing crooked."

"*Da*," she said, "but you did not learn to sing crooked and today I will like to sing with you."

I said, "What about Mal? It doesn't seem fair to leave him out."

"Ne," she said. "He is boy. He cannot sing. He can take photograph with mobilfon."

Zveta and Dora came in on Rosa's note and then started wandering, but never very far. A third, a minor fourth at most. Then began Lubka, straight and steady, cheek by jowl with me so I wouldn't lose my note. *Slance zayde.*

> *Go down, bright sunshine, hide your light.*
> *Trees, weep for your leaves*
> *And I will weep for my youth.*

It gets me every time.

She said, "It was jolly good sing. For sure this baby did hear you. Now he will grow big and strong."

I said, "*She*, if you don't mind."

CHAPTER
FORTY-THREE

Right now I should be in Seattle getting a full leg wax while Mal fields interview requests. But I'm in San Jose, in the Good Samaritan Pre-Natal Unit, trying to think calm, encouraging thoughts. We were on our way to Mendocino when it happened. At first I thought it was Dora's rose petal jam. Lubka made me eat a spoonful a day to make sure I got a girl. I told her, if my understanding of biology is correct, it's a bit too late to influence that outcome but she still insisted. She said if it's a boy rose petal jam could only improve it. Then I started to get these cramps.

They say it's very common. I'm what they call an elderly primigravida. They say it's really great that I knocked off the tranks and cut down on the uppers and the cigarettes practically as soon as I realised. They say it might not be anything to do with my age and if we don't get a good outcome this time around there's no reason to think I couldn't conceive again. But that wouldn't be the same. That'd have to be planned and organised and now I consider, I kind of prefer things this way. The chance hit.

When I told them I wasn't feeling so good everybody started flapping. Poor Mal. Stuck on a bus with five

322

headless chickens and a gynaecological emergency. But Lubka took charge. She told Dora to start praying to motherofgod and Rosa to lead the singing in the event of her not making it to Mendocino in time for the gig. Then they transferred me to Einstein's limo.

Mal said, "I feel I should offer to come with you."

But Lubka said, "Ne, is lady business. Is better I go. You stay with Grannies, keep eyes on idiot Neno. You are boss now."

Einstein drove her to the showground after she'd seen me into my hospital bed. She got there with half an hour to spare. Mal said even with the rain and the mud it was a great show. He said with the Tutrakan and the Ursari alongside them the old magic came back. I wish I could have been there. I wish I could have had another look at those Ursari boys, to try and remember his face.

They said they couldn't actually stop me flying to Seattle but they most strongly advised against it. Dabney Apple said they might even be able to organise a video link to my hospital bed, which would have been somewhat cool. But I had a better idea.

I said, "Mal, you're going to represent me at the Urbies."

He said, "Do I have to make a speech?"

I said, "Nobody makes my speeches for me. Your mission is to take Lubka to Seattle, buy her a red carpet outfit and squire her to the awards. When the moment comes, she goes up, gets the award, smiles. You bring

Lubka and my obelisk back here and as soon as I'm fit we all go home."

Buying the outfit has taken a great number of phone calls, what with Mal's lack of experience and Lubka's magnetic attraction to pastels.

I'd get a call from him, "We're in Bentall's." Or, "Now entering Barney's."

Whispering, like they're in a funeral parlour. Like they're in Westminster fucking Abbey.

I said, "What's wrong? A thousand-dollar budget, don't tell me you can't find something for the diva in one of those stores."

He said, "I think it's the way the sales staff look at her. I think it's her size."

They went to Lowell's for a mid-morning refuel and the waitress suggested they try the Plus-Size section in Nordstrom. Then things really hotted up. She apparently made straight for a plain silk tank dress with a matching long-sleeved lace duster coat but in the picture Mal sent me it looked like an unpleasant shade of eraser pink.

I said, "Steer her towards something that makes a strong statement. Keep in mind at all times who she's representing."

He said, "I am trying."

God, I so wished I was there. But if I was there Lubka wouldn't need a dress.

The shortlist:

1. A full-skirted black with a bateau neckline, three-quarter length sleeves and a microscopically

small, tasteful, frankly why bother, beaded waistline trim. Too severe.

2. A sleeveless Calvin Klein, kind of coppery-bronze with a halter top and a full-length swishy skirt. Possible.

3. A metallic blue mid-calf sheath with a pleated tulle overskirt, plus black mesh open-toe slingbacks and an ombre sequinned clutch purse. Yes!

I just talked to her.

I said, "Are you happy?"

She said, "Only I will be happy when baby is hundreds per cent."

I said, "The baby is hundreds per cent. Another twenty-four hours they say I should be okay to fly. Are you happy with your dress?"

She said. "Is most beautiful dress what I ever had. But we have spended three hundred dollar. Is too much?"

Sweet Jesus, I've spent that on a jar of face cream.

I said, "It's a bargain. But I hope you'll wear it when you get home."

"*Da*," she said. "When you bring baby in Bulgaria we will make big jolly party. Then I will wear."

I don't have the heart to tell her Bulgaria doesn't really feature in my future travel plans. I'm thinking Oahu, or Necker Island.

I said, "Don't wait for big jolly party. Wear it to feed the chickens. Give Gorni something to talk about."

She said, "Next I go to hairdress saloon. At seven and half clocks we go in car to ceremonies."

I said, "Are you nervous?"

She said, "Nervous, what is?"

I was a fool to ask.

She said, "I will tell you a thing of this place. Is one not nice thing."

I said, "Don't you like Seattle?"

She said. "Is okay place. I like quite much. But they have statue of Lenin. Why they do have statue of Soviet murderer in United State of America?"

I've seen that statue. It's just across from a burritos franchise in Fremont. A darned great bronze thing. Some guy mortgaged his house to buy it and ship it and then he died and his folks were stuck with it in their front yard. Much the same way Dorothy's could be landed with fifty pounds of shortening and a garage full of dog kibble that rightfully belongs to another family.

I said, "It's just kind of a joke. Sometimes they put lights on it and stuff at Christmas. It doesn't mean anything."

"Ne," she said, "I do not understand. Let them melted this statue. That will be better joke."

I called Corcoran.

He said, "Whatever it is, I don't want to know. It's nothing to do with me any more."

I said, "I got Lifetime Achievement."

"Oh Buzz," he said, "that's terrific. I'm chuffed for you. Sincerely. Well-deserved. So if Spam Javelins come through you're in for a great night. It is tonight?"

I said, "It is. Trouble is, I won't be there. I'm in bed with a threatened miscarriage."

"Oh," he said. "Bummer. I'm sorry to hear that. I didn't realise you were, you know?"

I said, "You didn't realise what, Dave?"

"Well," he said. "That you were involved with anybody. Somebody."

I said, "I'm not."

"Right," he said. "Test-tube, was it?"

I said, "No. Just the luck of the fuck."

He laughed.

He said, "Not mine is it? Just kidding."

One thing about Dave and Hunt, when it comes to infantile humour they're neck and neck.

He said, "So who's at the Urbies? Is Madson picking up the award for you?"

I wouldn't let Hunt Madson pick up my gum wrapper.

I said, "One of my Bulgarians is doing it. She's had a totally shit life through no fault of her own so I thought I'd give her a treat before she goes home."

He said, "Buzz Wexler, fairy godmother? I wouldn't have believed it. It must be your hormones."

He sounded kind of down. He's been talking to someone at a Nostalgia label called Yesterday but his heart isn't really in it. How could it be? What kind of a loser name is Yesterday?

I said, "My advice, don't rush into anything. All your experience in the business, you're a valuable property."

"Yeah," he says, "I'm the crown jewels, me. Actually, I'm thinking of a real change. Go back up north, do something different. I might buy a little shop. Sell golf clubs. No need to ask you what your plans are. Stone the crows, Buzz, the way you party I always thought you were hoping to die before you got old."

I said, "*Used* to party, Dave."

"Well yeah," he said. "In your condition I suppose you have to watch your step. I suppose you've got to think of the future. Now you'll have a kid in college when you're sixty."

CHAPTER
FORTY-FOUR

The limos are pulling up. The flashlights are popping.

"Buzz, Buzz, over here. Lifetime Achievement. How does it feel?"

"It feels very good indeed. Just don't run away with the idea I've finished achieving, okay? They may have to think up a new award for me ten years from now."

"Any comment on Spam Javelin's decision to stay away from the Urbies?"

"What's the latest? Did they save the world yet? You know they're a terrific band. They deserve to win tonight. But it's a sad day when stars forget what they're paid to do."

Tonight, at the Fisher Pavilion, Seattle, The 2004 Urban Music Panel Awards.

Nominations for Best Emerging Band: Refried Beaner; Duck Butter; Evil Marsupial.

Nominations for Best Extreme Metal Album: Nazi Vegans for *Global Dimming*; Kickinthenuts for *Off the Grid*; Mach 10 for *Bleeding From the Ears*.

Nominations for Best Industrial Album: Banana Bubbles for *Rat Dance*; Spam Javelins for *Flying While Muslim*; Latchkey Hamsters for *Armageddon-Compliant*. And the winners are . . . Spam Javelins!

Now, at the top of the night, the industry's highest accolade, UMP's 2004 Lifetime Achievement award goes to that tireless talent-hound, the legendary and awesomely dazzling Buzz Wexler!

Two minutes of applause. Count it. They're on their feet. Take your time, Buzz. This is your night. Three minutes. Take your time going up to the platform. Greet people as you pass their table.

"Hi, Don!"

"Scott! Looking fly!"

"Madson! Go get a spoon and eat my ass!"

Applause dies down. Wait for it, wait for it.

I say, "Well, they *say* it's been twenty-five years. Doesn't seem that long to me but I guess there's somebody at UMP who can count. To me it seems like only yesterday I was the kid from Troy Hill, Pittsburgh, hanging out in the Bowery, watching to see where music was going after Sid and Nancy."

No, leave Troy Hill out of it. Maybe something like, "I'd sure love to know who started this rumour that I'm old enough to have been in the business twenty-five years."

Pause for laughter. Yeah, pause.

Now let us stop to consider what is meant by Lifetime Achievement. The discovery of new talent, rooting it out like a truffle pig, panning for it like a gold miner? Certainly. Not everyone can do that. Seeding new trends? That too. Kids today think tongue studs just dropped out of the sky? They think ripped fishnets just happened to happen, like spontaneous combustion? Some people change the world. Like Elvis. Or the guy who split the atom . . .

A phone rings. They shouldn't allow interruptions when a person is delivering a speech.

Mal says, "Intern reporting. The obelisk has docked."

I think I must have been dozing.

I say, "Is it beautiful?"

He says, "It's . . . unusual."

I say, "Is my name engraved on it?"

He says, "Yes. Beryl Eunice Ermengild Woxler. Oh no! Don't worry, I'll make sure they correct that. They can scratch a little line across the o and it'll look like Wexler. Not really. I was joking. Also, Spam Javelins won Best Industrial Album."

Of course they did.

He said, "And Lubka got the biggest ovation of the night."

Lubka? What's she doing getting ovations?

He says, "They loved her. The minute she opened her mouth."

But there was no requirement for her to open her mouth. Rise, accept award, shake hand, descend, those were her instructions.

He said, "What was I supposed to do, go up there and drag her off? She was great. She said she didn't know exactly what the award was for but she knew you deserved a prize because you'd just spent a month touring with five old nuisances and you'd been kind and patient nearly all the time, even when you had problems of your own."

She said all that?

He said, "That was the gist of it. By the way, obelisk is the same word in Bulgarian. And then she told them why you're in hospital, and where we bought her outfit and what she thinks about that statue of Lenin. She really got them going. I've had requests from two radio stations to interview her tomorrow. She's recording a piece for a World Music show that goes out once a week from Everett, and then, listen, you're going to like this, she's going live on KOBZ-FM and the show's called The Buzz. Oh yes, and at the end of the ceremony Hunt Madson came over and introduced himself. He said Starburst likes to keep its artists happy and if ever she has any problems all she has to do is pick up the phone."

Yeah, right. The two-faced oily creepster scumbag.

He said, "Are you still there? Are you okay?"

They gave me a sleeping pill, that's all. I had a couple more cramps around dinner time and I couldn't relax. As I remarked to the duty nurse, "How can I fucking relax when I've hardly like, breathed for the last five fucking days and this child still keeps threatening to bail out?"

He said, "Well try. Do some knitting. I'll see you tomorrow evening. I'll call the hospital when I get to LA, to make sure they're going to let you out. It's going to be sad saying goodbye to Lubka. I feel like I've known her for years."

Years and years. Before I knew Lubka I was Senior Vice Doohickey of something very important. It'll come to me momentarily. But life moves on. In recent weeks I have acquired new skills that will equip me to better face the great future behind me. I have learned to sing. At the Ronald Reagan Memorial Coffee Shop I sang with my friend Lubka. Usually she sings crooked but on that occasion she sang straight, to help me keep my note, and that's true friendship for you. Song is like, vibrations. Some people think everything is vibrations but I don't buy that, no sirree Bob. I hit this night table, this night table is vibrat*ing*, but it's more than mere vibrat*ions*. This night table is one hundred per cent wood effect, fully spongeable fibreboard.

I have also begun to study the craft of nikting garments of wools and I've already learned the very great importance of binding-off. If you don't do it correctly everything is liable to unravel and much of your life will have been wasted. Yarn is an interesting material. It can come from a sheep and possibly from other life forms. How it gets from the sheep to the yarn store is not immediately clear but I can look into this.

Dora's sheep just called to say I got Lifetime Achievement for knitting an afghan for the poor and needy. They announced it on the Titch Marsh Show and I have to go to Troy Hill to collect the jellybean jar.

I said, "I can't go now because the Rubber Queen dress is stuck and I'll never get it off in time."

Then Dad came on the line.

He said, "That's all right. But you better come tomorrow because it's made out of dog kibble and I don't know how much longer I can hold off the schnauzers."

He was very proud I didn't let Olga get Mom's polka skirts. It isn't everybody can do stuff like that.

He said, "I've said it before and I'll say it again, you're a bagdarn wonderful daughter. Now you get some sleep."

Which I can do. Because the cramps stopped and I am now in a state of intense, total okayness.

CHAPTER
FORTY-FIVE

From Sofia airport you head south. It's signposted for Samokov. CAMOKOB. Pretty soon I saw a Metro supermarket and a cinema, and then just as I was starting to get crazy ideas about this country being in the twenty-first century, I saw a woman in rubber boots and a babushka scarf trying to get her cow off the central reservation.

Lubka had warned me I wouldn't be able to drive right to the door because of the mud, so she'd meet me, help me carry all the stuff.

I said, "But where will I find you?"

"You will not," she said. "I will find you."

And just as I was wondering if I'd ever see such a thing as another road sign, just as the road dipped down and I lost sight of the lake for a minute, there she was, sitting on the right verge in a lawn chair, flagging me down with a rolled up copy of *Celebrity!* Her roots need retouching.

"Nushka!" she's yelling. "Let me see my Nushka!"

Anna was asleep. Even after Lubka had slung her chair in the tailgate and slammed the door three times, she was still asleep.

Mal and Freddie already arrived. Mal's staying at Dora's place and Freddie's staying at Zveta's. It has to be that way because in Gorni guys only share a bed if they're very closely related.

Lubka keeps saying, "We will go in Samokov, or Dupnitsa. We will find nice girls can be their sweets heart."

And I keep saying, "Lubka, Freddie *is* Mal's idea of a nice girl."

"*Ne*," she nods. "I do not understand."

The high road south from Sofia is good but once you've made the turn to Gorni it's full of potholes. We parked in front of the store. There were three men sitting outside at a card table, nursing empty glasses.

Lubka said, "You see old man in T-shirt of beer factory? Is Grozdan Gavrilov, husband of Dora."

I said, "I thought he was dying?"

"*Da*," she said. "Grozdan does all things very slow. You see old man with blue shirt and head like football? Is Danil Stoyan, husband of Stanka. Third man is waste of time from Zheleznitsa. It does not matter his name."

We all shook hands. Danil Stoyan walked over to the car and looked in at Anna. Then he walked away, didn't say a word. Muddy boots and a slow, rolling gait. A man who used to play chess by cell phone. The waste of time from Zheleznitsa kindly offered to haul the bags so I could push the stroller and Lubka could carry Anna who was still half asleep.

I saw a house just like Lubka's, a lifetime ago, in a book of fairy tales. That one was made out of gingerbread but Lubka's is made of stone and twisted, sun-blistered wood. It's on a rutted track off Main Street. There are apple trees out front, in full blossom right now, and pines behind it, across the far side of the river, rising up to the start of the Rila mountains. There's a rackety stair you have to climb to the front porch, and a satellite dish and a stork's nest on the roof, and off to the side in a small leaning shed, is the john, upgraded on Gorni Grannies royalties and fitted with a laminate door with a porthole window and a sign that says STAFF ONLY.

The word soon went round: stunning, unaccompanied red head staying at Lubka Lilova's place. Thursday morning when we walked down to visit with Stanka the entire male population was hanging out by the store. They didn't even pretend not to stare. Freddie got very jittery but as Mal pointed out, it wasn't *them* the guys were looking at. It was my residual breeding potential they were weighing up. Whether I have what it takes to repopulate Gorni. That, and the pedigree of my child.

In Gorni when someone dies they put up a flier, with the name of the deceased and a photo, and it stays there, pasted to the wall, till the weather fades it or the space is needed for somebody else. Lubka had warned me it would be there. Boyko Gyorgiev Stoyan, Yul 2006. I thought I wouldn't want to read it, but the picture was nearly bleached out and anyhow, when I looked at it I truly didn't feel a thing. He more than had his chance.

Stanka still insists he was killed in a car wreck and I guess that's close enough to the truth for an old lady. It's certainly difficult to stop your vehicle leaving the road once you have a bullet in your brain. As for the unfinished business he left behind, she doesn't want to hear about anything that sullies her image of Boyko, the light of her life. Not even a little one-night miracle. Anyway, Kichka muddied those waters. She told everyone she'd seen me receive a midnight visit from an Ursari boy while we were in King's Lynn. When Lubka wrote to tell me that story was going around I thought she'd never speak to me again. But she wrote back and said, "So you are not so clever lady. This I already know."

When I finally agreed to come to Gorni I said, "Stanka won't want to see me or my child, so please don't push it, okay?"

She said, "What is push it? Stanka will want."

Stanka and Danil's house is the same style as Lubka's; living quarters upstairs with a *chardak* porch, animal quarters downstairs, but theirs has been fixed up with some of that shady Stoyan money. Where Lubka has nothing but old feed troughs and the smell of cowplop, the Stoyans have a washer-dryer and a chest freezer. They were expecting us. There was a lace mat in the centre of the table and glasses and a bottle of apricot rakia.

I'd dressed Anna in a red plaid dress with a ribbon rosebud trim and matching Mary-Janes, which is a like, ultra-cute hostility-defying outfit, but she decided to accessorise with her clock-stopper scowl and even Lubka couldn't get a smile out of her. So we sat in Stanka's pine-clad living room, trying to push the conversation along and I was just about ready to give it up as a pointless exercise when the cuckoo-clock struck thirteen and try as she might Anna couldn't prevent a smile breaking through.

There was a time, in the early days, when I truly wasn't sure whose child she was. She has black curls and the least bit of sun she tans the colour of a little pecan, but then one day she smiled at me and the one-sided dimple kicked in. The dead giveaway. And not long after that her dark gray eyes gradually lightened to cat's-eye amber.

Danil saw the dimple too. "*Da*," he said, kind of resigned. "*Fnoochka*."

Granddaughter. And Stanka wiped away a tear and squoze my hand.

We're here for Anna's christening. She's three already and Lubka threatened me, bring her to Gorni this year or else. So we fixed it for St Lazar's Saturday, which Lubka says is a particularly good day for a *krishtenye* and then "big jolly party for Nushka and for name day of Lazar Lilov, dear departed husband."

Olga and Jerry drove down from Sofia on Saturday morning. Jerry's first time in Bulgaria too. He still does the occasional tour for Starburst but so far our paths haven't crossed again. They tend to use him for Easy Listening artists.

Olga said, "It was shock with me, when you have kept this baby. What of career?"

I said, "I manage."

We run through *au pairs* pretty fast but it's not like there's a shortage of replacements, and World Music's a more forgiving master than Cutting Edge. A lot of my artists these days, they're disappointed if I don't bring Anna along on a tour.

She said, "Howandsoever it can be big worry when you do not have good husband to bring home celery."

She's as smug as ever. It's just that in Olga's universe the all-wonderful Chairman Zhivkov has been eclipsed by Jerry. Literally, by the look of Jerry's waistline. She offers one-on-one Bulgarian classes for business executives but she doesn't get a lot of takers in Harpenden so mainly she's a home-maker. They're happy.

Dora and Grozdan came to the christening, and Stanka and Danil. Zveta was there, but Dimitar didn't make it out of his armchair and Rosa had work commitments. She was at a Home Show in Collinsville, Illinois, demonstrating a new can opener. Of the original Mickey Mouse Club only Kichka was missing. She told Lubka it was more than she dare do to leave her house for five minutes because somebody would come and steal tiles from her roof, guaranteed.

Lubka said, "Let them steal. Is no damages. Kichka Nikolova has nothing in her roofs. But in secret I am glad she will not come. We do not need old witch at *krishtenye* of my Annushka."

Mal stood as godfather, Lubka stood as godmother, and Aunt Mara officiated, for want of a priest. There's a tree growing through the roof of Gorni church and anyhow, clergy are hard to find now everybody in Bulgaria wants to be a millionaire. Anna was in a pink and lilac halter-neck christening bikini and her yellow firechief rain boots. They all waded into the stream and a herd of goats tiptoed down the other bank to watch. There was a smell of garlic and mint where their hooves had trampled, and then a sweet, rosy kind of smell from the oil Aunt Mara used to paint the sign of the cross.

We let Lubka's table down on ropes into the front yard and Freddie brought Zveta's table too, balanced it on his head all the way along Main Street. The Gorni guys'll be talking about that for years. Dora brought sausages and a salad of sour pickles in yogurt, Stanka brought bean stew and pink wine, Mal and Freddie broiled lamb chops two at a time on Lubka's pre-war cooker, Zveta brought stuffed peppers and everyone brought sweet *banitsa*. It was like the World Strudel Championship cook-off.

Lubka whispered to me, "Now we will sing. Now you will hear my Mara."

Aunt Mara is about nine hundred years old. She stands four-ten in her stocking feet and weighs nothing. Lubka reckons she's slowing up but these things are relative. She's come by every morning so far, riding a man's bike that belongs in a transport museum. She puts Anna on the crossbar and they weave their way to Dora's house to give Mal his wake-up call and bring Dora's sheep down to the pasture. Mara only speaks

Bulgarian and Anna speaks the London dialect of Age Three but they seem to find plenty to talk about.

Mara's voice is so clear and strong. She started the line and cocked her head on one side, listening for Lubka and Zveta coming in. She looked like a little canary with her beady black eyes and her yellow turtleneck. I seem to remember Lubka bought that at Filene's in Pittsburgh. They sang and sang. "Two Pine Trees", I remembered from Reno, and "A Golden Apple", that I heard for the first time in King's Lynn. Then "Go Down", specially for me, so I could join in. Danil took Anna to hunt for glow worms. They put them in an empty piggle jar and they obligingly glowed until she fell asleep on Stanka's lap.

Mal and Freddie leave tomorrow. They're going to the wetlands to look at pelicans. We leave on Monday.

Lubka says, "Why you must go? You stay in Gorni. Go crazy same as me."

I said, "I have to work."

I have this amazing Costa Rican jazz funk quintet I'm taking to Scotland and Belfast. Anyway, I think Lubka has given up her button-tufted headboard for quite long enough. She's a big woman to sleep on that settle in the kitchen.

She said, "How you can work when you have beautiful baby? You must get husband. He can be ugly but he must be good person with nice house. Why you did not get Jerry Driver? I think he did liked you. Why we did let him marry Soviet puppy dog?"

I said, "Please, no Jerry, no husbands. I'm fine. We're fine."

"*Dobry*," she said. "But still I will find wifes for Mal and Freddie."

I said, "Did you think any more about re-forming? All you have to do is say the word. A new CD, another tour."

The Gorni Three never really took off after the Gorni Grannies disbanded. Zveta was up for it but Neno's plans for Rosa's movie career kind of got in the way. And once they were back in Gorni they just slipped back into the old routine. They sing when they feel like it.

"*Ne*," she said. "Not yet. I will wait few years, till my Nushka can sing. Then we can be Gorni Two and Half."

Today is Holy Thursday, the day Lubka dyes her eggs ready for Easter. Right after breakfast they did the red ones. You make the dye from the juice of boiled beets. After lunch I took a little zizz up on the *chardak* and when I woke up my daughter was down below, sitting in the grass with a pot of cornflower soup, giving it the occasional stir and waiting for another batch of eggs to turn the magic shade of blue. Someone's goat had failed to notice the post and wire fence and wandered into the yard to see how the eggs were coming along.

Lubka shouts up to me, "You see this goat? Is pretty good goat. Perhaps I will keep."

I said, "I thought you were finished with goats?"

She laughed.

She said, "Buzz Wexler can change her minds. I can change my minds also."

Also available in ISIS Large Print:

Their Finest Hour and a Half

Lissa Evans

It's 1940, France has fallen, and only a narrow strip of sea lies between Great Britain and invasion. What's needed is a morale-boosting, heart-warming war film. As bombs start to fall on London, work begins on an almost-true tale of bravery and rescue at Dunkirk. But call-up has left the film industry with the callow, the jaded and the utterly unsuitable.

There's Catrin Cole, junior copy-writer turned romantic dialogue specialist; Ambrose Hilliard, third most popular British film star of 1924, currently available for all leading roles; Edith Beadmore, ex-seamstress at Madame Tussaud's and ex-Londoner, having been bombed twice in two months; and Arthur Frith, whose peacetime job as a catering manager hasn't prepared him for sudden elevation to Special Military Advisor. In a city visited nightly by destruction, they must work together to produce a slice of the purest entertainment . . .

ISBN 978-0-7531-8410-3 (hb)
ISBN 978-0-7531-8411-0 (pb)

A Boy of Good Breeding

Miriam Toews

Life in Winnipeg hasn't worked out so well for Knute and her daughter. But living with her parents back in her hometown of Algren and working for the longtime mayor, Hosea Funk, has its own challenges. Knute finds herself mixed up in Hosea's attempts to achieve his dream of meeting the Prime Minister — even though that means keeping the town's population at an even 1500. It's not an easy task, with citizens threatening to move back, and one Algrenian on the verge of giving birth to twins — or possibly triplets.

Full of humour and larger-than-life characters, A Boy of Good Breeding is a warm-hearted novel about families that have been split up but are inexorably drawn back together.

ISBN 978-0-7531-7860-7 (hb)
ISBN 978-0-7531-7861-4 (pb)